WHAT PEOPLE ARE SAYING ABOUT VICTOR GISCHLER'S WORK

"First, who wouldn't want to read a novel titled *Go-Go Girls of the Apocalypse*? Second, who could have guessed the book was even *better* than the title? Part Christopher Moore, part Quentin Tarantino, Victor Gischler is a raving, badass genius."

—JAMES ROLLINS, *New York Times* bestselling author of *Map of Bones* and *Black Order*

"If it's all going to go to hell, you might as well have some *Go-Go Girls of the Apocalypse* to go with it. Weird just doesn't say it for this one. Gischler gives weird a kick in the butt, sends it right over the edge of the abyss. Wild fun."

—JOE R. LANSDALE, author of *Lost Echoes* and *Bad Chili*

"*Go-Go Girls of the Apocalypse* is funny, mordant, crazed, riveting, sardonic—and despite all that, it's got a plot. Bravo for Victor Gischler."

—MIKE RESNICK, Hugo and Nebula Award–winning author

"*Go-Go Girls of the Apocalypse* proves, if proof were needed, that Victor Gischler is among the most demented, nimble, and flat-out hilarious American satirists working today. Listen closely: that sound you hear, somewhere out there, is Vonnegut's applause."

—SEAN DOOLITTLE, author of *The Cleanup*

"If Pynchon ever decided to write an insane action novel, this would be it. All-out sustained brilliance; nobody is writing the unique lunacy that Victor Gischler is."

—KEN BRUEN, author of *The Guards* and *American Skin*

GO-GO GIRLS

of the

APOCALYPSE

VICTOR GISCHLER

A Touchstone Book
Published by Simon & Schuster
New York London Toronto Sydney

Touchstone
A Division of Simon & Schuster, Inc.
1230 Avenue of the Americas
New York, NY 10020

First Touchstone trade paperback edition July 2008

TOUCHSTONE and colophon are registered trademarks of Simon & Schuster, Inc.

For information about special discounts for bulk purchases, please contact Simon & Schuster Special Sales at 1-800-456-6798 or business@simonandschuster.com.

Designed by Mary Austin Speaker

Manufactured in the United States of America

10   9   8   7   6   5   4

Library of Congress Cataloging-in-Publication Data
Gischler, Victor.
   Go-go girls of the apocalypse / Victor Gischler.
      p.   cm.
      "A Touchstone book."
1. End of the world—Fiction.   2. Satire.   I. Title.
PS3607.I48G47   2008
813'.6—dc22   2007033601

ISBN-13: 978-1-4165-5225-3
ISBN-10:   1-4165-5225-1

For Anthony Neil Smith and Sean Doolittle, who both assured me I had a good book on my hands even before I believed it myself

ACKNOWLEDGMENTS

I need to add some names to the list of usual suspects. David Hale Smith has been one hell of an agent . . . Thanks for catching everything I've thrown at you. Thanks to Zach Schisgal, Shawna Lietzke and the team at Touchstone/Fireside for keeping me on track. And extra thanks to my wife, Jackie, and son, Emery, for putting up with me. Last but not least, many thanks to all those readers who keep coming back.

When the people saw that Moses was so long in coming down from the mountain, they gathered around Aaron and said, "Come, make us gods who will go before us. As for this fellow Moses who brought us up out of Egypt, we don't know what has happened to him."

—*EXODUS 32:1*

1

This is how Mortimer Tate ended up killing the first three human beings he'd laid eyes on in nearly a decade:

A wreath of cloud lay smooth and still about the top of the mountain like bacon grease gone cold and white in a deep, black frying pan. The top halves of evergreens poked through the cloud, frosted from last night's snow. The final days of winter, not too cold—Mortimer Tate estimated maybe thirty degrees. The thermometer had burst in the third year, that most bitter winter when it had gotten to twenty below or more. The thermometer had been made in America by a small company in Ohio.

Nothing was made to last anymore, Mortimer's dad had been fond of saying.

Mortimer sat at the window of the cabin, which had been built directly in front of the cave. The cave stretched back deep into the mountain. Mortimer sipped tea brewed from ginseng and tree bark he collected and dried himself. The coffee had run out the first year. So many things had run out that first year.

Mortimer watched the men come up the mountain, had seen them rise up through the mist and had blinked at them, thinking he'd cracked up at last. But they were real, rifles in front of them, not trying too carefully for stealth, but neither shouting nor taking the mountain for granted.

He considered going back into the cave to the gun locker, maybe getting the twelve-gauge or even something deadlier, but then he'd lose sight of the men and he didn't want to emerge from the cave again only to find they'd gone or had spotted the cabin. And anyway he had the police special in the pocket of his army-surplus parka. That should be enough. He wanted to talk, not shoot, but of course he had to be careful.

He didn't figure they'd seen the cabin, obscured as it was by the pines and two months' snow. It was possible he could sit right there, and the men would pass by and never be seen again. Nobody had been up this far before, at least nobody Mortimer had seen. Maybe they'd hunted the game out farther down and were up after meat. Mortimer himself had killed a big buck three weeks ago and had eaten venison four nights in a row before drying out the rest for jerky.

Goddamn, he was sick of jerky.

I'm stalling, Mortimer thought. He didn't want the men to pass without speaking to them. Now that he saw them, he was desperate to find out, get news of the world below. But he was afraid too. There were three of them.

He could call out to them right now and be safe holed up in the cabin. They couldn't get at him there. Not even if all three came at once. They'd have to climb up the rocks and snow and he could pick them off easy with the police special. But then they'd know about the cabin and the cave. They could come back with a dozen or a hundred, and that wouldn't do.

He'd have to slip down the side and try to catch one on the flank, open up a dialogue, and then maybe they could find out about each other. Maybe things were back to normal. The portable radio had devoured all the spare batteries so fast, ran out even before the coffee, but it had all been bad news, and when the last batteries had finally given up the ghost, Mortimer wouldn't have replaced them even if he'd had more. He hadn't been able to stand it, couldn't stomach another minute, the play-by-play of the world shaking itself to pieces.

It had been a long time, and maybe things had stabilized. That was a thought, and it turned into a hope; Mortimer found himself sliding down the incline from the thick plank door of the cabin and ducking into a stand of trees. The leftmost of the men was just on the other side. Mortimer went through quietly, not showing a weapon. Strike up a conversation. Sure. Maybe they'd be happy to see him.

He weaved and ducked among the pines, finally caught sight of the first man, ruddy cheeks, dirty red hair with a red-brown beard. Patched denim pants and work boots, thick corduroy coat, also patched. A red band around one sleeve. He held a deer rifle, bolt action, .308 caliber. Mortimer was so close he could see the rifle was a Remington.

Mortimer had one hand in the pocket of his parka, wrapped around the police special. He raised the other hand in greeting.

"Hey—" Mortimer's own voice surprised and startled him, and he cut off the greeting. Mortimer marveled momentarily at the strange voice, his own voice, how loud and croaky it sounded in the still morning. When was the last time he'd uttered a single syllable? He only pondered it a split second, because the stranger had already turned, big-eyed, mouth a shocked O of surprise, and was bringing the deer rifle around.

"No!" Mortimer threw up his free hand in a "stop" gesture. "Wait!"

But neither of them could wait. The rifle barrel had swung even with Mortimer's belly, and he thrust the police special forward and squeezed the trigger. The shot split the winterscape with a crack, white down exploding from the hole in the parka's pocket. The bullet caught the stranger high in the left side of the chest, a splash of red arcing and spraying and landing around him, harsh and bright in the smooth white terrain.

"Harry!" Another shot whizzed past Mortimer's ear.

Mortimer pulled the revolver, moved sideways among the trees as the other two ran toward him, snow crunching. He huffed breath, loud in his ears, steam billowing from his open mouth, eyes and nose wet from the cold and exertion. He fired once and the two guys slowed into a crouch, one going to a knee and shooting. The shot rent Mortimer's sleeve, more down swirling in his wake. They got up again and ran at Mortimer, who ran back at them, throwing everything into the encounter, howling and jerking the trigger three more times.

Two shots went high. The third took the kneeling shooter in the left eye, which popped and gushed blood and goo and shredded eyeball. His scream cut off in a strangled gulp, and he fell back.

The last stranger turned and ran, and this alarmed Mortimer more than when they'd shot at him. He couldn't let him bring others. He crunched in the snow after him. "Wait!"

They both ran faster.

"Wait!"

He didn't wait.

Mortimer fired. The shot caught the fleeing stranger between the shoulder blades. The man's arms flew out, the rifle tumbling into the snow. He fell face forward. Mortimer kept running until he was right up next to the body, dropped to his knees. "Oh, no." He turned the man over, but he was dead. "God damn it."

The first human beings he'd seen in nine years.

"Typical."

Using the sled he'd made to haul firewood, Mortimer took the bodies a mile or so away for burial. If the strangers had friends, Mortimer didn't want the blame for the killings. It had not been his fault, he'd convinced himself. He'd wanted to talk, and they'd drawn on him.

He still felt sorry about it.

Mortimer soon developed a little routine. He flailed at the frozen earth for a few minutes with shovel or pickax. Then he'd catch his breath by the small fire he'd built and search the pockets of the dead men. They carried precious little. One had a condom in his wallet and nothing else. *That's optimistic,* Mortimer thought. He discovered that each man had only one bullet in each rifle and carried no other ammunition. They could not possibly have been coming for him and must have been hunting.

All three wore red armbands.

He'd exhausted himself by the time he put the first two into shallow graves, covered them back over with dirt and rock. Another heavy snowfall would completely obscure the deed.

He leaned the third body in a sitting position against a young pine. He liked the look of this guy, the same brown-red facial hair except his moustache had been curled up into friendly handlebars. The face was pudgy and jolly in spite of the fact that all life had gone dark in the eyes, which were wide open, round and glassy.

"I'm sorry I had to do that," Mortimer said. "It was the other guy, almost got me with that deer rifle. Just wasn't anything else I could do."

Mortimer nodded and shrugged as if listening to the corpse's reply. "I know, I know. I should've yelled at you from the cabin instead of creeping up on you. But see it from my point of view. I had to make sure you guys were square first, right?"

The man's dead eyes appraised him unblinkingly.

"You were surprised to see me up here," Mortimer said. "A good place to hide, this far up. I'm probably the only fellow in East Tennessee who was ready for it."

The fire crackled. Mortimer put on another fistful of sticks. Nothing stirred on the mountain.

"If it hadn't been for my wife," Mortimer admitted, "I'd have never come up here. It took both the end of the world and Anne riding my ass to sign those divorce papers. One wasn't enough to run and hide. At the time, the divorce seemed worse. Can you believe that? I guess because it was personal to me."

Mortimer took the pickax and started on the third grave, stopped when he felt winded again and threw more sticks on the fire.

Mortimer resumed the conversation. "Her name was Anne. She wanted a divorce. I didn't. We were both angry. We didn't know why, just that our unhappiness had to be the other's fault, and damned if I was going to pay her one goddamn cent of alimony, you know? I was raised to work things out."

He got up, dug some more, came back to the fire.

"Anyway, you could see it all coming. I don't think anyone really thought it was the end, not the absolute *final* end, but just that it would be bad. And so I found the cave and started getting it ready. But really, I was leaving Anne. I was going to take the top of this mountain for myself and let her have the whole rest of the world, and all the trouble was just sort of an excuse. And I would just be *gone,* you know? And if she wanted those divorce papers signed, she'd damn well have to come find me. She'd have to earn it."

He finished the hole, but didn't put the body in right away. He still wanted to talk. He realized he was practicing. It was a time for talking again, and he wanted to remember how, wanted eventually to talk to someone who would talk back. The crushing loneliness had crept up on him so gradually that he hadn't even noticed it until he'd stood over the men he'd killed. He could have asked them so much, and maybe they'd have known some jokes and he could've laughed.

Mortimer laughed out loud to see if he recalled what it sounded like. It felt fake and tin in his throat, and he seemed to remember that a legitimate laugh came up from the belly. He decided not to practice laughing.

He conjured Anne's face in his mind, the sharp angles and bright, alert eyes, hair a rich brown. Skin so clear and white. "Huh."

Mortimer kept talking as he grabbed the man by the wrists and dragged him toward the hole. "I don't guess any of this makes a damn bit of difference to you. I wonder if you have a wife. I sure am sorry for her if you do."

Mortimer dropped him in the hole. "Again, sorry." He covered him up.

III

In back of the cabin was an opening four feet high and five feet wide that led into the cave. Mortimer stopped at the gun locker first, took the keys hung on a string around his neck, picked out the correct one and opened the locker. He reloaded the police special.

It was a big gun locker, long guns on top, ammunition and pistols in the drawers below. He had two more police specials in case something happened to the first and a thousand rounds of .38 ammunition sealed against the elements. He had a twelve-gauge pump shotgun, a lever-action .30-06, a .223 Ruger Mini-14 with two thirty-round banana clips. There was also a 9 mm Uzi that Mortimer had converted to full auto with online information, when there had been such a thing as the Internet.

Mortimer had maxed three credit cards stocking the cave with canned goods and medical supplies and tools and everything a man needed to live through the end of the world. There were more than a thousand books along shelves in the driest part of the cave. There used to be several boxes of pornography until Mortimer realized he'd spent nearly ten days in a row sitting in the cave masturbating. He burned the dirty magazines to keep from doing some terrible whacking injury to himself. There were also books on survival, books showing how to use the many tools he'd brought, books revealing the secrets of the land, how to skin and dress game, how to produce various medicines from plants and animals.

In the farthest reaches of the cavern, an underground stream ran through a deep chamber. Mortimer had secured a ladder down to the chamber and had rigged a system of buckets and pulleys to haul water. The cabin/cave combination was fortress, refuge, sanctuary and home. He had been relatively comfortable and safe these nine years.

Nine years. It seemed an impossible amount of time.

He dug into a cabinet and came out with a shaving mirror. He didn't shave anymore and had put the mirror away. He took the mirror out to the cabin window so he could see himself in the light. He gasped at his reflection, the haunted eyes glaring red-rimmed from the bushy hair, and beard and eyebrows gone awry. He remembered he was now thirty-eight years old, but he looked like some old, wild hermit, streaks of gray in his black hair and beard.

Many of the books Mortimer had stashed in the cavern were novels. He'd anticipated having a lot of time on his hands. In *Treasure Island,* there was a character named Ben Gunn who'd been stranded on an island and had gone half insane lusting for cheese. Mortimer imagined that's how he looked. No wonder the stranger had swung the deer rifle on him.

He fetched water up from the stream and heated it with a Coleman propane stove. He didn't have much propane left, but he didn't build fires in the cave because there wasn't any way for the smoke to vent. He rummaged the storage boxes until he found a disposable razor and a can of shaving gel. Rust ringed the bottom of the can.

He splashed warm water on his face and lathered up, but the

razor balked at his thick and tangled beard. He went back into the cabinet and found scissors. He cut away the beard in big patches. The hair collected around his ankles. He tried the razor again and shaved close, nicking himself around the chin. He wiped the blood with the bottom of his shirt. He cut his hair with the scissors. He surprised himself by doing a good job. Nine years had taught him patience with tedious tasks.

He went into the cabinet one more time and found the brush. He looked at it a moment like it was some alien artifact. In relearning these simple acts—shaving, brushing his hair—he was really learning to be human again. He planned to go down the mountain, and he was getting himself ready.

Mortimer brushed his hair and looked at his new sleek reflection and considered what he'd take. He would take the police special and the lever-action rifle. He wanted to protect himself but didn't want to appear hostile and thought the Uzi might be a bit much. He'd need food and a medical kit, but he'd also need to travel light. When first outfitting his refuge, he'd flirted with the idea of a horse, but he wasn't sure he'd be able to keep it alive. He'd sold insurance in a previous life and knew little of animal husbandry.

So he'd start down the mountain on foot. He'd go in the morning at first light with all his gear. He also decided to take three bottles of booze from the stock he'd kept unopened. Trade goods, if there was still such a thing as trade.

Trade goods. Weapons. He would not be able to get quickly back up the mountain if he needed something. He decided to pack the sled, extra weapons and the two cases of Johnnie Walker Blue, a third case of Maker's Mark. He could hide the sled at the bottom of the mountain, retrieve whatever he needed.

He realized there would be no McDonald's, no Holiday Inn, no Exxon station. Traveling would not be a lark. He did not know what it would be like except that it wouldn't be the same. He could not guess what awaited him down the mountain, but it was time to find out.

He dabbed at the blood on his chin.

IV

Among Mortimer's books were science fiction novels, some of which supposed the details of the apocalypse. Mortimer had selected these with wry irony. Popular methods whereby the world would snuff it: aliens, collisions with comets or meteors, plague, nuclear holocaust, robots rising against their masters, various natural disasters and so on and so on. Mortimer's favorite: space bureaucrats demolishing Earth to make way for a hyper-space bypass.

No single thing had doomed Mortimer's planet. Rather, it had been a confluence of disasters. Some dramatic and sudden, others a slow, silent decay.

The worldwide flu epidemic had come and gone with fewer deaths than predicted. Humanity emerged from that long winter and smiled nervously at one another. A sigh of relief, a bullet dodged.

That April the big one hit.

So long feared, it finally happened. The earth awoke, humped up its spine along the San Andreas. The destruction from L.A. to San Francisco defied comprehension. The earthquake sent rumbles across the Pacific, tsunamis pounding Asia. F.E.M.A. immediately declared its inadequacy and turned over operations to the military. The death toll numbered in the millions, and nothing—

not food nor fuel—made it through West Coast seaports. The shortages were rapidly felt across the Midwest. Supermarkets emptied, and no trucks arrived to resupply them.

Wall Street panicked.

Nine days later a Saudi terrorist detonated a nuclear bomb in a large tote bag on the steps of the Capitol building. Both houses of Congress were in session. The president and vice president and most of the cabinet were obliterated.

The secretary of the interior was found and sworn in. This didn't sit well with a four-star general who had other ideas. Civil war.

Economic spasms reached the European and Asian markets.

Israel dropped nukes on Cairo, Tehran and targets in Syria.

Pakistan and India went at it.

China and Russia went at it.

The world went at it.

It was pretty much all downhill from there.

V

Mortimer Tate started down the mountain, a rope over each shoulder as he pulled the sled behind him, another army surplus tote over his shoulder, police special in the pocket of his parka like usual. He carried the lever-action Winchester across his body. His pace was steady, and he puffed steam and his naked face went pink in the cold.

The base of the mountain sprawled across a high pocket wilderness that had been a state refuge. If he kept going down, Mortimer anticipated crossing one of the old hiking trails. If they hadn't all grown over.

The slope eased, the descent becoming more gradual by midday. Mortimer paused, leaned against a tree and took water, ate jerky. He turned his head slowly, listening to the forest. Not a bird nor a whisper of wind. He was still within the limits of what he considered his own territory, but the simple knowledge he'd be going farther made the forest appear alien to him.

He rested five more minutes, then began hiking again.

By nightfall he had still not crossed one of the hiking trails. He spun in the waning light, tried to get his bearings. Had he veered in the wrong direction, or was the distance simply farther than he remembered? In the morning, he'd look again with better light.

He considered a small fire but was afraid it would be seen. He pitched a low, sleek one-man tent made of light synthetic material, crawled inside and wrapped himself in a blanket. He fell asleep almost instantly.

He dreamt he was trapped in the tent, flickering light casting hellish shadows on the thin material, the sounds of stomping feet all around. He tried to stand and run, still wrapped in the tent like a burial shroud, faceless assailants circling him. Tangled in the tent material, unable to reach the police special, hands grabbing him, lifting and twisting and bearing him away.

Mortimer awoke with a gasp, freezing, hair sweat-soaked. He crawled out of the tent, stiff, aches in every joint. He had not slept on the ground in a long time, the thin blanket under him offering little comfort.

He squinted, looked around. Color had been bleached from the world, the sky a uniform gray. Even the evergreens were stark black against the white snow in the weak morning light, making the land appear like a two-dimensional charcoal sketch. He packed up the tent and built a fire, didn't care if anyone saw the smoke. He needed to thaw the ache from his bones. He heated water and made a cup of tea.

When the light grew strong enough to distinguish individual pine needles, he began the day's hike.

An hour later he crossed the first hiking trail and followed its winding path to the entrance of the refuge. There was still a brown sign with yellow lettering guarding the entrance: NATIONAL POCKET WILDERNESS.

He parked the sled behind a stand of trees, covered it with pine branches. He put a whiskey bottle in his knapsack. He'd put it in bubble wrap to keep it safe.

A hundred more steps and he stood on paved road.

He stood there awhile. An unfortunate sentimental streak rose up in Mortimer and he considered the road with misty eyes. Here was the asphalt thread that wound its way down the mountain to civilization. Or, at least, where civilization had stood once upon a time.

Mortimer rubbed his hands together, stamped his feet in the cold and considered his options. If he recalled correctly, the road ran down one side of the mountain to Evansville and the other way to Spring City. His first urge was toward Spring City, where he'd lived before with his wife, where he'd sold insurance and gone to the Methodist church every third or fourth Sunday. He couldn't decide if he was afraid to find his wife or if he'd be disappointed if he failed to find her.

He'd left her. Abandoned her. His wife. Whatever their problems might have been, Anne was still Mortimer Tate's wife. And a man doesn't shirk that kind of responsibility and not feel it in his gut.

He turned and headed toward Evansville.

He felt strangely happy and expectant. He longed to see buildings, a town, and most of all people. But his heart sank at the thought of the three hunters he'd killed. Mortimer put his head down and hiked into the wind.

He paused at the first house, stood a long time hoping for someone to come out. The dark windows without curtains looked like the wide eyes of a corpse. All quiet. The same thing with the next five houses he passed, and the sixth was hollow and blackened from fire. No people.

When he reached the Luminary Firehouse, another memory surfaced. The first Monday night of every month, the firefighters had put on a spaghetti dinner fund-raiser. It had all seemed very down-home and Americana when he and Anne had come up the mountain a few times to strap on the feedbag.

Now the idea of hot pasta and meatballs and garlic bread dripping butter almost gave Mortimer an erection. He found himself unconsciously walking toward the firehouse, the memory of fat men in denim overalls slurping spaghetti drawing him on.

He stopped short, blinked at the pale face in the window. It didn't move, wide eyes unblinking, and for a moment, Mortimer mistook it for a face on a poster, maybe an ad for Pepsi Cola or Life Savers. It was immobile, so pale and lifeless. But then a hand appeared, a wan wave.

Mortimer felt something tighten and then flutter in his chest. This time he'd do it right. No accidental murders as with the three hunters up the mountain. He slung the rifle over his shoulder, held his hands palms-up and away from his body. "Hello."

The face withdrew into the shadow.

"Wait!"

Mortimer fast-walked toward the firehouse, the small side door next to the closed garage. He turned the knob, entered slowly. "Hello? It's okay. I just want to talk." He pushed the door open all the way, the sliver of sunlight widening into a brilliant yellow cone, spotlighting the young girl backed into the corner of what must have been the firehouse office. "It's okay," he said again.

He looked about the shabby room. A calendar hanging faded and askew. The ratty remains of a desk against the wall. A pallet of rags and straw that must've been used for a bed. The girl herself was maybe sixteen, pale bruised legs coming out of a threadbare flowered dress. She stood in a pair of hiking boots at least two sizes too large. Frayed laces. A dark blue navy peacoat with holes in the elbows. Her full lower lip hung open and moist. Dark circles under green eyes. Dishwater hair. She was small and thin and the world had squashed her flat.

"I—I . . ." Mortimer didn't know how to start. He wanted to do it right, remake contact with the world, and he'd start with this girl. He trembled. What to say first? What to ask?

Something struck the back of his head. Bells went off. Lights flashed. He teetered, lurched forward but didn't go down. Another sharp shot below his left ear. He spun, saw a blur of boots, a big furry thing. Then his eyes went fuzzy and he hit the firehouse floor.

VI

Mortimer awoke naked and shivering. The girl lay on the pallet ten feet away, her legs in the air, dress up past her waist. She whimpered, her head back, glassy eyes fixed on the ceiling. A big man, maybe a full foot taller than Mortimer, grunted and heaved on top of her, thrusting mercilessly and without grace. His jeans bunched around his ankles. He wore some kind of coarse, black fur coat that made him appear like a prehistoric beast.

Mortimer twisted. His head swam. He was bound at the wrists and ankles with thin twine. He writhed, strained against his bonds. No good. The beast continued to thrust. Mortimer tried to sort out what had happened. He'd been hit from behind. He'd been too stupid and eager, let his guard down.

The Beast shuddered and howled, then pulled out of the girl with a nasty wet sound. He was flushed and sweating, rolled off her and reached for something. It was one of Mortimer's bottles, Johnnie Walker, half full. The Beast took a swig, wiped and smacked his lips. His black shaggy hair and beard matched his coat except for the gray at his temples and the corners of his mouth.

The Beast saw Mortimer, grinned, slugged back another hit of Johnnie Walker. "Well, well. Santa Claus is awake." He toasted Mortimer with the bottle. "Thanks for the goodies, Santa." Another thick gulp.

The girl was already curling into the corner, smoothing the dress back over her thighs. Her face was as blank and white and distant as the moon.

The Beast lurched to his feet, reaching for his jeans, his rapidly deflating pecker and balls swinging in a salt-and-pepper thatch. "I'm glad you're awake. Got some questions for you." He fastened his pants, drank more whiskey and nudged the girl's ass with his boot heel. "Sheila."

She turned her head toward him. Her eyes remained unfocused.

"Food."

She nodded once, got to her feet and went away.

The Beast turned his mad grin back at Mortimer. "Now we have a chat." He stepped forward, stood directly over Mortimer. The reek off of the Beast was formidable, a yeasty, pungent cologne of sweat and grease and sex. He shook the bottle of Johnnie Walker in Mortimer's face. "Any more where this came from?" His eyes gleamed like wet, black river stones.

Mortimer said nothing, eyes wide and round and waiting.

The Beast chuckled from deep in his throat and drank the rest of the Johnnie Walker, hiccuped and belched. He squatted next to Mortimer, sniffed. "You smell like soap, and you look clean."

You smell like a turd covered in feta. Mortimer tried twisting out of his bonds again.

"You down from Knoxville? I hear they got power on in Knoxville, but I thought it was just talk."

Mortimer now recognized the Beast's black coat as a bear skin. Mortimer remained silent. This was not defiance. *Don't provoke the scary man.*

The Beast tossed the bottle over his shoulder, and it clinked and tumbled without breaking. "Cat got your tongue, huh?" He unzipped his pants, fished inside and came out with his pecker. He leaned, grunted and squirted, the piss splashing against Mortimer's face.

Mortimer sputtered and coughed. The piss was warm. An ammonia taste. It stung his eyes. He gagged, stopped short of vomiting.

The Beast laughed. "Drink up, beautiful." He shook off his pecker, zipped up and left the room.

Once the piss cooled on his skin, Mortimer shivered.

The Beast returned and squatted next to him. He held the bubble wrap that Mortimer had used to protect the whiskey. He held it close to Mortimer's face, turned it over. Mortimer didn't understand what he was supposed to see.

"You taped this," the Beast said.

Mortimer frowned. "Yeah."

"You fucking *taped* it?"

"So?"

The Beast's hammy hand swatted Mortimer's cheek, the slap loud and sharp. A thousand hot needles in Mortimer's skin.

"Where the fuck did you get Scotch tape, dipshit?"

"What?"

Another quick slap from the Beast, and Mortimer yelled. Ringing in his ears.

"You gonna tell me you just went down to the Walgreens and picked up some goddamn Scotch tape?"

It clicked in Mortimer's head, a realization sliding into place, the slow understanding. Where the hell did you get Scotch tape after the apocalypse? Something so commonplace, but who would make more? Scotch tape and underarm deodorant and hairspray and antacid and toothpaste and aluminum foil and dishwashing liquid and roach spray and all of civilization's bright conveniences. Would anyone ever make those things again?

"I found the tape in an old house," Mortimer said. "I was scavenging, and I found it."

"Well, ain't you just the luckiest goddamn scavenger ever." The Beast made a noise in his throat, then spit in Mortimer's face. "You found tape and ammunition for both your guns and food and whiskey and . . . and fucking *bubble wrap*?" He stood, kicked Mortimer hard in the gut.

This time Mortimer did vomit. He rolled his face toward the floor and heaved once, twice. The third time brought up bile.

"Tell me where you got this stuff," the Beast said.

"I . . . I found it."

"You found it, huh?"

The Beast stomped the heel of his boot into Mortimer's forehead. Mortimer grunted.

"I know you fucking found it, cocksucker. Now tell me where."

Mortimer shook his head. "A long way from here. I've been gathering it up, saving it."

"Bullshit." The Beast lifted him a foot off the floor by a fistful of hair. "Nobody carries that much food and booze and doesn't eat and drink it. What? You just like lugging it around?" He brought his other fist down hard, knocked Mortimer's head around.

Mortimer blinked, colored lights dancing in front of his eyes and a hot buzz in his ears. He tried to curl into a ball, but the Beast still held him fast.

"Where'd you get it? Someplace close, right?"

Mortimer shook his head.

The Beast punched again, and Mortimer felt his lips flatten against his teeth, skin ripping. He spit blood, coughed.

"Shit." The Beast let go, and Mortimer's head knocked against the floor. The Beast left the room again.

Mortimer lay on the cold floor, reeking of piss, face throbbing. This had been a mistake, coming down the mountain, trying to reconnect with whatever remained below. He'd been safe, comfortable. There had been no need to leave his sanctuary, only the imagined necessity of human companionship, only the vain notion that he must know what had become of the world.

The world had broken, and there was nothing left of humanity but the dregs, dumb sons of bitches in bear skin.

Mortimer opened a swollen eye, saw the girl standing over him, her face expressionless.

"Help me," Mortimer pleaded.

She stood frozen.

"Untie me," he croaked. "I'll go away. I won't do anything, I promise. I'll just go."

She didn't say a word, didn't blink. A few moments later she started at the Beast's return and slunk away.

The Beast knelt next to Mortimer, held up a gleaming bowie knife. "Like it? It ain't quite as sharp as I'd like, so the cut won't be clean. I'll have to saw a bit." He grabbed Mortimer's bound hands, pulled them close to his thick body.

Mortimer gasped, tried to jerk away.

The Beast shifted, pinned Mortimer's wrists under his arm. Mortimer tried to squirm away. The Beast selected the pinkie finger on Mortimer's left hand, stretched it out. Mortimer tried to make a fist and pull away, but the Beast was too strong.

"P-please." Saliva flew from Mortimer's lips. He shook so badly he couldn't talk.

"I think we're gonna have a more productive conversation after this." The Beast put the blade against the finger. Mortimer renewed his struggles, but the Beast held him.

"Here we go." The blade bit deep, dark blood flowing over the metal.

Mortimer howled, kicked, screamed. The Beast sawed the blade back and forth. So much blood. Within ten seconds he was down to bone. The Beast leaned his weight into it, sawed bone. The finger came off, blood squirting over both of them.

Mortimer lay covered in sweat, limp in the Beast's lap, like a spent lover deep in swoon. The Beast splashed water on Mortimer's face, shook him until he woke.

"Okay," the Beast said. "Let's take it from the top."

VII

The Beast led Mortimer on an eight-foot length of thin rope back down the road toward the entrance of the pocket wilderness. The girl walked silently behind them like the dead, wagless tail of an old dog.

Mortimer had lain on the office floor of the dilapidated firehouse and told the Beast all, his secret cabin and the cavern and his storehouse of old-world commodities. The Beast demanded to be taken there. Mortimer had agreed, lying there bleeding and weak.

But now, treading the frozen road, Mortimer burned with hate and humiliation and plotted the Beast's demise. The wind tore at his eyes, face and ankles. A six-foot length of hickory lay across his neck, his wrists tied to the wood in crucifixion fashion. He wore his boots and his pants and shirt. The Beast had taken his parka and socks, marched in front of him holding the rope in one hand, the police special in the other.

The Beast wore his bear skin over the parka, and walking along the road, Mortimer on the leash, they looked the grotesque reverse of some old-west traveling carnival act, the dancing bear leading his trainer. Mortimer desperately looked for his opening but did not expect one. He'd have to make some kind of move before they reached the cavern. The Beast would not want to keep and feed Mortimer after he'd been led to the stash.

Even in the worst throes of torture, Mortimer had kept his weapons stash a secret. Somehow he'd make a break for it or maybe fake needing to take a shit. If Mortimer could just get his hands on the Uzi, he'd chop the Beast in half with a spray of nine millimeter.

They had taken Mortimer's medical kit too, the iodine and hydrogen peroxide and bandages. They'd used none of it to bind Mortimer's mangled hand. The girl had splashed the wound with dirty water, wrapped the finger stump in a tattered pink rag. His hand throbbed but bothered him less than the biting cold. He staggered and shook and lurched forward at the Beast's insistent yank on the rope.

Mortimer took another fifty steps, shivered and collapsed.

"Get up." The Beast yanked the leash.

Mortimer shook his head, panted. He didn't have the energy to form words.

The Beast took two quick steps toward Mortimer, then kicked hard, caught Mortimer in the ribs. Mortimer wheezed and heaved dry.

"I said get up." The Beast drew his leg back for another kick.

"Stop."

The Beast froze, looked for the source of the new voice, which had echoed along the mountain road. Mortimer looked up too. What now?

"Show yourself!" the Beast yelled.

Forty yards up the road, a man stepped out of the bushes, planted himself in the center of the road, legs apart. Mortimer blinked, not sure if he was seeing right. The newcomer wore a black cowboy hat, long leather coat swept back to reveal a pair of pistols hanging on his hips. A blue bandana pulled loose around his neck. A forked beard yellow as the sun, long hair the same color, hands hovering dangerously over the pistols.

The Beast squinted. "What the fuck are you?"

"Cut that man loose," ordered the cowboy.

"Kiss my ass." But the Beast's eyes flicked to the man's twin six-shooters.

"Mister, I'm gonna tell you just one more time." He eased forward as he spoke, one deliberate step at a time. "Let that man go and piss off. That's your only chance to live."

The Beast dropped to the ground, rolled, came up behind Mortimer in a kneeling position. He grabbed Mortimer's face and pulled him close until the two were cheek to cheek. He pulled the police special, put it against Mortimer's head. "I don't know what your interest is in this guy, but I'll splatter his brains all over the mountain if you don't stop right there." With his arms spread along the length of hickory, Mortimer provided good cover. Only half the Beast's face and a bit of shoulder showed.

The cowboy froze. He squeezed his fists so tight, Mortimer heard the knuckles crack. They all waited for something to happen.

A split second later it did.

The cowboy dropped into a kneeling position, one six-shooter flashing from its holster. His arm shot out straight, and he sighted along the barrel, one eye mashed closed, biting his lip in concentration. It all happened in a heartbeat.

Bang.

The Beast screamed, a high-pitched mix of surprise and pain. He stood, staggered, blood trailing from his shoulder. He swung the police special to return fire.

The cowboy was already on his feet. He fanned the six-shooter's hammer twice, and the Beast fell dead in front of Mortimer. Blood pooled in the Beast's empty eye sockets.

The girl, Sheila, who'd been twenty paces behind the whole encounter, turned and screamed back up the road and out of sight.

The cowboy trotted to Mortimer and knelt next to him, began to untie his wrists. "Hold on, mister. We'll get you free shortly." He had a yellow handlebar moustache to go with the forked beard.

"Thanks," Mortimer said. "Who are you?"

A smile across the young face, under thirty years old. "Who do I look like?"

"George Custer."

The smile fell. "Damn. I was going for Buffalo Bill."

VIII

After Bill had cut him loose, Mortimer lay in the road, groaning and rubbing the circulation back into his wrists. His finger stump throbbed. The cowboy squatted next to him muttering encouraging things like "You'll be okay, partner" and "Live to fight another day" and so on.

Mortimer didn't mind. He'd give Buffalo Bill a big wet kiss on the lips if that's what he wanted. Mortimer Tate was alive. He'd escaped the Beast.

He stood, looked down into the Beast's hollow and bloody eyes before taking back his parka and other belongings. He kicked the dead man into the shrubs on the side of the road, tossed the bear skin on top of him.

"This yours?" Bill held the police special toward Mortimer butt first.

Mortimer hesitated. If this insane cowboy had wanted Mortimer dead, then he'd already be dead. He took the pistol. "Thanks."

They stood in the middle of the road among the frayed rope and the splotches of blood and the cold wind lifting the cowboy's yellow hair.

"Now what?" asked Buffalo Bill.

"You tell me," Mortimer said.

"I'm going to Spring City."

"I was thinking Evansville," Mortimer said.

Bill shook his head. "Red Stripes on that side of the mountain. Not too many. Enough to worry."

Mortimer frowned, recalled the three men he'd killed up the mountain who wore red armbands. "Red Stripes?"

"Jesus, you don't know about them? What? You been in a cave for nine years?"

"As a matter of fact . . ."

"It might snow soon." Bill squinted at the dark clouds gathering overhead. "Maybe we should find a roof."

"I need to get something first," Mortimer said. "It's not much farther."

"Okay."

Bill retrieved a battered backpack from behind a stump, and both men set off toward the entrance to the pocket wilderness. They walked in silence, and at last the snow began to fall gently, silently dusting their heads and shoulders.

Mortimer broke the silence first. "Why did you save me?"

"Can't let an innocent man be dragged along like an animal. Ain't right."

"How do you know I'm innocent? Maybe I'm a criminal. Maybe I was being taken to trial. I could be a murderer."

Bill's head jerked around to look at Mortimer, eyes wide. This possibility clearly hadn't occurred to him. "Hell."

"Don't worry." Mortimer grinned. "You did the right thing."

Bill exhaled, shook his head. "Damn. It's a hard world to be good in."

. . .

The snow was a foot thick on the ground by the time they reached Mortimer's stash. He cleared away the shrubs and accumulated snow, pulled the tarp off the sled.

Bill whistled appreciatively at the weapons, and Mortimer assumed Bill was looking at the formidable Uzi, but the cowboy reached for the lever-action rifle. Bill stopped mid-reach, raised an eyebrow at Mortimer.

"Go ahead."

Bill picked up the rifle, ran his hand over the stock. He looked right holding it, like it completed his costume.

"Take it," Mortimer said.

"What?"

"It's yours. Least I can do after you saved my ass."

Bill grinned big, worked the lever and sighted along the barrel. He held the gun in both hands, held it away from his body, looked at it like it was a sacred relic. "This is how the world was built, and how it was destroyed, and how it'll be built again." He cradled the rifle in one arm like a puppy. "You got shells for it?"

Mortimer handed him a box of ammunition, then showed him a bottle of Johnnie Walker. "Help me pull this sled, and I'll buy you a drink."

"Amen to that, brother."

They found an abandoned house, all the windows broken out, but there was a large fireplace. They hauled in wood, started a fire. Soon it was dark, snow falling thick outside, wind blowing the ragged curtains in the windows like the wispy nightgowns of ghostly orphans.

Mortimer had cleaned and wrapped his finger stump with the extra first aid supplies from the sled.

They sat on a fake leather couch and passed the bottle between them; the whiskey lit up amber in the firelight. The house creaked in the moaning wind.

"Goddamn, that's good," Bill said. Another big slug and he held it in his mouth an extra moment before swallowing, smacked his lips.

"I miss Burger King." Mortimer took the bottle, drank. It was so warm and good going down, Mortimer marveled he'd been able to leave the bottles unopened for nine years. "I like Whoppers."

"SONIC," Bill said. "I liked to pull up and eat in my car, listen to the radio and eat foot-long chili dogs. I could eat two and Tater Tots in the space of an Avril Lavigne song."

"Do people still drive cars?"

Bill shook his head and took the bottle back, sipped. "Gasoline goes stale after a while and nobody's refining anymore. Horses are coming back. Man, I'd love to get me a horse."

"Coming back?"

"People ate them."

"Jesus."

"You really don't know any of this?"

Mortimer shook his head, took the bottle and gulped.

Bill said, "Goats too. Dogs and cats. Rats. Meat is meat. I heard tell they turned cannibal in some places, but I don't know if that's true or not."

I could turn around right now, thought Mortimer. *I could go back to the cave. There's no Burger King down the mountain, no world I remember.*

"Why are you dressed like a cowboy?" Mortimer was curious as hell.

"Does it seem weird?"

Mortimer shrugged. "I don't know the standard of weird anymore."

"I'm always afraid people will think it's weird."

"Do they?"

"Yes."

"You don't have to tell me if you don't want."

"I don't know why I did it at first," admitted Bill. "I always liked westerns, John Wayne and Jimmy Stewart, you know? Think about what a cowboy is, what he represents. The new order rolling across the prairie, right? Even when he was slaughtering buffalo and red Indians, he still left civilization in his wake, towns and railroads and all that. I guess maybe I thought we needed cowboys again. Maybe not. Hell, I don't know. Probably sounds stupid."

"No it doesn't." Yes it did.

"Anyway," Bill said. "Everyone else looked like a refugee, dressed in rags. Everyone looked lost, like they've got no place to go. If you're a cowboy, you're not a refugee. You don't need anyplace to go. Cowboys are supposed to drift, ride off into the sunset. If you're a cowboy then you ain't lost."

The man had found his purpose through costuming. Sure. Whatever helps a guy cope. Buffalo Bill was an un-lost non-refugee.

"I want to find my wife." Mortimer belched. It tasted like barfy booze.

"You didn't take your wife into hiding with you?"

"It's complicated."

"No it's not," Bill said. "Everything's real simple now. She's either alive or dead."

Mortimer thought about that. Outside the wind howled. Inside the fire crackled and snapped. Mortimer's eyelids grew heavy, and he faded into whiskey dreams.

IX

"You okay?" There seemed to be genuine concern in Bill's voice.

Mortimer leaned into the rope, trudged in the shin-deep snow, one foot in front of the other, every step an effort of titanic proportions. His head throbbed. His stomach rebelled. He had not been this hungover in . . . how long?

A decade.

Abruptly, Mortimer dropped the rope, dashed to the side of the road and went to his knees. Heaved. The puke was acidic, made his eyes water. He hurled three times in quick succession, splattering the snow. Steam rose. He wiped his mouth on his sleeve.

"I'm a little fuzzy myself this morning," Bill said.

"Get bent," Mortimer muttered, then spit.

"What?"

"I said I'm fine. Let's go."

They made their way down the mountain. Landmarks began to look familiar. A flood of memories. Mortimer found himself hurrying. He wanted to see his town, his old office, his old house.

His old life.

The gas station and convenience store at the bottom of the hill was a charred husk, blackened and hollow. He'd bought beer and newspapers there. Toilet paper, Slim Jims, ice cream, unleaded. In an odd way, Mortimer was relieved. He would have felt like a grade-A jackass if he'd hidden in a cave for nine years and then come down the mountain only to find the convenience store selling cigarettes and lotto tickets like nothing had happened.

"I want to find my old house," Mortimer said.

"Wait!" Bill grabbed Mortimer's sleeve and tugged, pointed at the side of a brick building across the street. "It's true. They have one here. Thank God. I didn't know if it was true or not."

Mortimer looked at the wall. Spray-painted in three-foot, neon-pink letters were the words JOEY ARMAGEDDON'S SASSY A-GO-GO. An arrow painted underneath pointed toward downtown.

Mortimer squinted at the sign. "What the hell's that?"

"Paradise, partner, paradise. Come on." Bill began to pull the sled in the direction indicated by the sign.

"Wait." Mortimer pulled back on the other rope. "I told you I want to find my house."

"Just for an hour." Bill dug into his pockets, came out with a handful of silver coins. "I'll buy you a drink. I have six Armageddon dollars."

Mortimer's stomach pinched. "I don't want a drink."

"Just for an hour."

"No."

"Thirty minutes."

"I said no."

Bill dropped the rope, turned on Mortimer, pointed at him. "Listen, pal. The only people who don't want to go to Joey Armageddon's are those who've never been to one. Ten minutes. You won't be sorry."

Mortimer admitted to himself he'd like to see downtown, the little Norman Rockwell Main Street, the storefront where he'd sold insurance. He wondered if he'd recognize the town he'd lived in. His old house had waited nine years. It could wait a little longer.

"Okay," Mortimer said. "Lead the way."

"You'll love it."

"Just pull the sled."

Spring City was the kind of sleepy small town high school kids vowed to leave for the big city. Before the Fall there had been a bank and a post office, various stores. A blinking stoplight. Old men had stood in front of the greasy diner, thumbs hooked in denim overalls as they discussed the Volunteers' football season and the doings at the First Baptist Church. A Laundromat. Feed store. Hardee's.

Now, as Mortimer and Buffalo Bill pulled the sled toward the old armory, vague faces watched them from dirty windows. There was an eerie caution in their expressions. Mortimer asked Bill if they should be worried.

"Not in town," Bill said. "We're safe enough. I think they have a militia here."

A militia. The idea made Mortimer feel nervous instead of safer.

The armory had been transformed. A sign above the double doors in bright pink, professionally stenciled, not the rough spray-paint job they'd seen on their way in, declared the place JOEY ARMAGEDDON'S.

Mortimer raised an eyebrow. This had been a place for high school dances, city league basketball and town hall meetings. What was it now?

They walked inside, Bill leading the way, excited like a little kid going to a birthday party. Mortimer did not recognize the interior of the armory. Tables and chairs were scattered throughout it, a hodgepodge mismatch of booths and other furniture clearly looted from various restaurants and pubs. At the far end of the auditorium, a long pine bar; behind the bar and slightly elevated, a stage. What looked like two enormous birdcages flanked the stage on either side. Strings of unlit Christmas tree lights crisscrossed the ceiling, hanging low.

"Will the sled be okay outside?"

"Nobody pulls shit within five hundred yards of a Joey Armageddon's." Bill beelined for the bar.

Mortimer followed.

As he approached the bar, Mortimer noticed a dozen men at a pair of picnic tables along the far wall. They wore dirty clothes and spooned a thick, brown stew into their scruffy faces. Next to the picnic tables was a line of stationary bicycles, a cumbersome wad of wires and cables leading from the bicycles to a metal box.

He caught up with Bill at the bar, where the cowboy had caught the bartender's attention.

"Is the beer cold?" Bill asked.

"Sure," said the bartender. He was fat and bald, a large tattoo of a black spider in the middle of his forehead. "The kegs are outside in the snow. Cold beer in summer, that's the real trick."

"Great. You have the house special microbrew? Chattanooga Brown?"

The bartender shook his head. "Ran out three nights ago, and the Red Stripes are fucking up the supply wagons coming north. We got Freddy's Piss Yellow."

"Never heard of it."

"Remember Pabst Blue Ribbon?"

"Yeah."

"Not that good."

"Two mugs," Bill said.

Spider-face leaned on the bar. "Let's see the color of your money, friend."

Bill put the silver coins on the bar. Spider-face took one and pushed the rest back. He pulled the tap and filled two mugs with foamy, bright yellow liquid and set the mugs in front of Bill and Mortimer.

"You got any rooms?" Bill asked.

"Five coins a night."

Bill frowned. "That's pretty steep. It'll clean me out."

"That's with electricity and plumbing. You'll think you're at the fucking Marriott."

"Let me think about it."

Spider-face shrugged and went about his business.

Bill lifted his mug. "Cheers."

Mortimer tasted the Freddy's Piss Yellow. It tasted more or less like beer. Beer somebody had used to wash his balls. But after his third sip, Mortimer felt his headache ease a little. Hair of the dog.

"Can I see one of those coins?"

"Sure."

Mortimer turned one of the coins over in his hands; it was heavy, maybe lead or nickel with a shiny silver coating, smaller than a silver dollar but bigger than a fifty-cent piece. Primitive stamping. It had ONE ARMAGEDDON DOLLAR on one side, a picture of a mushroom cloud on the other.

"What the hell is this?"

"Armageddon dollar," Bill said.

"Yes, the words *Armageddon Dollar* printed on one side tipped me off."

"They're used as currency at all Joey Armageddon locations."

"The place has its own money? How many locations are there?"

Bill shrugged. "If I were you, I'd exchange that sled of trade goods for Armageddon dollars right away."

"Why would I want to do that?"

"For one thing, carrying a bag of coins is easier than pulling that damn sled everyplace. Which, by the way, is getting kind of old."

"What if I want to shop somewhere other than Joey Armageddon's?"

Bill chuckled, sipped beer. "There isn't anyplace else."

Mortimer asked Spider-face where he could trade his goods for money. The bartender pointed through a door.

"Be right back," Mortimer told Bill.

Mortimer went to the sled, made sure no one was looking, then took one of the Johnnie Walker bottles from beneath the tarp and carried it back inside, went through the door the barman had indicated.

A small man sat behind a wire-mesh cage, a little window in front of him, like a bank teller. Sitting on a stool in a corner was a three-hundred-pound black man in army fatigues and a purple fez. He looked grim and dangerous. The M16 machine gun in his arms didn't help him look any friendlier.

The white-haired man behind the cage wore a thick pair of glasses, a pencil behind his ear. He regarded Mortimer with little interest. "Yes?"

Mortimer cleared his throat. "I'm here to trade."

The white-haired man yawned. "Buying or selling?"

Mortimer put the Johnnie Walker on the counter. "Selling."

The man's eyes slowly widened. "Is that real?"

"Yes."

"We had someone in here before." A warning tone in the man's voice. "He drilled the top and filled the empty bottle with home mash. After we beat him, the mayor sentenced him to a month on the bicycles. I'll ask you again. Is it real?"

"It's real," Mortimer said. "As are the other thirty-five bottles out on my sled."

"Thirty-five?" The man trembled. "Mister, if you're telling the truth, you just became the richest man in town."

"I have other things too." Mortimer listed the items.

Sweat beaded on the man's forehead as he copied the list into a little notebook with his pencil. "Can I get your name?"

"Mortimer Tate."

"I'm Silas Jones, Mr. Tate. And may I say you are a most welcome and valuable customer here at Joey Armageddon's."

The tally came to seven thousand Armageddon dollars, and Mortimer took the Emperor's Suite on the second floor of the brick building attached to the armory. Two rooms, a double bed in each. A bathroom.

Mortimer Tate took his first crap on a working toilet in nine years.

He took a shower. A hot shower. Dried himself with a clean towel. Put on a terry cloth robe. A knock on the door.

It was the clerk, Silas Jones.

"I trust everything is to your satisfaction, Mr. Tate."

"Completely."

"I have been authorized to give you this."

Silas Jones handed him a pink card. It had been laminated. On the front was a mushroom cloud exploding upward into a pair of breasts. On the back were Mortimer's name and the words *Platinum Member*.

"What's this?"

Jones gasped. "What's this?" He looked surprised. "Why, Mr. Tate, this is one of the most sought-after status symbols of the new world. This is a Joey Armageddon's Platinum membership. It entitles you to special treatment at any of our fine locations."

"How many locations is that?"

"I don't know," admitted Jones. "Last count was something like twenty. I think."

"What kind of special treatment?"

"Alas, I don't know that either, since I myself have not been fortunate enough to achieve Platinum membership."

Uh-huh.

Buffalo Bill emerged from one of the bedrooms. He wore only his boots, his hat and a towel. "Jesus H. Christ, it's like Buckingham fucking Palace." Bill was middling drunk, having worked halfway through a complimentary bottle of Freddy's Piss Vinegar Vodka. (Bill had asked for a bottle of Major Dundee's Slow-Motion Gin, but the most recent shipment was rumored to have been hijacked by Red Stripes.)

Bill slung an arm around Mortimer's shoulders. "I saved this motherfucker's life. Best thing I ever did." He slurped vodka, gagged, and it trickled down his chin.

Silas Jones cleared his throat. "Quite."

Bill sniffed one of his own armpits. "Damn, I stink. Better shower." He stumbled into the bathroom.

"Mr. Tate, if I may offer a suggestion," Jones said. "You are now in possession of a staggering number of Armageddon dollars. You'll probably want to take steps to secure their . . . uh . . . security."

"Is there an open bank in town?"

"The First Armageddon Bank of Spring City is an authorized subsidiary of Joey Armageddon's Sassy A-Go-Go. I happen to be the head teller."

"Thanks. Sign me up. Where can I get some food?"

"The kitchen downstairs at Joey Armageddon's will be open in an hour."

"I'd like some new clothes."

"The selection downstairs in the trading post is top notch, and Joey Armageddon's has a tailor on call. I can send a runner for him if you need alterations."

"So is Joey Armageddon's the only store in the world or what?"

"Mr. Tate, with all due modesty, I think you'll come to find that Joey Armageddon's *is* the world."

X

Mortimer left Buffalo Bill snoring in the Emperor's Suite and smelling like Dial soap.

The Emperor's Suite had come with Dial soap and Pantene shampoo and a small tube of Aim toothpaste. The suite was normally one hundred Armageddon dollars a night. For Platinum members it was only sixty.

Mortimer trudged the ten blocks from the armory to his old neighborhood. He wanted to find his old house before nightfall. A few people passed him on the street. Nobody said hello, but nobody seemed terrified either.

Some houses looked perfectly normal. Others were clearly abandoned, and a few had been burned down to the foundation. But there was something else. Mortimer couldn't quite put his finger on it. He stood in the middle of the street, turned three hundred and sixty degrees trying to figure it out.

No cars. None driving, none parked in the driveways or along the streets. The gas might have gone stale, but where did the cars go?

He kept walking.

He turned onto his street, spotted his house about halfway down. It came into focus as he trudged closer. The windows were dark, but so were all the windows along the street. No power. His house looked dirty and unpainted. The shrubs grown long and wild. It hadn't been such a bad house, three bedrooms, two baths, a fireplace. Now the gutters hung loose at one end. He stood watching the house for ten minutes but didn't see or hear any signs of life.

He climbed the three steps to the front porch. The wood creaked under his boots. Someone had painted graffiti on the front door, a blue circle with a triangle of three dots inside. Some gang?

Concern for Anne suddenly welled up inside him. What had happened to her? Did she make it okay when the world went crazy?

He knocked on the door. It felt strange, even after all this time, to knock before he entered his own home. He pushed the door open and entered.

The living room was nearly barren, a sofa with stuffing oozing out of the cushions and a beanbag. He stood there trying to remember the good times with Anne, long nights in front of a cozy fire. Mortimer's eyes grew misty as the past formed a picture in his mind.

The old screaming woman with the frying pan in her hand broke the spell.

"Whoa!" Mortimer flinched, backed away.

She was wild eyed, gray hair exploding in all directions. She rushed at Mortimer, the frying pan swinging savagely. Mortimer threw up his arms, tried to duck away. A glancing blow on the tip of his elbow shot hot pain up his arm.

"Lady, please. Jesus!" Mortimer attempted flight, tripped backward over the beanbag.

The old lady loomed over him, mouth a feral, toothless grimace, ragged dress billowing around her like the tattered cape of some obsolete superhero. "My house. The place was empty, so I puts my mark on the door. Them's the rules." She lifted the pan over her head for a killer blow.

"I'm sorry, I'm sorry." He reached into his pocket, came out with a handful of coins and tossed them at the old woman's feet. "Here, take them."

She stepped back, blinked at the glittering coins on the floor. "Are those . . . ?" She knelt, picked one up and held it in the light. "It is. Armageddon dollars!" She scooped them into her trembling hands. "Thank you. Oh, my God. Thank you."

Her head came up suddenly and she met Mortimer's gaze, one eye half-milky with cataracts. "Wait a minute. I know what this is about."

"It's not about anything." Mortimer struggled to his feet. "I'm sorry I barged in."

"A strapping young buck like you. I know what you want from a woman."

"Oh, shit." He backed away, headed for the door.

The old woman ripped open the front of her dress, buttons flying. "Take me, you randy bastard. I'm bought and paid for." Her breasts flopped into the open like deflated hot-water bottles.

Mortimer screamed and dashed for the door, made it outside and kept running.

"You goddamn pussy," she called after him. "Come back here and deliver the sausage!"

XI

Back in the Emperor's Suite, Mortimer found Bill's vodka bottle. Empty. He sniffed, and the fumes scorched the inside of his nose. "Hell."

Bill walked in from the other room, tucking in his shirt. He looked alert and no longer smelled like a campfire after his shower. "Sorry, all gone."

"I need a drink."

"Sounds good. Let me get my boots on."

Mortimer squinted at the empty vodka bottle. "You can handle it?"

"I never get sick," Bill said. "Or hung over."

"Come on, then."

They went downstairs. Things had changed with evening. Half the scruffy men along the far wall now pedaled stationary bikes while the other half sat on them and leaned on the handlebars. All huffed breath. Sweaty. Christmas tree lights zigzagged the ceiling of the hall. It looked like a dystopia-themed high school prom. Music leaked tinnily from unseen stereo speakers.

"That sounds familiar," Mortimer said. "What is that?"

"It's Tony Orlando," Bill said. "'Knock Three Times.'"

Mortimer shook his head. "Jesus."

"No, Tony Orlando."

A bell went off, like a doorbell chime. The resting guys on the stationary bicycles started pedaling, and the half who'd been pedaling rested. The Christmas tree lights dimmed momentarily during the changeover, Tony Orlando's voice stretching into slow motion, then picking up speed again.

Talk about a shitty day job, thought Mortimer.

A man appeared in front of them wearing the worst tuxedo in history, neon orange with a ruffled shirt. He sported a handlebar moustache, and his slicked-down hair was meticulously parted in the middle. It looked like he'd escaped from a psycho ward's barbershop quartet.

"Gentlemen?"

"I want to get a drink," Mortimer said.

He sniffed. "We're switching over to our dinner shift. You'll have to wait."

Bill stuck a finger in his face. "Who the hell are you?"

"I am Emile, the maître d', and I'm sorry, but—"

"Show him the card." Bill elbowed Mortimer.

Mortimer produced the Platinum card. "This?"

Emile's eyes widened; the ends of his moustache twitched. *"Sir!"*

The maître d' turned abruptly, snapped his fingers. Burly men appeared from nowhere. They frantically prepared a table down near the stage, white tablecloth, a candle. Emile ushered them to the table. There was much bowing and hand wringing.

"I humbly and abjectly apologize most profusely," Emile said. "I didn't recognize you, Mr. Tate."

"Forget it."

"Of course, of course. You are obviously a most generous and forgiving—"

"He told you to forget it, friend," Bill said. "Now rustle us up a bottle before I stomp your foppish ass."

Emile's smile strained at the edges. "Yes. Certainly."

"Bring us some vodka and some clean glasses."

Emile left, bowing and muttering under his breath.

"You don't have to be so hard on the help," Mortimer said.

"Hey, you're an important guy now. You can't let these peons piss on your boots."

Mortimer blew out a ragged sigh. "I need that drink."

Bill leaned forward on the table, lowered his voice. "You okay?"

"I went to my house."

Bill nodded. "Let me guess. Your wife wasn't there."

"No."

"It happens."

"A toothless old lady wanted me to fuck her."

"You need a drink."

"Yes."

Emile the neon maître d' returned with a bottle of vodka and two mismatched glasses. He poured as he bowed. He was obsequious as hell. "The waitresses have yet to come on duty, but it is my delight to bring your bottle myself so you don't have to wait."

Mortimer tossed back the vodka. It burned his throat. He tried to thank the maître d' but erupted into a coughing fit instead.

"Mort says thanks, now fuck off," Bill told Emile.

Emile left the bottle on the table, rolled his eyes as he walked away.

"This tastes like kerosene," Mortimer said.

"Don't be ridiculous. Did you ever drink kerosene before?"

Mortimer admitted he hadn't.

"Then don't talk crazy." Bill tilted the bottle, filled up Mortimer's glass again.

They both drank, winced, filled their glasses again.

"I don't know where my wife is," Mortimer said. "If she's even alive."

Bill nodded, slurped booze. "It's tough to keep track of kinfolk in the new world."

Kinfolk. Bill's cowboy act got cornier the more he drank. Mortimer didn't mind. He liked Bill. He liked drinking with someone again. If he let his eyes glaze over and listened to the music and forgot how toxic the vodka was, Mortimer could almost believe he was enjoying happy hour after work with coworkers from the insurance company, that he'd go home a little drunk, make love to his wife. Anne. Where was she?

He grabbed the bottle. Shook it. Empty. "Damn."

Bill snapped his fingers. "Another bottle, you greasy bastard!"

Emile returned. A frown had replaced his strained smile. He wasn't even pretending anymore. "What?"

Bill returned the frown. "Keep a civil tongue, you . . . you . . ."

"Varmint," Mortimer suggested.

"Yeah! You motherfucking varmint asshole."

"What do you want?" demanded Emile. His moustache had drooped. The maître d's haughty air had been completely defeated by the Platinum card. All he could do was endure.

"Booze!"

Emile slunk away, and Mortimer watched him go. He couldn't summon any pity for the man. Mortimer was too wrapped up in his own thoughts, too enamored by the fuzzy Christmas tree lights, too light-headed from the vodka. What would he do now? How long could he sit here drinking poison before he was forced to determine what happened next? Mortimer Tate had not considered what his life would be at the bottom of the mountain.

Emile paused to talk to a skinny, dark-eyed man leaning in the doorway. Mortimer thought him familiar. Emile nodded at the newcomer, pointed toward Mortimer's table. Had Buffalo Bill's rude behavior caused trouble? Where the hell was that bottle? Mortimer still thought the skinny man looked somewhat familiar.

"Your wife might not even be alive," Bill said.

Mortimer flinched at the statement. "What?"

"I remember getting lost in the food riots back then. It was rough. I found my way home, found my dad in the living room, blood all over the place. Somebody had smashed his head in with a pipe or something. The house had been ransacked. I waited and waited by his body for my mom to come home, you know? I never did find out what happened. Never." Bill's eyes were focused someplace far away, years into the past. "I thought later, you know, what if she'd come home and found Dad dead? What if she'd just left and saved herself and didn't wait for me? I always thought—" Bill's voice caught; he shook his head, cleared his throat. "Where's that fucking bottle?"

Emile came back just in time, filled their glasses from the new bottle. Bill drank quickly, eyes down, face clouded with dark memories.

Mortimer could see Bill didn't want to talk about it, but Mortimer couldn't help himself. He peppered the cowboy with questions. How many had died? Was anything being done? What was this world they now lived in? Did people still vote? Was there still an America? The answers were all the same. Everything had changed.

Emile bent to speak softly into Mortimer's ear. "Professor Coffey wonders if he could join you for a drink."

Mortimer lifted an eyebrow. "Who?"

"The owner, sir."

"Uh . . . okay."

The name, the face. So damn familiar.

The lanky man came over and sat in between Bill and Mortimer. "Hello, Mort. I thought it was you."

Recognition snapped into focus. "Pete Coffey!"

Bill raised an eyebrow.

"This is Pete Coffey," Mortimer said. "We were on the baseball team in high school together."

Bill nodded. "How do."

"Last I heard you were an English professor at Georgetown."

Coffey shrugged. "I taught classics. Georgetown is radioactive rubble now. I was home for my mother's funeral, or I'd have bought it with the rest of my department."

"I'm sorry to hear it," Mortimer said. "Your mother, I mean."

"It's okay."

"You're the owner of this place?"

A smile flickered across the professor's face. "Half owner. Joey Armageddon owns half of all the places. Some local guy—in this case, me—owns the other half."

"Where's the government?" Mortimer blurted.

"Once in a while we get something on the short-wave," Coffey said. "Some air force general in Colorado Springs claims to represent the government. Then other times we hear about some low-level cabinet secretary holed up in Omaha saying she's constitutionally in charge." A shrug. "It doesn't really matter."

"Doesn't matter?" Mortimer poured vodka, shook his head. "I can't believe it."

"You're drinking that?" Coffey asked.

"It's—*hic*—good," Bill said.

"No, it's not," Coffey said. "It's a shortcut to the Hershey squirts. Like washing out your bowels with battery acid." He waved at Emile, and the maître d' was at Coffey's elbow in an instant. "Bring the Bombay from the safe in my office. And the lime juice. Silas knows the combination."

Bill gaped. "You got limes? Where'd you get limes?"

"Nobody has limes," Coffey said. "We got six little cans of lime juice in trade last month, and I've hoarded them for myself. The Bombay too."

"I miss oranges." Bill sounded wistful. "Any citrus."

"Nothing comes up from Florida," Coffey said. "Not for a year now."

Emile arrived with a half-full bottle of Bombay Sapphire, a can of lime juice and a bucket of ice cubes. Coffey mixed the drinks, poured the gin like he was handling nitroglycerin, careful not to spill a drop. He made sure not to pour Bill or Mortimer any more than he poured for himself. At last, they drank.

Contented sighs. All three men closed their eyes, let the booze ease down.

"Damn, that's a hell of a lot better than the vodka, all right," Bill said. "I don't feel like I'm going to die at all."

They sat quietly. The gin demanded respect, so they sipped, didn't talk. Mortimer glanced around; more patrons had crowded into Joey Armageddon's. The song playing now was "Things to Do in Denver When You're Dead" by Warren Zevon. Above the stage, men lowered what looked like shark cages on steel cables. The Christmas tree lights began to blink. Mortimer noticed something else. Something important.

Women.

Scantily clad women moving among the tables, taking drink orders. Some wore tank tops with the hems tied into a knot above the navel. Others wore bikini tops or lace bras. Tight cutoff jeans seemed to be standard.

Mortimer Tate had not had a woman in nine years. Something stirred in his pants, fluttered in his gut. He gawked openly.

Coffey told his story. He'd survived the worst times, helped hold the town together. It was a small town, people knew one another. They'd banded together, fended off marauders from without, despair from within. Coffey was mayor now. More important, he was half-owner of the Spring City Joey Armageddon's. He might as well have been royalty.

"Anne," Mortimer said. "Is she . . . do you know what happened to her?"

Coffey nodded slowly. "Of course. I'd forgotten. Naturally you'd want to know. Sorry, Mort. I really am."

Oh, no. Mortimer's heart froze. *She's dead. How? What happened?*

"I'm truly sorry," Coffey said again. "But I had to sell her."

"No, no, no. It can't be true. It can't. . . ." Mortimer blinked. "Did you say . . . *sell* her?"

"Hey, it wasn't my idea," Coffey said. "Believe me, I wanted to keep her. The customers loved her. She could really shake her ass in the cage."

It was reflex. Mortimer shot out of his chair, knocked it over behind him. His fists came up. This son of a bitch was talking about his wife.

Mortimer froze when he felt the cold metal under his right ear. He turned slightly, saw the big man with the shotgun pushed up against him. *Where did he come from?* He felt something else sticking hard into his ribs on the left side. He unclenched his fists and held his hands up. "No problem here."

"Let's have a seat, sir. Nice and calm." It was Emile, who held a small silver revolver against Mortimer's ribs. "There's a good gentleman."

Mortimer eased down, and somebody slid his chair underneath him.

Emile looked at his boss, raised an eyebrow.

"I think we're okay here," Coffey said. "Mort, you'll behave, right?"

Mortimer nodded, his teeth clenched. The gunmen withdrew. Bill eased his grip on one of the six-shooters. Mortimer noticed Coffey's fist on the table next to his drink. It clutched a little nickel derringer. The saloon owner slowly tucked the pistol back into his belt.

"That was insensitive," Coffey admitted. "I forgot you don't know how things work now."

Mortimer glared outrage. "Selling women as sex slaves? Is that how it is?"

"Don't think of it that way. It's like when the Red Sox trade an outfielder to the Yankees. The new location needed an experienced girl. Anne was happy, Mort. It was a promotion."

"Where did she go?"

"I don't know."

"You're a liar."

Coffey frowned, sighed. "I'm going to try to understand how you feel. I'm going to overlook that you're rude."

"Kiss my ass."

Coffey sighed and stood. "Things have changed, Mort. Adjust." The Christmas lights went wacky, and the music cranked a notch. "Looks like the show's about to start," Coffey said. "You boys enjoy. I have to make the rounds. Check with you later."

The shark cages lowered from the ceiling, and the music

boomed. "Raspberry Beret." There were women in the shark cages. Dancing women.

Naked women.

They thrashed and shook and tossed their hair, an hourglass blonde with big tits in the close cage. Across the stage in the other cage a willowy, athletic redhead undulated and twisted. Joey Armageddon's had filled with hooting, drunken men. It had become hot, a musty, boozy smell filling the place, mixing with musk and tobacco smoke. Mortimer's head swam. Sensory overload. He fumed, but naked women demanded his attention. He reached for his glass of gin, found it empty. The Bombay had disappeared, replaced by another bottle of the lethal vodka.

Mortimer drank. The world blurred.

He heard Bill shouting at him; his voice seemed so far away. Mortimer squinted, looked at the cowboy. One of the waitresses had found her way into Bill's lap. "What?"

"I said loan me some of them Armageddon dollars," Bill shouted.

Mortimer went into his pockets, came out with a handful of coins and shoved them across the table. He reached for the vodka bottle, couldn't quite grab it. His depth perception was in the toilet.

Mortimer felt himself floating, felt he was leaving his body, drifting amid the swirling colors of the Christmas tree lights. He could not make his eyes focus, could not hear specific sounds, the noise and music and conversation all boiling into a single, messy soup. But on some level his brain was working, reaching a new plateau of knowing and understanding and determination. He knew what he would do. He was having an epiphany, a spiritual awakening.

He glanced again at Bill, made his eyes focus. Bill had the waitress's top down, one erect nipple in his mouth. The waitress's hand reached below the table into Bill's lap, pumped.

To hell with spiritual awakening, Mortimer thought. *I want a hand job.*

XII

In his dream, Mortimer smelled coffee.

His eyes flicked open. He rolled over, heaved, launched a stream of acidic puke over the side of the queen-size bed. He lay back, sank into the pillow. Where was he? He tried to focus. Gnomes with miniature sledgehammers were trying to pound his eyes out of their sockets from the inside. He felt like unholy shit. Perhaps if he puked again . . .

He rolled over. Puked again.

The smell of puke made him puke a third time.

Beyond the sour smell of vomit, Mortimer could have sworn he still smelled coffee. Wishful thinking. A nice dream.

Bill burst into his room, holding a ceramic mug. "Wake up, sunshine. Time to— Jesus H. Christ, what happened in here?" He went immediately to a window and opened it wide. The cold wash of air took some of the stench away, felt good on Mortimer's slick face.

Mortimer summoned the energy to say, "Go away. I'm dying."

"If you die, you'll miss the train." Bill shoved the coffee mug at him. "Drink this. You paid enough for it."

Mortimer struggled, grunted, sat up in bed. "What are you talking about?"

"When you bought all that stuff last night. You got some coffee too. Three hundred bucks a pound." Bill shook his head, laughed. "I guess there ain't no more bean boats coming up from Colombia."

Three hundred dollars a pound for coffee? Bill had said he'd bought some things. Mortimer had been so very drunk . . . had spent so much . . . had Bill said . . . ? "What train?"

"It was your idea. When Mr. Coffey came back and said he knew where your wife—"

"Anne! You know where my wife is?"

"Hell, you really don't remember, do you?"

"God damn it, Bill!"

"Mr. Coffey said he felt bad so he asked some questions and found out your wife went to Chattanooga, to the main Joey Armageddon's there. She's going to be head girl or something."

"Christ."

"So you said you were going to get her and bought a bunch of supplies, ammunition and food, and you booked us passage on the Muscle Express."

"The muscle what?"

"The train."

Mortimer looked around the room. He remembered a blur of women, half expected to see one in his bed. "Did I have any company last night?"

"Well, you could have," Bill said. "When they all found out you were the richest guy in the place, you became right popular. But you drank so much. I don't think you could've gotten Mr. Willie to work."

Damn.

Bill lifted the mug again. "This is getting cold. You want it or not?"

"Hell yes." Mortimer took the mug. "I paid for it."

His sipped the coffee. Mortimer's eyes slowly widened. Every molecule in his body came alive. His bones hummed with electricity, the caffeine flowing the pathways of his body, a latent memory in his veins moaning ecstasy, seeming to say, *Oh, yes. This is good. This is right.*

Bill looked alarmed. "You okay, man? What is it?"

Fat tears rolled down Mortimer's cheeks. "Could you leave the room please, Bill? I'd like a moment alone with the coffee."

Once upon a time it had been a whistle stop, an insignificant knot in the great tangle of the American railway. Now, like a thriving port in the endless deserts of the old west, the Spring City train station writhed with activity, a score of stout men loading crates of trade goods (including three hundred gallon-jugs of Freddy's Stain Your Tongue Purple Merlot). The very few passengers who could afford the fare disembarked, looking sore-limbed and happy as hell to be off the train.

The only two people who could afford the fare south were Mortimer and Bill. They stood in the snow next to their gear, hands in pockets, stomping to keep their feet warm. Mortimer swayed in the biting wind, only the caffeine in his veins keeping him upright. His finger stump ached with the cold.

Silas Jones found them, puffing and red faced. He'd run all the way to the station. "I thought I might miss you before the train left, sir. Thank goodness I caught you."

Mortimer belched, and it tasted like death. "What is it?"

Jones presented him with a sheet of paper marked up in pencil. A row of numbers swam before Mortimer's eyes. He looked away. Reading the numbers made him nauseous. "Just give me the gist of it."

"Your final bill," Jones said, handing Mortimer a pen. "If you'll just sign at the bottom, we'll deduct it from your account."

Mortimer took the pen, glimpsed the total at the bottom of the page as he signed. He gulped. Mortimer had spent over two thousand dollars. His newfound wealth would evaporate in a week if he kept spending at this pace. He mentally vowed not to let that happen.

Pete Coffey appeared at Mortimer's elbow. "You look green."

"Don't worry about me," Mortimer said.

"I hope you find her," Coffey said. "Seriously."

"You didn't have to come see me off."

"I didn't. I'm mayor, remember? I always make sure the train goes out on time. I also want to make sure my boys get aboard." Coffey indicated a dozen men climbing aboard the flatcars. All held rifles and looked ready to use them.

"Red Stripes down the line, maybe. Can't take chances."

Mortimer touched the Uzi hanging from its shoulder strap. "I hear you."

"They're bringing the handcar out now," Coffey said. "So you'll be pulling out soon."

"Handcar?"

"Sure," Coffey said. "How do you think we pull the train? It's not like we got a big fat diesel engine. No fuel."

Mortimer shook his head. "Whoa. Wait. You mean guys are going to hand-pump that thing and pull three flatcars and all that cargo? It'll take a hundred years to get to Chattanooga."

"Getting started is the hard part. Once they get into a rhythm, you'd be surprised. Here come the pumpers now."

Now Mortimer saw why they called it the Muscle Express. The eight men designated to operate the specially modified hand-car were brutes, hulking, shirtless men with rippling muscles. The smallest was just over six feet tall, three hundred and fifty pounds.

"Four rest while four pump," Coffey explained. "Doc!"

"I'm here." A frumpy man with disheveled gray hair waddled forward, clutching a black doctor's bag dangling from a gnarled hand. He fished an inoculation gun out of the bag and zapped each muscleman in the arm.

"Speed boost," Coffey said.

The musclemen flexed, their faces turning red, grunting and posing, a light sheen of sweat on their muscles. It looked like a really angry Chippendales show.

"They'll be ready to go now. Better climb on," Coffey said. "Once those guys get going, they don't let up."

Buffalo Bill had already tossed the gear onto the nearest flatcar. He jumped up and held out a hand for Mortimer. "Let's get a move on, partner."

Mortimer took the cowboy's hand and let himself be heaved onto the flatcar. He broke out in a sweat from the minor exertion, the wind sending a chill to the marrow of his bones. He sat on the flatcar, looked back at Coffey, who stood waving. The train was inching forward, almost imperceptibly slow at first. The pumpers heaved and grunted and leaned into the hand pump, their muscles bulging, faces turning red.

Belatedly, Mortimer returned the wave, the Spring City train station shrinking behind them. The grunts and groans from the hand pumpers finding a rhythm, the meaty machine, a new-world locomotive narcotic-fueled and lubricated with sweat.

THE MUSCLE EXPRESS

XIII

Mortimer noticed the cars straight off, half-buried in snow, the old metal husks like beer cans of the gods, crushed and tossed without heed along the roadside, the debris of some cosmic tailgate party. Others seemed obscenely new, bright fiberglass bodies sitting on the rotted remains of tires. The old junkers had been cleared out of Spring City, but now, as the Muscle Express glided the rails parallel to Highway 27 south, Mortimer remembered how it had been, the millions of automobiles plying America's roadways. Where did you want to go today? The store for milk, Sunday church, take the kids to Disney World? It had all been so close, so possible.

An hour and a half's drive to Chattanooga would now be a three-day walk. The world had grown smaller and smaller until it exploded into bigness again, distances stretching, horizons meaning something.

But Mortimer and Bill weren't walking. The Muscle Express had picked up speed, the cold wind stinging his eyes.

"How fast, you think?" asked Mortimer.

Bill squinted, tried to judge. "Maybe thirty miles per hour. Not more than that. Pretty good though. Better than hoofing it."

Mortimer leaned out, looked ahead to the handcar. Four brutes pumping, four others resting. No more unleaded for cars, no more diesel for locomotives. He wondered how many Armageddon dollars it would be worth if he salvaged a steam engine.

Somebody had bolted four movie theater seats at the back of the middle flatcar. Bill and Mortimer occupied two of them, Mortimer slouched low, trying to ignore his stomach. The cowboy thumbed shells into the lever-action rifle.

A slender figure appeared atop the crates in front of them, looked down on the two passengers in the theater seats. The newcomer's face wasn't clear at first, a dark silhouette against the morning sun. Mortimer held up a hand, shaded his eyes to get a look. A woman.

"Don't puke on my train," she said.

Mortimer looked down, closed his eyes. It took too much energy to hold his head up. "Your train?"

"I'm Tyler Kane. I'm the train captain."

She hopped down from the crates, and Mortimer got a better look at her. Athletically thin, hard body like a track star. She wore black leather pants and a matching leather jacket too light for the cold, a white turtleneck underneath. A nickel-plated revolver sprung from her waistband. Her hair was a burgundy red, cut close on the sides and spiked on top. A black patch covered her left eye, and a thin white scar leaked from under the patch and ran straight down to the edge of her angular jawline. Her one eye was bright and blue as an arctic lake. She had the palest skin Mortimer had ever seen on someone still alive.

"You're paying passengers, so you don't have to do anything except stay out of the way," Tyler said. "If we're attacked, be prepared to help repel boarders. If you vomit, stick your head over the side. Any questions?"

"When does the stewardess come around to take my drink order?"

Tyler's upper lip curled into a half-smile, half-sneer. "You make me laugh. I'll make sure you land on something soft if I have to toss you over the side."

She leapt past them onto the third flatcar.

"Nice," Bill said. "I think she likes you."

Mortimer only grunted, sank lower in his seat. It was too fucking cold. He climbed down to the backpacks, went through the gear until he found the down-filled sleeping bag. He curled up on the floor of the flatcar, the clattering ride rocking him to sleep.

In the dream, the man's scream was a shrill steam whistle, and the train traveled over water instead of land. Somehow the train floated. Pirates rowed toward them in Viking longships, oars dipping into water, prows beating against the wake left by the train. They fired a cannon. The train shuddered, waves coming over the side.

Mortimer's body shook and shook.

"God damn it! I said get your ass up right fucking now!"

Mortimer's eyes flashed open, panic shooting up his spine.

Tyler Kane had a tight grip on his jacket, jerking him away. Mortimer sat up, found he was clutching the Uzi to his chest. Gunshots. Screams.

"What is it?"

"Can you use that thing?" She nodded at the Uzi.

"Yes." He had only fired it once to test it. But it was a simple weapon.

"Then come on!" She dragged him up, and they climbed onto the cargo crates. "We've got to get forward."

Mortimer saw Bill crouched behind the theater seats. He worked the lever action, fired into the buildings along the railroad tracks. It looked like Evansville. Men on the roof and at windows fired at the train. Mortimer caught a glimpse of a red armband.

They were going too slow. Targets like the sharpshooter game at a carnival.

They stood, jogged at a crouch along the flatcar's cargo crates. A bullet whizzed past Mortimer's ear like a subsonic hornet.

Tyler grabbed Mortimer's elbow and jumped, pulling Mortimer down with her. They landed between two crates, crouched behind the cargo while she took something from her jacket pocket.

Bullets ricocheted. Mortimer's heart thumped up into his throat.

"Why are we going so slow?"

"We were coming into the station," Tyler said. "Evansville is a scheduled stop. The Red Stripes jumped us, but the pumpers are exhausted."

Mortimer saw what she'd taken from her pocket, the inoculation gun the doctor had used to juice the muscle guys back in Spring City.

"You've got to cover me," she said. "I need time to power up the guys again. Man, you've got to shoot that thing and keep those fuckers off me. You get it?"

Mortimer tried to speak but found his mouth too cottony. He nodded.

She slapped him on the shoulder. "Let's go!"

They climbed up again, made their way forward to the end of the flatcar. He cocked the little machine gun, thumbed off the safety. One of the train guards hung limp and dead between the flatcar and the handcar, the back of his head wet and bloody from a large-caliber slug. They leapt over him and landed with a thud on the big handcar.

The stink of sweat slapped Mortimer in the face. The muscle guys pumped, hot, wet skin steaming in the freezing air. A shot caught one of them in the head, brain and skull and blood exploding red and gunky. He toppled over, hit the deck of the handcar with a meaty thump and rolled off.

Tyler punched Mortimer in the shoulder. "Shoot!"

He brought the Uzi up and sprayed the buildings along the track, shattering windows, gouging holes in brick. Wherever he saw a Red Stripe pop his head up, Mortimer squeezed off a burst and sent him back into hiding. He ejected the spent magazine, slapped in a new one. The muzzle smoked. His palms and fingers tingled from gripping the gun so tight, the pinkie stump throbbing.

He glanced over his shoulder and saw Tyler placing the inoculation gun against thick shoulders, injecting the narcotic boost. It took only a few seconds. Veins pulsed along necks. Eyes bulged. Faces clenched. They pumped harder.

They picked up speed.

"Up there!" Tyler pointed ahead of the train.

A narrow pedestrian bridge crossed low over the railroad tracks. At least a dozen Red Stripes jogged across the bridge to take up positions. Mortimer edged around the pumping musclemen, ran to the front of the handcar and knelt at the very edge of the train. Cold wind stung his eyes. He brought up the Uzi. The men on the bridge leveled their rifles.

The Uzi bucked in Mortimer's hands.

Red Stripes along the bridge clutched themselves, toppling over, their death screams filling the air. Mortimer looked back as the handcar and the first flatcar passed under the bridge. A handful of surviving Red Stripes leapt from the bridge onto the middle flatcar.

Tyler had finished drugging the pumpers and motioned to Mortimer. "Come on. Let's get them."

Get them? Fuck you. But he followed her.

The half-dozen Red Stripes were locked in hand-to-hand combat with the surviving few train guards. Mortimer climbed atop the cargo crates, leveled the Uzi but couldn't get a shot. It was an erratic weapon, and he was as likely to hit the guards as the Red Stripes.

He saw Bill jump up from the theater seats and swing his rifle butt at the head of a Red Stripe, who ducked underneath and tackled the cowboy. They both hit the deck. Mortimer dropped the Uzi and drew the police special.

They were out of the town now, the train rolling along much faster. Tyler and Mortimer ran along the top of the crates, the rocking train threatening to toss them over the side. They hit the melee just as one of the guards took a knife in the stomach and dropped off the speeding train.

Tyler put her revolver against the back of a Red Stripe's head, pulled the trigger. Half the Red Stripe's head flew away into the wind, the body falling.

Mortimer went for the Red Stripe on top of Bill, but another stepped in swinging a club. It caught Mortimer in the gut. He whuffed air, tumbled over and hit the crates hard. He turned, fired his police special vaguely in the direction of his attacker.

The blast shattered the Red Stripe's ankle. He yelled hoarse and agonized from the throat, hopped on his good leg for a moment before the train lurched and tossed him over the side, trailing blood.

Mortimer climbed to his knees, sucking breath and gagging. He probed his side with tentative fingers but found nothing broken.

He looked around. All of the train guards and Red Stripes were dead. Bill stood over his bloody opponent, Bill's right eye swelling where he'd taken a punch.

Tyler stuck the revolver back in her waistband. "I think we're past the Red Stripes for now." She wiped sweat from her face. "If we can just get through the cannibals, I think we'll make it."

XIV

"I'm sorry." Mortimer blinked. "But did you just say *cannibals,* or have I gone crazy?"

"I'll explain later. Right now the pumpers are overdosed and I have to bring them down before they all have heart attacks." She dashed off in the direction of the handcar, her perfect balance a tribute to long experience on the rocking flatcars. *Train legs instead of sea legs.*

Bill flopped into one of the theater seats. "I'm out of shells for the rifle."

"You okay?"

Bill nodded. "Guy jumped me before I could get the pistols out."

"Stay here. I'll see if she needs any help."

Mortimer climbed forward after Tyler. He noticed the train had slowed again to the pace of a fast walk. He reached the handcar and found most of the musclemen slumped on the deck, eyes closed, massive chests rising and falling with shallow breaths. Greasy piles of meat. Only two of the big brutes remained to work the hand pump.

Mortimer watched Tyler put two fingers to a man's throat, shake her head and roll him off the train.

"What happened?"

"His heart exploded," Tyler said. "I couldn't dose him in time. The two pumping are on a half-dose of downer juice. When they get tired, I'll wake up two more to take over. Best we can do for now."

"Can't we just stop for a while?"

She shook her head, squinted up at the sun. "At this pace, we won't reach our destination in daylight. It's dangerous to run at night, but worse if we stop."

Mortimer remembered she'd said something about cannibals. He gulped. "Right."

"I need your help now," she said. "Get to the back end of the train and keep watch. We don't want anything crawling up our tailpipe while we're going this slow."

He flicked her a two-finger salute and headed back the way he'd come. He picked up the Uzi along the way and paused to tell Bill he'd be guarding the back of the train.

"I'll keep my eyes peeled here," Bill said.

Mortimer went into the gear and found a box of 9 mm ammunition, winked at Bill and headed back.

He sat with his feet dangling over the back of the last flatcar. The track dwindled behind. Forest had cropped up on either side, although he occasionally glimpsed a stretch of road or power lines, a small abandoned house. A barn. He thumbed new shells into the Uzi's magazine, reloaded the police special. He wished he had cigarettes. Mortimer had never smoked, but lighting up a Lucky seemed like something soldiers on guard duty did in the movies.

Miles and hours crept away, never to be seen again.

In spite of the cold wind on his neck and ears, Mortimer started to drift, the rocking train easing his eyelids down. He slumped, the Uzi heavy in his lap. With the adrenaline rush from the attack fading, the aches and nausea of his hangover seeped back into his body. He'd pay a hundred Armageddon dollars for three hours back in the hotel bed.

Joey Armageddon's, the hotel, the food, the drink, the lights. It had all fooled Mortimer, lulled him into forgetting the world was now a wild and broken place. Could Anne survive out here? This savage country where women were bought and sold like cattle. She seemed far away, and here was Mortimer inching along on a train powered by sweaty men. Mortimer had read those Conan the Barbarian novels as a teenager. It took a barbarian to live in such a world, someone brutal and ruthless with the survival instincts of an animal. Mortimer wasn't a barbarian. He was an insurance salesman. He felt suddenly small and fragile. He needed Starbucks and Krispy Kreme and Jiffy Lube.

Mortimer dreamed of Anne in a metal bikini like the one Carrie Fisher wore in *Return of the Jedi*. But she wasn't chained to Jabba the Hutt. She was chained to Arnold Schwarzenegger, but not the Conan Schwarzenegger. It was Arnold from *The Terminator,* the flesh peeled away from half his skull, revealing the metal underneath. One eye glowing red.

This is my woman now, said the Terminator.

No! That's my wife.

Take him away, barked the Terminator.

Men grabbed him, took him to the Thunderdome, where Mad Max tried to kill him. No, not Mad Max. Mel Gibson handing him a big wooden cross. *Carry this.* He stuck a crown of thorns on Mortimer's head. The thorns tore flesh, blood running into his eyes.

Mortimer looked at the blood in the palm of his hand. The

blob of blood became a glowing light, blinking red. Michael York grabbed his arm. *Run! Run!*

Mortimer ran. He was in a bright city. They were chasing him. He ran and ran until the world was a blur, a forest, then a desert, then the ruined buildings of a deserted town. Anne! Anne! Where was she? And even if he found her, then what? How would they live? Where would they go? Mortimer thought he was rescuing her. He couldn't even save himself.

He felt somebody grab him, looked up at Kurt Russell with long hair and an eye patch. *Come on. We've got to escape from here.*

Leave me alone. I'm too tired.

"I said wake up." The voice had become feminine but with a hard edge.

Mortimer started, blinked. Kurt Russell's face morphed into somebody else. Only the eye patch remained.

"You'd better not be falling asleep," Tyler warned.

Mortimer dug the sleep out of his eyes with a thumb. "No, of course not."

"Uh-huh." Tyler looked doubtful. "It's going to be dark soon, and I need you on your toes."

"I hate to even ask this, but when you say *cannibals,* are you being figurative? I mean, is it a gang that calls themselves the Cannibals or something?"

Tyler leaned down, pinched the flesh of his cheek. "They'd fry you up and serve you with little red potatoes, man. Now stay awake." She went forward again.

"They'd find me very chewy," he shouted after her.

Great. I'm going to be an entrée.

The train crawled along like an anemic box turtle. The sun

sank, and in the final orange fuzz of daylight, Bill came back to the end flatcar, sat next to Mortimer. He cradled the lever-action rifle, the last rays of the sun making his complexion ruddy and outdoorsy. He looked like the cover of a Louis L'Amour novel.

"She wants you up front," Bill said.

What now?

He clapped the cowboy on the shoulder. "Stay awake."

He made his way forward, moving more easily this time, getting used to the sway of the train. He found most of the sleeping meat snoring on the deck of the handcar, except for the two at the hand pump. Tyler waved him over, handed him a big, heavy flashlight.

"Get up to the front of the train. It'll be full dark soon. I don't usually like to run at night, but it can't be helped. I need you to watch for obstructions."

"Right." He started for the front.

She grabbed his arm tight, looked down at the flashlight. "I'm not even going to tell you what a flashlight and rechargeable batteries cost. You drop it over the side and—"

"I know, I know. You'll toss me over and feed me to the cannibals and blah blah blah."

"Just so you understand."

He took his position up front. The sun finished its escape, and the night went dark and cold quickly. Mortimer flipped on the flashlight, and the beam stabbed out far and strong, lighting up the track a good fifty feet in front of the train.

Mortimer kept his eyes on the track but allowed himself a glance at the sky. The stars hung bright and vivid in the deep black of space. With the wind in his hair, the light out front, Mortimer almost felt like he was flying, the train gliding along smooth and straight.

The forest widened, the trees falling away on both sides. They were on a long bridge. Mortimer fished around with the flashlight. They were crossing over a river. It must have been one of the dozens of middling-sized rivers that fed the Chickamauga. It would be deep and cold with mountain runoff. Mortimer leaned over the edge, looked down, the flashlight beam playing over the running water. He estimated it maybe twenty-five feet down. His gaze came back up, away from the river.

A face, slack jawed, haunted eyes.

It startled him. Mortimer gasped. It had only been a second, a glimpse. But Mortimer was sure he'd seen a pale figure, greasy haired, standing on the bridge at the edge of the track. He leaned over the side, shined the light back the way they'd come.

Nothing. Had he imagined it?

He swung the light back forward again. A gap in the track, twenty feet away, the metal rails twisted and scorched as if from a blast. Mortimer's eyes shot wide. He drew breath to scream a warning.

Too late.

The handcar dove into the gap, jammed and jerked to a halt, the flatcars piling up behind. The crash was a shattering mix of splintering wood and groaning, clanging metal. He heard a number of screams, the loudest his own as he flew headlong onto the railroad track ahead of the train. He landed hard, the wind knocking out of him. He rolled and tumbled.

Then he was flying, wind flapping his clothes. Stars flashed over him, then his breath was taken away by the freezing sting of impact. The river closed over him like a cold tomb. He bounced against a rock, kicked, paddled, surfaced. He had time for one ragged breath before the river took him down again.

Mortimer spun and tumbled in the dark water, the current sweeping him an unknown distance in time and space, the cold searing him to the bone with white-hot pain. His lungs burned. He broke the surface again, gasped and gulped breath, taking in water too. He coughed and picked a direction in the implacable night, kicked and stroked for the bank. The icy water had sapped him.

He was about to give up when he touched bottom, dragged himself onto the land and flopped on his back in the patchy snow and mud. He lay a moment, chest heaving as he sucked air. Every limb screamed murder.

The ripple of orange along the water made him sit up. He'd come down the river farther than he'd thought, the current so swift. In the distance, hellish light bathed the bridge. The Muscle Express burned, the flames reaching into the sky.

It must have been visible for miles and miles.

XV

Shivering, aching and cramped from the cold, his wet clothes clinging to him, it took Mortimer nearly an hour to pick his way along the steep bank until he stood almost directly below the blazing train. He stood in its heat, let the warmth spread through him.

Had Tyler been aboard? Bill? He shuddered to think of them burning alive.

But there had been no fuel. The train had been powered by muscle. What had caused the fire? Or who? The same people who'd sabotaged the track. An ambush. He jerked his head around, scanning the tree line. Nobody.

He had to get ankle-deep in the water again to make his way to the other side of the bridge. He found crates busted open. The train had been looted. His eyes raked the water and the far bank. No bodies. Where were the muscle guys? Had Mortimer been the only one thrown clear? The bodies had been taken.

Cannibals.

A shiver crawled up Mortimer's spine that had nothing to do with the cold.

Turn around and walk the other way.

But he didn't. At the very least he owed Bill. He had to know, had to see. He started walking upriver, keeping close to the bank, clueless where else to go.

. . .

Soon he'd have to stop and build a fire and damn if anyone saw. Hypothermia was fast becoming a bigger worry than cannibals. But Mortimer had no matches, and if he did, they'd be soaked. He could rub sticks together until doomsday and never get a fire. Everything near the river was snow-soaked and muddy.

Why had he come down from the mountain? There was no point in continuing. He'd lost the Uzi. The police special was at the bottom of the river. He couldn't rescue Bill even if he was still alive. All of Mortimer's possessions were lost, even the Armageddon dollars.

He'd have traded every last Armageddon dollar he had for dry clothes and matches.

A cup of hot coffee.

He marched on. *Lie down and sleep. Go ahead,* his body said. *Slip into that final dream without thought or pain.* The idea was so seductive. That he could give up, curl into a ball and simply drift off forever.

A hamburger would have been nice.

Through the dense trees up the bank, Mortimer glimpsed a flicker of orange. He jogged toward it, wove a crooked path among the trees. The fire was farther than it had seemed at first, and Mortimer soon slowed to a ragged walk, stumbling in the dark, tree branches scraping his face, roots catching his toe.

He tripped, fell face-first flat into cold leaves and mud.

Mortimer sighed, heaved himself up on his elbows and summoned the energy to get to his feet.

He heard the scream and went flat again.

The second scream was worse than the first, a panicked, terrified, agonized howl.

Mortimer could not make himself move forward. Petrified.

The screams came again, a series of hopeless cries mixed with indistinguishable pleading and sobbing, each wail turning his spine into jelly.

Even worse than the screams was the chanting, low and guttural. Mortimer couldn't quite make it out, but it seemed to be the same word over and over again. He had to know, had to find out. Even as he told himself *Run,* he found himself slinking forward, crawling on his belly like a lizard, slithering through the dead leaves and the sparse undergrowth.

It seemed to go on for hours, the hideous screaming and chanting, Mortimer's edging closer an inch at a time. It must have only been twenty minutes.

A lifetime of pain and evil could be packed into twenty minutes.

Mortimer was close enough now to hear the many voices chanting.

"Meat. Meat. Meat."

Turn around. Run, you dumb son of a bitch.

"Meat. Meat. *MEAT!*"

Another scream punctuated the chant. The crowd paused to raise an ugly, jeering cheer before resuming. "Meat. Meat. Meat."

Mortimer flattened himself against a fallen tree. *Raise your head and look. You wanted to see this. Look.*

He raised his head but suddenly squeezed his eyes shut tight. He could feel the heat from the bonfire on his face. *Open your eyes. Do it. Look now. Do it.*

Mortimer opened his eyes.

It took him a long moment to completely realize the scope of the horror.

He looked into a large compound, a group of Appalachian savages swaying and pumping fists around a big bonfire. *Meat meat meat.* They all wore ragged denim, many in overalls. Beat-up hats pulled tight on greasy heads. Some macabre version of the Hatfields and McCoys. Some held rifles, but many others clutched crude spears with heads of jagged metal.

Just to the left of the fire, several figures had been tied to poles stuck in the ground. Like a captured safari party in a bad Tarzan movie. He saw two of the musclemen and Tyler. Bill was there too. Even at this distance, Mortimer recognized their terror-stricken expressions. They waited to be eaten.

Much closer to the fire, a table made out of a large wooden door had been propped up at a forty-five-degree angle. One of the muscle guys had been tied spread-eagle on the table. A splash of red gore stained the table where his left leg used to be. He stared vacantly into the night sky. Catatonic.

Mortimer realized he was watching the whole scene through some sort of makeshift fence only three feet away. A closer examination turned his stomach. The fence had been constructed of old, bleached bones. Toothy skulls capped the posts. How many gruesome meals did those bones represent?

A loud voice snapped Mortimer's attention back to the bonfire.

A tall figure, gaunt, hands raised like some savage priest's. Dark paint around his eyes, making him look like a raccoon. "We have conquered the train that dares invade the clan's territory!"

A cheer from the crowd.

Mortimer propped himself up on the fallen tree, craned his neck for a closer look.

The priest wore a large necklace of finger bones. A wide black belt from which hung a rusting cavalry saber. High black boots. A black cape, probably looted from some costume shop. He'd have looked almost comic if not for the glint of fire reflecting in his demon eyes.

The priest's voice carried over all. "We are the clan, and we absorb the strength of our enemies through blood. Nothing is forbidden us!"

Another cheer.

"Bring forth the butcher! Take the other leg!"

Wild cheering, followed by the chant. *Meat meat meat!*

A hairy brute emerged from the crowd. A short man but wide, a bulging fireplug. He wore a stained leather apron, various knives and cleavers dangling from his belt. An orange Tennessee Volunteers cap. He clutched a gleaming hacksaw in his thick hand and approached the muscle guy strapped to the table.

Dear God . . . But Mortimer couldn't turn away. He watched, transfixed.

The butcher bent over the muscle guy's leg, prodded it with thick, stubby fingers, nodding to himself, egged on by the chanting crowd. The muscle guy still stared ahead at nothing, deep in his horror-induced trance. The butcher set the saw's teeth against flesh, high up the thigh.

Meat meat meat!

The saw blade bit deep, the butcher leaning all of his weight into it. Bright blood fountained. The muscle guy was yanked back to reality, screamed and thrashed against his bonds, eyes bulging. The butcher was relentless, sawing back and forth with long, hard strokes. Blood sprayed his apron and face.

Mortimer turned away and vomited.

At last, the screams stopped. Perhaps the muscle guy had passed out, or maybe he'd simply died from shock and blood loss. Mortimer poked his head up again, fearing what he might see.

The legless muscleman twitched and drooled, eyes hollow, seeing nothing. The butcher carried the leg to a small group of cannibals who already had the other leg lashed to a spit attached to two long poles. Once they'd attached the other leg, the cannibals held the legs over the fire. The smell of roasting human almost made Mortimer throw up again.

"Break out the fermented blood," the priest shouted. "Tonight we party!"

The most enthusiastic cheer yet. A group of cannibals produced instruments: mandolin, guitar, harmonica and bongo drum. They played—something between bluegrass and adult contemporary. Some danced around the fire. When the meat had cooked, portions of leg were sliced off and passed around. Lips smacked. The butcher brought the arms and torso to be cooked.

Mortimer went flat on his belly again. He couldn't watch any longer. He crawled around the camp trying to edge closer to the prisoners. The thought he could free his friends was laughable. But he had to see, had to be able to tell himself in the deep dark of future restless nights that he'd tried.

The music, the hellish orange of the bonfire, the chanting and dancing and occasional scream all mixed to form a portrait of hell that would have made Dante piss his pants.

Mortimer belly-crawled until the cold and wet and the long night sapped all that was left of him. He curled against a stump, clapped his hands over his ears in a futile attempt to keep out the nauseating racket of the vile barbecue only a hundred feet away. He lay exhausted and defeated. *Sorry, Bill.*

Sleep took him finally, and he dreamed of unspeakable things.

XVI

Soft voices woke him. Mortimer's eyes pried themselves open.
Darkness. He blinked a few times, and shadows took shape. The
bonfire had dwindled, but there was just enough light to see after
his eyes had adjusted. His subconscious had mercifully padlocked
the nightmares into an unused corner of his mind. Still, a vague
dread weighed heavily on him.

He lay perfectly still, listened. The cannibals' party had waned
and finally petered out. But those voices, somewhere close in the
night. He tilted his head only slightly. The voices were just around
the other side of the stump, two women.

The first voice: "I'm so tired. Some party."

The other: "Yes. Roger's sleeping it off."

"Isn't it your anniversary? I thought Doris was on guard duty
with me tonight."

"She's not feeling well, and Roger couldn't get it up anyway.
He had *so* much fermented blood."

"I get a little tired of the fermented blood sometimes."

A pause. "Really?"

"It seems so long since I had a nice glass of wine or a Dr. Pep-
per."

"You really don't like the fermented blood? Seriously?"

"Oh, I like it. Don't get me wrong. The fermented blood is
great. Love the fermented blood, but . . ."

"A little bit overkill with all the human flesh and everything?"

"*Exactly*. Sometimes I'd trade it all for a nice green salad and a glass of Shiraz."

"I hear you. But you wouldn't give it up. The blood and the human flesh and the whole lifestyle. You don't mean that, do you?"

"No, of course not. All my friends are here."

As the women spoke, Mortimer had stealthily slunk around the stump, froze when he saw a pair of slim legs wearing pink-and-black cowboy boots stretching away from the stump. The women appeared to be leaning against the stump, facing back toward the compound. They probably should have been facing out instead. A little luck at last. Now Mortimer could slink away without their seeing. He prepared to do just that, when one of the women stood and stretched.

"I'm going to take a wee-wee. Back soon." She picked her way through the bushes and out of sight.

Mortimer changed his plan, hardly even thought about it.

He circled the stump and grabbed the remaining woman, pulled her toward him. She drew breath for a scream, but Mortimer quickly clapped a hand over her mouth. His other arm went around her throat. She struggled, kicked.

Her hands came up, tried to claw his eyes, but he pulled her down, squeezed. He wanted to end it quickly, crushed her windpipe with his forearm. She went stiff briefly, then limp in his arms. He put her back in front of the stump, arranged her to look as if she'd curled up asleep. A crude spear leaned against the trunk and he grabbed it, darted back to his hiding place on the other side of the stump.

His hands shook; his breathing was shallow, verging on hyperventilation. He'd never killed anyone with his bare hands before. Up close. A woman.

He held the spear, squatting and ready to spring.

A long way off an owl hooted.

The other woman returned.

"Jesus, Lydia, you're not supposed to sleep on guard duty. What if . . . Lydia?"

Mortimer went for her, spear held out front. He saw this one's face and almost balked. She looked young, dark hair in a ponytail, expression wide-eyed and innocent like the naïve daughter on a feminine hygiene commercial. Her mouth fell open, and Mortimer struck.

The spearhead caught her square in the throat. Blood bubbled out of her mouth. He yanked out the spear, stabbed her again in the chest. She sank to her knees, coughed more blood and fell on top of her friend.

These hadn't been the cannibals Mortimer had expected, not drooling savages with bones through the nose. They could have been members of the PTA. Soccer moms. *God, forgive me.*

Then he remembered the grotesque cookout only a few hours earlier.

He knelt next to the bodies, searched them. The one he'd speared had a good bowie knife with an eight-inch blade. He took it, strapped it to his belt. He coveted their dry clothing, but they were both too small. He checked their pockets, had hoped for the miracle of a book of matches. No luck.

Without thinking, Mortimer headed for the sleeping camp.

There was a gap in the bone fence wide enough for one person to walk through at a time. Mortimer went in, crouching low and grasping the spear with tight, nervous hands. The stench of scorched flesh mixed with campfire smoke still hung in the air.

In the dim, dirty orange light, Mortimer now saw a line of shabby huts on the other side of the compound, crude dwellings pieced together from mismatched scraps of wood. His eyes darted in all directions. Presumably, there were other guards. Mortimer kept to the shadows as he crept toward the poles where the limp bodies of his friends were still tied.

He went to Bill first, lifted his head, slapped his face lightly. *Come on, man. Wake up.*

Bill's eyes creaked open slightly, regarded Mortimer at half-mast. When Bill saw who it was, his eyes shot open with surprise and hope. He opened his mouth to speak, and Mortimer put a hand over it, shook his head. Bill's eyes slowly moved back and forth. He remembered where he was and nodded his head.

Mortimer sliced through the ropes with the bowie knife, and Bill collapsed to the ground. He silently began to rub the circulation back into his legs and wrists.

Tyler's bright, clear eye was already open and alert. She wordlessly urged Mortimer to hurry. He cut her down, and she fell also, a grimace across her face as she bit back a groan. Being tied to a post for hours obviously hadn't been very comfortable.

Mortimer freed the two muscle guys. One of the big men wept openly, and Mortimer shot him an angry glance, mouthed the words *Shut up.* Soon they were all on their feet, headed back for the gap in the fence.

Yells from behind, the whole camp suddenly and angrily rousing from sleep.

"Run!" Mortimer shouted.

He sprinted for the fence, the others staggering behind. Soon they were in the forest, running blind, tree branches lashing them in the darkness. Mortimer stumbled, righted himself, kept running. He risked a glance over his shoulder.

The glow of torches, shouts of pursuit.

"Scatter!" Bill yelled.

Mortimer didn't wait to see where the others went. He picked a direction and ran, his arms and legs shouting hatred at him, his face and arms stinging from a dozen shallow cuts. He ran until the glow of torches faded. He ran until the shouts faded to a muffled murmur and then finally to nothing at all, until his own breathing and his own heartbeat pounding in his ears were the only sounds in the world.

And then he ran some more.

LADIES

XVII

Like so many nightmares, this one involved falling.

First he fell into water, deep and dark and cold, so far into the depths he thought he'd fallen to the center of the earth. But then he splashed through the other side, fell through the branches of a huge tree.

Aching limbs, sopping clothes.

Then something cottony soft broke his fall. Mortimer felt warm and dry. The nightmare feeling ebbed. Perhaps he was dead. That would be a relief. A soft light above him. A clean bright face, blue eyes, blonde hair glowing soft and gold like a halo. Clothed in raiment of white.

An angel. Taking me to Heaven.

She spoke, but Mortimer couldn't understand. Maybe it was Latin. Ancient angel language.

What is it, little angel? Speak to me in your holy tongue.

"I asked if you wanted some soup," the woman said.

Mortimer propped himself up on one elbow, rubbed a knuckle into his eyes. He lay in bed. Clean sheets. He looked around the room. Almost like a hospital room but softer, less sterile, flowered curtains, personal belongings, books and things spread about.

He looked at the woman, who was young and fresh faced. No more than twenty. She wore clean white pajamas. No, not pajamas. Hospital scrubs.

"Where am I?"

"Saint Sebastian's of the Woods," she said, her voice soothing, calm.

A hospital, thought Mortimer, *or some sort of clinic.* Thank God. He'd been found, or some good Samaritan had brought him. He flirted with the brief fantasy that the past nine years had all been a coma delusion, but that was going too far.

The room's heavy curtains were drawn. The light came from a bulb in an overhead fixture.

His many cuts and scrapes had been cleaned. A bandage over a deeper slash under his left eye. A fresh bandage on his pinkie stump. He'd been bathed and wore a clean hospital gown. He ran a hand down the soft cotton.

"Your clothes are in the washing machine," she said.

Washing machine. The words were almost alien to him. He remembered his first washer and dryer, a gift from Anne's parents. It seemed the ultimate luxury when they no longer had to make those weekly trips to the Laundromat.

"Who are you?"

"Ruth. Who are you?"

"Mortimer. How did you find me?"

"Not me," Ruth said. "Mother Lola. She said it was fate to find you just in time."

How far had Mortimer fled in his blind panic? Five miles? More maybe. He remembered being dizzy, pressing on. He didn't remember finally collapsing but figured he must have dropped from exhaustion.

"Did she find anyone else? I was with some other people."

She shook her head. "Just you."

Mortimer felt a pang of regret. He wondered if he'd see Bill again. Found that he hoped he would. The cowboy was the closest thing Mortimer had to a friend.

"It's mushroom soup," Ruth prompted.

He was hungry, famished in fact. "Okay."

She smiled, childlike, as if she'd accomplished something by getting him to eat. "I'll be right back." She left, closed the door behind her.

He sat up, arranged his pillows.

Another woman brought a tray with his soup. She was older, sagging white skin and frightened brown eyes. She approached tentatively, set the tray gently on his lap.

"Thanks."

She gasped, jerked back.

"It's okay," Mortimer said. "I didn't mean to startle—"

She yelped and ran from the room, waving her hands in the air.

Mortimer blinked. "What the fuck?"

He shrugged and picked up the spoon, filled his mouth with mushroom soup. He spooned fast and slurped. In three minutes, he'd finished the whole bowl. He belched and wiped his mouth on a white cloth napkin.

Ruth entered, smiled at the empty bowl. "Oh, my."

"I was hungry."

She held a glass and handed it to him. Water. He drank. It was cool and clean.

Ruth asked, "Is there anything I can get you? Anything you need?"

"I'm trying to think of what to ask," Mortimer said. "Where is this place?"

She frowned. Not angry. A little kid confused. "I told you. Saint Sebastian's of the Woods."

He laughed. "But where is that? I know we're south of Evansville, but I don't know how far."

She offered a blank look in return.

"I was on my way to Chattanooga."

One of her eyebrows went up. "I've heard of that town."

"Uh . . . maybe I'd better talk to . . . who did you say was in charge?"

"Mother Lola."

"A nun?"

The frown again. "None of what?"

"I think I'd better talk to Mother Lola."

"Oh, that won't be any problem at all," Ruth said. "She wants to speak with you too. She says you've been sent to us. You're the talk of the society."

"What society?"

"*The* society. All that is everything. Together we are all the society."

"And when exactly can I see Mother Lola?"

"When she returns."

"Returns from where?"

"From without the society."

"Listen, do you have any drugs or whiskey or anything I can have?" asked Mortimer.

"Do you have pain?" Ruth looked alarmed. "I can treat it with acupuncture. I've been reading a book on how to do it."

"Never mind."

The frightened woman stuck her head in the door again, mouth hanging slightly open as she eyed Mortimer with trepidation.

"It's okay," Ruth said. "You can come in."

She darted in, set Mortimer's clothing on the foot of the bed and scampered out again.

"She'll talk your ear off if you let her."

Ruth laughed.

"Thanks for the soup. I feel better. I think I'd like to get dressed now."

"Of course." She didn't budge.

Mortimer made shooing motions.

Ruth looked toward the door, then back at Mortimer. "Oh." She left, closed the door with a loud click.

He stripped off his gown, naked underneath, and began to dress. He paused, examined his pants and shirt. They were laundered and pressed. Rips had been sewn with fine stitching. Even the socks had been bleached. Boxers lightly starched. He put it all on and felt like a new man.

His boots hadn't been returned to him.

Mortimer went to the window and swept the curtains aside. The boarded-up window surprised him, wide planks fastened snugly crossways. Only a thin slice of light between planks told him it was daylight. He wondered how long he'd been asleep. No clocks in the room.

In the bathroom, he urinated, washed his hands and splashed water in his face. He dried himself with a fluffy white towel. The towel smelled fresh, like a meadow, with just a hint of bleach.

He opened the door and found Ruth waiting for him in the hallway. Fluorescent lights, a slight antiseptic odor. It seemed like any hospital he'd ever been in.

"Feeling okay?" she asked.

"Where are my boots?"

"We don't like to track dirt in from the outside," Ruth said. "They're in storage."

Mortimer noticed Ruth wore fuzzy white bedroom slippers.

"If you're feeling up to it, I can show you around," Ruth offered. "I sensed you were curious about the society. I can show you how we live."

"Sounds good. I am a little curious."

Her smile radiated innocent pleasure. "This way." She motioned for him to follow.

They walked the long hall, passed rooms with closed doors. Sleeping quarters, Ruth explained. A woman Mortimer hadn't seen before passed them, pushing a cart full of clean laundry. She was tall and haggard, late forties with dark circles under her eyes. She wore the same white scrubs and slippers as Ruth. Mortimer wiggled his fingers in a friendly wave. She returned only wide-eyed silence.

They found a stairwell and went down two levels, came out in a wide main corridor.

Mortimer asked, "How big is this place?"

"Three main floors, and then two five-story towers on either side of the garden," she said. "There are two sublevels, housing the kitchens, laundry and other maintenance facilities, including the power station. Sixty-three thousand, five hundred and sixty square feet all together."

She sounded like she'd memorized a brochure. Maybe she had.

Ruth led him through a set of wide double doors into a sudden open space, sunlight pouring down on them. Mortimer estimated it was only just after noon. Trees and plants, fat, ripe tomatoes in ceramic pots surrounded by a chest-high wire fence. The temperature was mild, and Mortimer realized they weren't outside. A huge glass dome arched over them. It was some kind of gigantic arboretum. Completely enclosed, walls rising all around. Mortimer could see blue sky and the towers on either side, but that was all.

An ancient woman tended a dozen goats. There were also chickens and a few ducks. The old woman wore a loose, flowing white gown of light cotton and walked barefoot among the animals. She spotted Ruth and Mortimer, approached and curtsied, her old joints creaking.

"Hello, Ruth. Hello, mister." Her voice sounded like a rusty hinge.

Ruth smiled. "And how are the goats today, Felicity?"

"My mommy says if I milk them all before dinner I'm to have a treat."

Mortimer stared at the old woman. *What the . . . ?*

"You're a good girl, Felicity. Run along and make sure the goats stay out of the tomatoes this time."

Felicity trotted back to the goats, tittering, a creepy burlesque of a little girl's giggle.

Mortimer looked at Ruth. "Is she okay?"

"She has a good way with animals," Ruth said. "Come on. I have so much to show you."

Mortimer followed, a little dazed. *What is going on here?*

They passed through a storage area marked RECREATIONAL EQUIPMENT. Croquet mallets, a Ping-Pong table, Frisbees, horseshoes, a soccer ball and other sporting gear. Mortimer noticed three large archery targets but neither bows nor arrows.

Ruth took him to the first sublevel, where a big hydroponics setup impressed Mortimer. Ruth explained that they grew a variety of sprouts as well as carrots and other vegetables. They had several books on gardening and hydroponics in the hospital library. Gardening had been considered very good therapy during the hospital's heyday, and they'd started with a good variety of seeds.

They paused to watch a young girl about Ruth's age plant seedlings into small plastic pots lined in neat rows. She had bland brown hair, pale, sickly skin and bone-thin arms and legs. And white bedroom slippers.

"Hello, Emma."

"Hello, R-Ruth."

Ruth said, "This is Mortimer. He's been sent to us. I'm showing him the ways of the society."

Mortimer nodded. "Hi."

Like the others, Emma looked at him like he was from Mars. "H-hello."

"What have we here?" Ruth picked up one of the seedlings, squinted at it.

"B-banana p-peppers," Emma said.

"Emma has quite a green thumb." Ruth passed the seedling to Mortimer.

He looked at it briefly before setting it back on the table. "Great."

A panicked, high-pitched noise popped out of Emma's mouth. She bent over the seedling, lined it up exactly with the rest of the seedlings in the row. She examined it from every angle, making sure it was perfectly aligned.

"She likes things just right," Ruth said.

Mortimer smiled weakly. "Who doesn't?"

She showed him through the kitchens, then took him down another level. She opened a big steel door, and Mortimer balked at the darkness and the damp smell. But Ruth took a lantern hanging from the wall and flipped it on. It hummed and buzzed to life, casting a blue glow on the rough cavern walls beyond. She led, and he followed.

The tunnel's low ceiling was a mere two inches from his head, but it soon opened into a wide cave. The sound of rushing water. She held up the lantern, showing Mortimer the pool of water, the underground river flowing in one side and out the other. Mortimer thought of his own caves, where he'd hidden from the world for so long.

"We catch fish here," Ruth said. "This isn't the drinking water. The hospital has a system fed by a very deep well. But we have plans to put in a hydroelectric waterwheel here if the solar panels on the roof give out. There are complete diagrams for how to build a waterwheel in a book in the hospital library."

She took Mortimer through the rest of the hospital, showing him inconsequential nooks and crannies. The entire time something about the place nagged at him, something beyond the general strangeness of the people he'd met. He couldn't quite put his finger on it.

"How many live here?" Mortimer asked.

"Eighty-eight," said Ruth. "Fewer than in the old times."

"The old times?"

"Before. The time before the society."

Right.

A large room with many shelves and books was obviously the hospital library. Ruth credited the written knowledge within for a good portion of the society's survival. Everything anyone needed to know, she claimed, was written down in one book or another. How to make soap or repair a furnace or catch fish or set a broken arm or . . . well . . . anything.

Mortimer wandered while Ruth chattered on about the wonders of the library, her bubbly voice fading to background music. He drifted toward a wall where several framed newspaper articles hung. The newspaper had yellowed almost to brown. He scanned the headlines and photos.

A man in a hard hat and a business suit breaking ground with a ceremonial golden shovel. Another photo dated almost twenty-four months later, of a sharply dressed woman cutting a ribbon. Various headlines:

GROUND BREAKS ON INNOVATIVE CARE CENTER.

SECLUDED WOMEN'S HOSPITAL A RETREAT FOR THE WEARY.

RENOWNED PSYCHOLOGIST TO JOIN SAINT SEBASTIAN'S STAFF.

Mortimer scanned the articles, frowned as other headlines and bits of story jumped out at him.

DEPRESSION UP AMONG WOMEN, CLAIMS SAINT SEBASTIAN'S DOCTOR.

SAINT SEBASTIAN'S TO OPEN NEW WARD FOR VIOLENT PSYCHOTICS.

KNOXVILLE WOMAN WHO MURDERED FAMILY TO GO TO SAINT SEBASTIAN'S.

Something cold and leaden sagged in the pit of Mortimer's stomach. He glanced sideways at Ruth, who still gestured airily at the many volumes. *Oh, hell,* he thought. *I'm in a nuthouse.*

Mortimer cleared his throat. "Uh . . . well, this has been fun. If I could just get my boots, I really need to hit the road."

Ruth tilted her head, frowned at him. "The road?"

"I want to leave. Thanks for the soup."

She shook her head. "Nobody leaves. This is the society. We are within, safe from the outside. No one leaves. Ever."

Mortimer suddenly realized what was so strange about the hospital. He'd not seen a single open door or window.

XVIII

He burst from the library and headed down the hall at a fast walk, Ruth trailing behind and looking confused. His eyes darted in every direction looking for a door to the outside or a window. There wasn't even an EXIT sign.

Mortimer spotted a hall branching off, turned on his heel and jogged down it.

"Not down there." Ruth trotted after him. "Nobody goes down there!"

The hall was dim, every third or fourth fluorescent bulb burned out overhead. Cobwebs in the corners.

"Stop!" she shouted. "You'll get us in trouble."

He ran faster. "Why? Is this where the door is?" he shouted back. "Is this the way out?"

"Please!" Distress high in her voice. "Stop!"

"Get away from me, wack-job."

A door at the end of the hall snapped into focus, and Mortimer ran for it. As he got closer he saw the DO NOT ENTER sign across the front, the yellow police tape crisscrossing the doorway. A large padlock.

Above the door was another sign, spray-painted in rough, juvenile lettering. HOLY OF HOLY.

He heard more footsteps stomping up behind him.

Mortimer ripped aside the yellow police tape. He kicked the door hard, rattling the padlock. The shock traveled up his leg, hurt all the way to his hip. He ignored the pain, kicked again.

Ruth screamed.

Mortimer tried to turn, but white-hot fire struck him in the side, bathed his nervous system in electricity. He fell, twitched and slobbered, tried to turn his head.

The last thing he saw was a man in a dress.

"Hit him again with the stun gun," he said.

ZAP.

When Mortimer came around, he was tied spread-eagle on an operating table. Bare-ass naked. He felt slightly queasy, his whole body still humming from the massive zap, all his nerve endings buzzing and raw. It was cold, and Mortimer shivered.

He blinked the blur from his eyes, saw the rows of faces above him like some grim jury. He realized the operating room was theater style, a place where surgeons could demonstrate complicated procedures to student cutters.

Mortimer worried what they intended to demonstrate on him.

The women in the gallery were of every variety, tall, short, fat. Women with haggard horse faces. Younger women with open, timid expressions. Old crones crazy eyed and wrinkled.

Some regarded Mortimer like a new species of insect to be logged and dissected. Others had an eerie, hungry look, like Mortimer was raw red meat.

"Some hardly remember what a naked man looks like." The voice behind him was gruff and low. "A few have never seen one at all, not quite like this."

Mortimer twisted, tried to turn his head. All he could see was the suggestion of a big, dark shape behind him.

The voice rose for the benefit of the gallery. "Fate has sent us this man. His seed will ensure the survival of the society. The lucky chosen shall bear children, and we will know life again."

Murmuring from the gallery, a mix of excitement and anxiety.

"For years have we lived in harmony and peace and safety," the voice continued. "We need not have any contact with the world outside. The world poisoned and destroyed by men. We happy sisters live and prosper here in our sanctuary of Saint Sebastian's. Only one thing do we need: the seed of life. It is the ultimate irony that those who would destroy the world would also hold the essence of life, the seed. But destiny has provided this man. We will take his seed, and we will *live*!"

Halfhearted applause from the gallery.

The voice walked around the table until it came into view. Mortimer gasped. It was the man in the dress, a flowing black gown with a high neck. He was tall, broad-shouldered. He had a potbelly and big arms bulging beneath the silky sleeves, a five o'clock shadow on an anvil chin, an Adam's apple the size of a baseball. The blonde wig was some sort of cabaret nightmare.

He leaned in close, his hot breath like bad cheese on Mortimer's face. "You're going to get it up, little man. And you'd better perform."

He turned back to the gallery again. "Let the breeding begin!"

A door slid open on the bottom level of the amphitheater. Mortimer lifted his head, watched the newcomer enter between his feet. A silhouette against the harsh light from the hallway. She came into focus as she entered the operating room.

Ruth.

Mortimer was suddenly angry. Sweet, naïve Ruth shouldn't be made to sex up a stranger in front of an audience of nutballs. To hell with these women and their wacko society. Ruth didn't know any better. She could only have been a little girl of nine or ten when the world went boom. She didn't know how men and women lived.

Still, if it had to happen . . . well, Ruth would be best. She was shy and innocent and gentle. Under other circumstances it would even be pleasurable.

Ruth stepped aside and ushered in a woman with the biggest ass Mortimer had ever seen. Fat flat lips that looked like they were pushed up against a window. She had short black hair and many chins.

Oh, shit.

Mortimer arched his back, pulled at his restraints until they dug too painfully into his wrists. No use.

He felt the transvestite's hot breath on his ear again. "You're not going anywhere until you put out, lover boy. Now get some lead in that pencil."

The corpulent brood mare approached the table and dropped her white robe. Naked beneath, a wide, thick torso, a thick thatch of hair in each armpit. A big mole at the corner of her mouth sat there like a lost kidney bean. She climbed on the table, hovered over Mortimer.

"Wait," Mortimer said. "This isn't a good idea. You don't want my seed. I have bad DNA."

She grabbed his cock too roughly and Mortimer winced. The mix of sweat and love juice radiated from her, smacked Mortimer in the face. He had never been more uninterested in sex, hung limp in the woman's fist.

She looked in confusion at the transvestite. "Mother? He's not ready to put the seed in me."

"Get him hard like I showed you," Mother said.

She nodded, started yanking Mortimer's prick with hard, sharp jerks.

Mortimer winced, shut his eyes tight and turned away. He opened his eyes briefly and saw Ruth watching, horror and fascination at odds on her childlike face.

"That hurts," Mortimer said. "For God's sake, you're bruising the shit out of me."

"Stop," said Mother.

The breeder ceased her sadistic jerk job on Mortimer's pecker. He sighed relief.

"Clear the operating theater," Mother said. "His body hasn't recovered from the stun blast."

Muttering among the women. They began to file out.

The ogre on top of him slumped in disappointment, slid off him and grabbed her robe. Soon only Mother Lola and Mortimer remained. Mother paced around the operating table, her high-heeled boots echoing off the sterile tile, pouring derision onto him with a vicious expression.

"If you know what's good for you," the transvestite said, "you'll get Mr. Johnson into the ballgame. You take my meaning?"

"I'm not used to doing it as a spectator sport."

"Tough shit," said Mother Lola. "You think I'm doing it this way for perverse jollies?"

"Seems like it."

Mother Lola shrugged. "Okay, maybe a little. But it's more important they all see. This is a very special group of people with special needs. You think it's easy leading them?" He snorted.

"Fat chance. I know you'd rather have privacy, but we can't have a few privileged breeders while everyone else is left out in the cold. That's the perfect way to foster discontent. No, they must *all* be involved, even if it's only as spectators for many. That's the sort of unity that keeps our society together. Unity keeps us strong."

"I thought it was fear," Mortimer said. "Fear of the world outside the front door of this hospital. What lies have you told them to make them so terrified to leave? That's how you stay in control, right?"

"And what of the cannibals? Are they a lie?"

Mortimer's eyes grew wide.

Mother Lola nodded, chuckled softly. "You think I don't know? I don't need to make up fairy stories to keep my girls in line. The truth is devil enough."

"It's still a lie," Mortimer said. "Acting as if they have no choice is a lie."

"They are children and need leadership. But all of this . . ." She shook her head and tsked. "All this talk is of no concern to you. Your function here is biological, not philosophical."

"It might be a little easier to make with the semen if the first one up to bat wasn't some slobbering hog."

"Yes, I'd forgotten how important arousal is to the process for you men. It's not enough to know you're creating a new life. It's all about getting your rocks off, isn't it? Fine. If that's what it takes." Mother Lola slipped the black dress slowly off one shoulder, then the other.

Ohhhhhhhh no no no . . .

Mother Lola let the dress drop, stood naked, arching her back in an unfortunate pose.

"Uh, listen," Mortimer said, a slight tremor of panic in his voice. "You don't want the other girls to think you're getting special privileges, remember?"

"They don't need to know. It'll be our special moment."

Mortimer tried to stop himself, but he couldn't help it. He looked. What he saw made his stomach churn.

Mother Lola was not a transvestite. The oversize breasts were obscenely tight and perky compared to the sagging flesh on the rest of the body. Clearly the work of a surgeon with more ambition than skill. A hairy crater like some abomination against anatomy itself sat where there should have been balls and a schlong.

Mother Lola moved closer, her sweat and musk filling the operating theater.

He/she put a loving hand on Mortimer's flat stomach, caressed downward.

"Listen," Mortimer said, his nerves making his voice an embarrassingly high squeak. "I've been thinking. Why don't you bring the other woman back? I'm pretty sure I can fill her up with seed. Seriously, let's get her back in here."

"Don't be shy," Mother Lola said. "I know you want it." She brought her fingers to rest in Mortimer's pubic hair, curled it playfully around her pinkie. She bent in low for a kiss, her breath like greasy meat.

Mortimer convulsed and vomited.

Mother Lola screeched and flung herself backward, the puke barely missing her as it splattered the operating table and floor, running down Mortimer's chin and chest.

"Asshole," spat Mother Lola. "You wouldn't know true beauty if it bit you on the ass. I would have rocked your world." She grabbed her dress, shimmied back into it, thrust her arms into the sleeves. "Ruth!" she yelled.

Fast footfalls in the hall, the door pushed open quickly. "Mother?"

"Ruth, clean this animal up." She bent over him, brought her face to within an inch of Mortimer's. "And you'd better be ready to perform this time," she growled. "Otherwise you're no good to anybody." She turned back to Ruth. "He's got an hour to rest." She stalked out of the theater.

Mortimer felt a cool, wet towel on his forehead, looked up into Ruth's concerned eyes. She dabbed at the puke on his chin, wiped his chest.

"I'm sorry," she said. "Mother Lola is only trying to keep the society safe and strong."

"Mother Lola is insane. She's not even a she."

"She—Mother Lola—she says if you finish with Mona—"

"Who's Mona?"

"The woman who tried to—she was on top of you before—"

"Oh, Jesus."

"Mother Lola says if you finish with Mona, that I could be, maybe after, I mean . . ." She wouldn't meet Mortimer's eyes, went pink in the cheeks. "I've read a book from the hospital library on how to pleasure a man." The pink went to deep red.

"You've got to listen to me, Ruth. This isn't right. You have to see that keeping me like this is wrong. Unshackle me. Please. You've got to show me the way out of here."

"I don't think . . . If Mother Lola . . ." She bit her bottom lip, shook her head.

Mortimer sighed, leaned his head back and closed his eyes. "How old were you when you came to Saint Sebastian's, Ruth?"

"Nine."

"Why?"

"I wouldn't talk to anyone. I was withdrawn."

"What happened?"

"I saw my parents burn to death in a fire."

"You're talking now. You seem okay."

She shrugged.

"You don't need to stay here, Ruth. That was a long time ago. Show me the way out and come with me."

Her eyes widened in surprise then narrowed to suspicion. "Mother Lola says it's dangerous outside."

The cannibals and brigands? Starvation and disease? Small potatoes. "You'd be free outside. Mother Lola doesn't want that. She wants to control you. Get me loose and we can go together. There are risks, yes, but that's what it means to be free."

She shook her head vehemently. "I can't."

"You can. Unbuckle the straps on my wrists."

"No." But her hands went to the buckles and loosened them. She moaned the whole time, as if the weight of rebellion caused her physical pain.

Mortimer sat up, rubbed his wrists, then bent to release his ankles. He slid off the operating table, the tile floor cold on his bare feet.

"I need my clothes."

"Mother Lola took them."

"Where?"

"I don't know."

Mortimer grabbed her by the forearms, and the sudden contact made her gasp. She went weak, going to her knees. Mortimer sank to the floor with her, shook her until she met his eyes.

"Listen to me," Mortimer said. "You've got to make a decision. What is it you want?"

"I want to go outside," Ruth said. "I want to go with you."

"Then show me the way."

"Take this." Ruth shoved something into his hand. "I saved it for you. I wanted you to know that I . . . that I was thinking about you."

He opened his hand, looked at what she'd given him. His pink Joey Armageddon's platinum card. "Thanks." His only possession in the world. "Ready to get out of here?"

She searched his face, then nodded slowly. "It's mealtime. If we're quick, we might get out without anyone knowing. Follow me."

Mortimer again confronted the words HOLY OF HOLY spray-painted over the door. The yellow police tape lay in tatters where he'd ripped it down earlier. He touched the padlock, looked at Ruth.

"Only Mother Lola has the key," she said.

"Why does it say 'Holy of Holy'?"

"Mother Lola says it holds the total knowledge of the society. Nobody but God should know all, so it's kept locked."

Mortimer walked down the hall, opened a glass door in the wall and came back with a fire extinguisher. He slammed it three times against the padlock until it popped open. He looked up and down the hall, but apparently no one had heard. He paused, then twisted the knob and entered.

The moldy smell hit him, the old, dusty odor of a room long unused. He turned around, looked back at Ruth still out in the hall. "Coming?"

She shook her head, took a step back.

The room was dark. Mortimer felt his way to a desk lamp and switched it on, the low-wattage bulb splashing its feeble light around the interior of the office. Desk, filing cabinets, bookcases. A big black leather couch along one wall.

A dead body on the leather couch.

He'd been dead a long time, his skin shriveled and dried. Most of his hair had fallen out. White lab coat with pens in the pocket. A plastic I.D. card with photo hanging from his neck. Mortimer noticed the corpse's pants were down around his ankles. A large pair of rusty scissors stuck out of a vacant eye socket. A mummi-fied fist clutched a pair of faded red panties.

You horny old bastard.

Mortimer examined the cabinets. Patient files. This was what Mother Lola must have meant about the total knowledge of the society. He brushed aside the temptation to look up Ruth's file. He was curious, but it was none of his business. It took ten min-utes of searching to find Mother Lola's file.

Unless there was more than one transsexual admitted to the hospital, it had to be her file. Lawrence "Lola" Jameson was a real piece of work. According to the file, he hated men and therefore himself. No wonder the sex change operation looked so shoddy. Lola had done it to herself, eliminating, according to the doctor's notes, "all that was male about herself." The doctor had allowed for Lola to be transferred to his care, theorizing that Lola might feel better among women. The doctor's scribbled notes went on to muse, "Lola blames men for the evils of the world, and sup-poses an all-female society as an ideal utopia."

Mortimer closed the file and returned it to the cabinet. He didn't want to read any more, and there wasn't time anyway.

He saw a door in the back corner of the room and went to it.

He turned the knob and went inside. A very small, dank-smelling bathroom. He closed the door, pissed and flushed.

A pinstripe suit hung from a hook on the back of the door. It was in plastic from a long-defunct dry cleaner. Navy blue with gray stripes, a blue shirt. No underwear or socks. He put on the suit. It was a half-size too big, but it would do. The pant legs were long, so he rolled them up.

He went back into the office and took the dead man's shoes. He left the socks. The shoes fit perfectly. He took the belt too, cinched up the loose trousers.

Ruth stuck her head into the office. "What are you doing?"

Mortimer ignored her, went to the desk and searched the drawers, hoping to find anything useful. Stationery, pens, paper clips, a calculator. In the bottom drawer he found a set of keys on a big ring.

He held them up so Ruth could see, jingled them. "What do these go to?"

"I don't know. Mother Lola never lets us—"

"Think, Ruth. There has to be a door out of this place."

She wrung her hands, looked back over her shoulder, then back at Mortimer. "There is this one place—I don't know if it's anything. It might not be—"

"Show me."

Her deep, pleading eyes met his. "You'll take me with you?" she whispered.

"I'll take you."

She nodded, finally deciding, grabbed his hand tight and led him from the office. "There's not much time."

They continued down the hall past other offices with doctors' names on the doors. The farther they went, the more obvious it became that the hall was unused, dusty, almost none of the fluorescent bulbs burning overhead. As far as Mortimer had observed, this was the only portion of the hospital that had fallen into such disrepair.

The hall terminated in almost total darkness. Ruth led Mortimer forward, her hand gripping his almost too tightly, her other hand held out in front of her as her steps slowed near a wall.

Mortimer's eyes adjusted. Fake potted plants in the corners, covered by years of dust; a cheap oil painting of a sailing ship on choppy waters hung in the middle of the wall. A dead end.

"What is this, Ruth?"

She shrugged, her eyes unreadable in the darkness. "I was hiding in one of the offices. Mother Lola came from this direction."

"Why were you hiding, Ruth?"

"I wasn't supposed to be here. I was looking in the offices. I was curious. Nobody is ever supposed to come down here." She latched suddenly on to Mortimer's arm. "Please, we have to go. If she catches us here . . ."

Mortimer shook his arm loose, stepped up to the wall, ran his hand along its surface. Knocked. The material was thin, flimsy. "This is cardboard painted to look like the wall."

Mortimer shoved, and the wall shook; the ship picture fell, frame glass shattering on the floor. Ruth started, yelped. He pushed the wall again, and the cardboard structure flopped over. Light streamed in, and Mortimer flinched. He pushed on, kicking the wall down until it was flat.

The hallway led to a glass door.

They went to it, pulled. Locked.

Mortimer looked for a place to try the keys he'd found in the doctor's desk. No luck.

Ruth put her hands flat against the glass, looked through to the other side. "What is it?"

"Some kind of reception area. Or maybe a security checkpoint," Mortimer said.

There was a counter, a phone and two cheap office chairs in a small waiting area. Half the lights still worked. Mortimer jerked on the door, but it wouldn't budge.

"I bet this is it," Mortimer said.

"What?"

"The way out. Wait here." He jogged back down the hall.

"Where are you going?" A hint of alarm in Ruth's voice.

"I'll be right back."

Back in the dead man's office, Mortimer picked up the fire extinguisher he'd used to bash open the padlock. He hefted it, feeling its weight. Probably he could smash through the glass door with it. He turned to run back down the hall. Paused. He set the extinguisher down, entered the office again.

He stared at the corpse, still clutching the panties, imagined a macabre smile of perverse satisfaction across the mummified face. Mortimer's gaze shifted downward, came to rest on the plastic I.D. badge hanging from a frayed cord. Mortimer grabbed it quickly, yanked, and it came loose. He ran back down the hall and found Ruth squatting small and quiet against the wall.

It only took Mortimer a second to find the slot. He inserted the plastic I.D. Nothing happened.

"What's that?" Ruth got to her feet, stood close to Mortimer. "What are you doing?"

Mortimer turned the I.D. card around so the magnetic strip faced the other way. He inserted it again. The slot buzzed sluggishly, a green light flickering and struggling.

"Come on!" He jammed the card in harder, slammed the slot with the heel of his other hand. "Work, you piece of shit!"

The green light buzzed. An audible click from the glass door.

"Get it. Quick!" ordered Mortimer.

Ruth pulled the door open and held it. Mortimer put the I.D. card in his pocket, raced through the door, pulling Ruth after him. "Come on!"

This is it, thought Mortimer. *The way out.* Mother Lola had kept it hidden, kept all her little subjects trapped in her morbid little kingdom. But they'd made it through. They ran down a long hall, Mortimer's heart thumping.

"Wait! What's that?" Ruth halted abruptly, pulled on Mortimer's arm.

They held their breath, listened.

From behind they heard movement, hard footfalls on a tile floor, muffled voices.

"Oh, God, they're coming." Ruth's eyes shot wide with animal panic. "Mother Lola knows. She's coming."

"Hurry!" Mortimer pulled her forward, ran down the long hall.

They turned a corner, saw a smear of daylight. Double doors leading to the outside. They ran. Ruth faltered, almost stumbled, but Mortimer jerked her upright and kept running. Flashlight beams behind them now, harsh shouts to stop.

They didn't look back, hit the doors at a run, bright sunlight washing over them as they erupted into the open.

"Run for it!" Mortimer let go of her wrist, ran full speed for open ground. "We can make it," he shouted into the wind. "Keep running!" He turned his head, expected to see her sprinting for her life.

She wasn't next to him.

He stopped, turned, saw her still only a few yards from the hospital entrance. "What the hell are you doing?"

"I . . . I can't . . ." She took three halting steps, then froze, shut her eyes tight, put her hands in the air as if fending off some unseen ghost.

Mortimer ran back, grabbed her, started running again. It was like pulling a sack of bowling balls. But then she jogged, tried to keep up, Mortimer pulling and urging her. Abruptly she fell to the ground, sliding out of his grip. She curled into a ball.

"Are you fucking kidding me?" He grabbed under her armpits, attempted to hoist her up. She went limp, dripped from his arms.

"I can't . . . I didn't know." She shook her head, the words coming breathless. "I didn't know it would be like this."

He grabbed her, ran sluggishly with her a hundred yards before they fell into a pile. Mortimer panted, gulped for air, his breath steaming in the cold. "What the hell is your problem?"

"It's too much," she gasped. "I didn't know it would be so big. I can't do it. It's so much. So open." She put her hands over her head like she was trying to fend off the sky, gigantic open spaces threatening to crush her into the earth.

Mortimer stood, looked back at the hospital entrance. Three women stood in the doorway. Mother Lola with a fox fur around her neck, two women flanking her. Both holding bows and arrows.

"Unhand her, vile abductor," bellowed Mother Lola.

Mortimer dropped next to Ruth, whispered in her ear, "We have to go *right now*."

"I can't. It's too much. There's nothing between me and . . . and . . ." She waved a frantic hand at the sky. "Everything." She staggered to her feet, ran for the hospital. "I have to get back inside."

"Are you crazy?" Mortimer leapt, tackled her around the ankles. They both went down, Ruth screaming.

She kicked at him, writhed, twisted from his grip. She was up again and running.

Mortimer started after her when an arrow landed with a meaty *thwock* in his upper thigh.

"Holy fucking shit, that hurts!" He hopped on one leg, gritting his teeth and uttering curses. He grabbed the shaft, pulled the arrow out with relative ease. A nonbarbed target arrow. It hadn't penetrated deeply, but it stung like a son of a bitch.

Mortimer yelled, "Ruth!"

She didn't turn, fled weeping into the arms of Mother Lola.

He stood a moment looking at the women and the hospital, vines creeping up the building on all sides as if the earth were trying to swallow it whole. He saw Mother Lola and Ruth disappear back into the darkness within.

Another arrow whizzed over his head.

"Okay, okay. I can take a hint."

Mortimer limped away as fast as he could. They didn't chase him. Maybe his seed wasn't so desirable after all.

XIX

The cold tore at Mortimer's bare ankles, whooshed up his pant legs to do fierce, shrinking things to his genitalia. He shivered and trudged, favoring the leg with the shallow arrow wound. The winding, narrow road twisted and curved through the forest away from Saint Sebastian's and toward nowhere he could guess. He assumed the asphalt would eventually take him to some village or town. He'd settle for a farmhouse where he might beg a scrap of food.

He could not shake the sick feeling in the pit of his stomach. Ruth. Poor girl. What should he have done for her? Ultimately another victim of the world's implosion. After growing up in her sterile cocoon, how could she possibly face the unyielding totality of an entire planet?

Or maybe she was just a wack-doodle.

Mortimer hugged himself tighter, trudged on, tried to keep his teeth from chattering.

He passed three dead farmhouses before he realized it might be a good idea to scavenge. Even if he didn't find food, he might possibly find something warmer to wear. He might even stay in one of the abandoned dwellings for the night and try to get a fire going somehow.

The next two farmhouses produced nothing of value. In the

third, Mortimer attempted to pull down a thick set of yellow drapes to use as a blanket, but the material disintegrated in his hands.

By evening, he was exhausted and starving. His feet hurt, and every muscle ached.

The next farmhouse had no front door, all the windows smashed out. He found only barren rooms and hard wooden floors inside. There was a fireplace but nothing he could use to start a fire. He'd read a number of frontier guides that demonstrated how to build a fire without matches, but he couldn't remember anything that would allow him to strike a spark out of thin air with his bare hands.

In the bathroom, he found a dirty plastic shower curtain still hanging. He tore it down and used it as a blanket. Mortimer spent a long uncomfortable night in the tub.

Every limb was sore and stiff when he awoke. The leg with the arrow wound was the worst. Not for the first time, Mortimer thought how much simpler and safer and more comfortable it would have been to stay in his cave. Or he could have stayed in Spring City, bought back his house from the crazy old lady.

The idea of tracking down his wife seemed useless and arbitrary now. And yet Mortimer could not quite picture himself turning back, living easily and without direction, drinking his fortune at the Spring City Joey Armageddon's.

He stretched, stomped the feeling back into his legs and hit the road again.

Two more farmhouses and still nothing. He felt he might soon eat his shoes if he didn't find food.

He arrived at a larger county road that crossed his at a T intersection. This would certainly lead to some kind of town, and

Mortimer brightened microscopically. Another farmhouse sat at the head of the T intersection. Maybe Mortimer would get lucky. He went inside.

The first thing he saw was the dead body.

Mortimer was still not quite used to seeing dead bodies.

The corpse sat at a desk. The desk faced the front door. The dead man had fallen forward. He clutched a revolver in his stiff, dead hands. He didn't look quite as mummified as the dead doctor back at Saint Sebastian's, but he'd clearly been there a long time. A brown-red bullet hole above his right temple.

He couldn't take it, and he shot himself.

Mortimer's eyes fixed on the gun. It was like finding a bar of gold. Next to the man's head was an ashtray with a book of matches in it. Fire! And what was that on the end of the desk? Ravioli. A fucking can of Chef Boyardee Overstuffed Ravioli.

Mortimer almost flew to the desk, arms outstretched.

The floor vanished out from under him. Falling. Flailing limbs. Rope tight across his face. He was tangled, swaying, bobbing up and down in the musty darkness.

After a few seconds, Mortimer stopped his struggling, tried to turn his head and assess his situation. He hung upside down in a large net. That much was obvious. A trapdoor must have dropped him into a net, and he now hung in the basement below. The only light came from the still-open trapdoor above. He craned his neck, tried to see what was in the basement.

Bodies. Dozens of dead bodies in a pile.

Oh . . . shit.

He heard something and froze. It had sounded like a bell. He struggled, heard the bell again and froze again. Experimentally, he twisted and shifted in the net. The bell sounded.

It's connected to the net, he thought. *Come and get it.*

He renewed his struggles more frantically. He had to get out before they came. Whoever the hell *they* were. Mortimer didn't want to find out. He managed to struggle right side up, reached up between the thick net ropes to see if he could feel how the thing was put together. Maybe he could untie it.

Footsteps up above, the wooden floor creaking. Mortimer held his breath. A black silhouette appeared against the square of light above him, stood at the edge and looked down at him through the trapdoor. Mortimer saw the vague outline of a firearm cradled in the man's arms.

"He got any weapons?" called a voice.

The silhouette turned his head to answer. "Nope. Go get him."

"Right."

Another set of footsteps crossed the floor. The sound of a door swinging on rusty hinges, followed by the muffled clomp of boots coming down stairs. A door swung open, and light flooded the basement. A man in jeans and a heavy flannel shirt approached Mortimer. He was pale, red hair, medium height, small black eyes and yellow teeth spread out with gaps. Late twenties. On his shoulder rested a wooden baseball bat.

"I'm gonna let you down, okay? You try anything, I'll bash you good with this." He hefted the bat. "You understand?"

Mortimer nodded.

The man looked up at the silhouette. "Bobby?"

Bobby shifted the firearm to point at Mortimer. "I got him covered. Go ahead."

The bat wielder went to the wall, untied a rope and slowly lowered the net to the basement floor.

"Untangle yourself."

Mortimer spread the opening in the top of the net, shimmied out of it as he stood.

More footsteps up above, the quick patter of high heels. A woman's voice. "Did you get one?"

The one called Bobby said, "Just stay back, Sue Ellen. We got it handled. Floyd's down there with him now."

Floyd said, "You want me to search him down here or bring—"

Mortimer bolted for the stairs, ignoring the pain of his leg wound. He got three steps before feeling the sharp smack at the base of his skull. He went to his knees, his head swimming, eyes going unfocused.

"I told you not to fucking do that, asshole." Floyd's voice sounded like it was down a well.

"You got him?" Bobby called.

"Oh, I got him all right."

Another smack to the back of the head and everything went black.

Mortimer awoke with the sensation he had only been unconscious a minute or two. The back of his head throbbed. He turned to look into the eyes of a sallow, glassy-eyed corpse. His suit jacket and shirt were off, and the cement floor was cold on his back. He was barefoot.

He raised his head, saw a woman holding his shoes.

"You must be Sue Ellen."

She turned, shouted up the stairs. "He's awake."

Mortimer wished he wasn't.

Boots hammered down the stairs while the girl looked down

at Mortimer. She was a sight. An emerald-green cocktail dress, a big white sun hat, black silk gloves, fishnet stockings, satin pumps. She looked like she was auditioning for a community college production of *Breakfast at Tiffany's*.

Her face, pretty in a flat, plain sort of way, was ruddy, her brown eyes dull, her expression a bit too slack-jawed. She blinked at Mortimer, still holding his shoes. She didn't seem very concerned that Mortimer was conscious.

Maybe that was because Floyd and Bobby stood next to her now, Floyd with his baseball bat and Bobby with what Mortimer could now see was a single-barreled shotgun. Bobby had thinning hair the same red as Floyd's but a sharper, angular face and hard, probing eyes of bright blue. Like Floyd, he wore jeans and flannel shirts in layers.

The three of them gawked at Mortimer like he was a farm animal with a mildly interesting disfigurement.

"What are you going to do with me?" Mortimer asked.

Bobby shrugged. "Don't know yet. Sue Ellen?"

"Nothing hidden in his shoes," she said. "And I already went through his pants pockets. I'll look in the jacket." She picked it up, started turning the pockets out.

"Let me go," Mortimer said. "I don't have anything you want."

"Shut up," Floyd told him.

"If nothing else we can put him on the bicycle line," Bobby said.

Floyd pointed at Mortimer's thigh with the bat. "He's got a bum leg."

"He'll heal up okay."

Sue Ellen squealed. "It was in his jacket pocket." She held up the pink plastic card she'd found. "Wow. A Platinum member."

Bobby sighed. "Hell. Okay, then. Give him back his shoes."

DINNER AND ENTERTAINMENT

XX

They all hopped aboard the wagon and started up the county road. For a while, Mortimer could not take his eyes off the mule pulling them. He'd seen no horses or cows or sheep or livestock of any kind. Perhaps the mule's mangy, decrepit state had kept it from being eaten. Even as starved as Mortimer felt, the animal did not look appetizing.

The wagon rocked back and forth. They clip-clopped up the road.

"Where are you taking me?" Mortimer asked at last.

"Joey Armageddon's," Bobby said.

"What? All the way back to Spring City?" The mule would never make it. Maybe he'd end up eating it after all.

"Hell no," Bobby said. "The new one in Cleveland. We just struck a deal with the owner to give a safe pass to members. You're a Platinum member, so we thought we'd better take you in the wagon. Otherwise, we'd have just let you walk it."

"We expect a lot more traffic through here when the new Joey's is up and running full speed," Sue Ellen said. "It's been dead around here. We ain't caught anyone in the net in . . . how long, Floyd?"

"Six months," Floyd said. "Maybe seven."

"It'll be nice to get commerce flowing again," Bobby said.

"More traffic means more people in the net?" Mortimer asked.

Bobby shrugged. "Got to earn a living."

"Seems a little gruesome."

"Hey, it used to be a lot worse," Bobby said. "Back when Daddy was alive we'd rob them and strip them and kill them. But I guess Daddy finally felt guilty about that because he shot himself. That was him you saw at the desk."

"Lovely."

"Anyway, folks are worth more alive now with the new Joey's. We put a sentence on them for trespassing and they work it off on the electricity bicycles. But members get a pass. You can't fuck with the customers."

Bobby mumbled, "Whoa," and the mule eased to a stop in front of a relatively well-kept brick house. "Floyd, I'm dropping you off here."

"What?" Floyd's voice leapt two octaves.

"Damn it, Floyd, we're the only people for ten miles with chickens. You want them stole while we're away? Now get out of the wagon."

"But I want to see the Joey Girls."

"Get out!"

Floyd grumbled but got out.

In a second, the wagon was on its way again.

"He's as good a brother as a man could ask for, but he's hornier than a damn jackrabbit. They only got four girls at Joey's and he's been at each of them maybe a half-dozen times."

Mortimer didn't have anything to say to that.

"But overall, I guess you could say we're relatively affluent here," Bobby continued. "We got chickens that lay good eggs, so we can trade. We got two hogs we're trying to breed, so if that works out we might end up being the pork barons of the whole damn state. I like to think big."

Mortimer's stomach growled. A plate of bacon and eggs would be heaven. And coffee. A cup of coffee.

A steak. He'd kill for a thick, red T-bone steak.

No, not kill. That kind of thing wasn't a figure of speech anymore.

"And I might be getting a job as a Joey Girl," Sue Ellen said.

Bobby snorted. "Hell, girl, that place is known for the hotness of its female employees. Why would they want your ugly ass?"

"You shut up, Bobby. A good brother would support his sister's career ambitions."

"You don't have no tits."

"I said shut up. You smell like cat piss. Shut up. Tits ain't the whole package. I'm refined. I dress nice."

Bobby nudged Mortimer in the ribs. "She found all these old clothes and thinks she's Elizabeth Taylor."

"I don't even know who the hell that is." Sue Ellen stuck her tongue out at her brother. "Shithead." She touched Mortimer on the shoulder. "You think I'm attractive, don't you, Mr.— hey, we never did get your name."

"Mortimer."

"Mortimer, you think I'm attractive, don't you?"

Please leave me alone.

Sue Ellen shook his shoulder. "Seriously, I'm pretty, right? Alluring."

Mortimer swallowed hard, cleared his throat and nodded. "You look nice."

Bobby brayed laughter. "Shit, Sue Ellen, he's a Platinum

member. He could have big-titty blonde whores out the ying-
yang." Bobby nudged him again. "Eh, buddy? All them choice
whores. Eh?"

"How much farther is it?"

"Oh, it's a ways. Get comfortable."

Clip-clop clip-clop clip-clop.

As in Spring City, the folks of Cleveland, Tennessee, had
decided to congregate downtown, fleeing the exposed suburbs for
the relative safety of brick buildings and narrow streets, almost
like a tightly clustered medieval village behind a palisade. Even
more than Spring City, the downtown had been made into a fortress, the roads blocked in a zigzag pattern with junk cars. Bobby
maneuvered the mule slowly but with ease through the narrow
path. A block from the courthouse, a pair of men with rifles rolled
aside a barricade made of scrap iron welded to supermarket shopping carts.

One of the guards waved the wagon through. "Who you got
there, Bobby? Somebody for the bicycles?"

"Not this one," called Bobby as he eased the wagon past the
barricade. "He's got a Platinum card."

The guard laughed. "You hear that?" He winked at his buddy.
"We got us a playboy in town. Hide your daughters."

Mortimer smiled weakly and waved.

They passed the courthouse, and Mortimer noticed two more
riflemen patrolling the roof.

"What's with all the fortification?"

"Red Stripes."

"What do they want here?"

"Same as always," Bobby said. "Food, weapons, clothing, women."

"And blood," added Sue Ellen, her face suddenly stern.

Bobby reined in the mule and they dribbled to a stop in front of a gigantic stone church. "In there," Bobby told Mortimer. "Sue Ellen, help me carry in these eggs."

Mortimer climbed out of the wagon, stretched and heard his joints pop. Every limb was stiff. He looked at the wide, closed double doors of the church, then back at Bobby. "In there?"

"In there."

Mortimer pushed the doors open and stepped into the church. It was cavernous within, and the footfalls of his wingtips echoed off the high walls and vaulted ceiling. The church had been cleared of pews. There was nothing but wide-open space between him and the altar. Mortimer recalled that medieval cathedrals had no pews. The peasants had to stand and kneel on the cold stone floor. That was when people were serious about religion. Hard people for a dark age.

Mortimer felt weak from hunger and fatigue, his head slightly dizzy.

The setting sun suddenly poured its light into the far windows, a fiery orange and red coming through the stained glass. It bathed Mortimer in holy light. It warmed him, drew him toward the altar.

At once Mortimer felt leaden, the weight of his journey, the accumulated fatigue of running from danger and into danger. Replaying the past few days' events in his mind, Mortimer could hardly believe he was still alive. Perhaps it was some form of miracle. Maybe the hand of God had directed him to this place. Maybe this was God reminding him, showing him that even in this desolate land, in these forsaken times, a higher power was still here, still taking some interest in the small creatures, this ridiculous humanity, crawling and hiding like insects over the earth.

Mortimer sank to his knees in front of the altar, the light nearly blinding him now, the setting sun at a perfect angle, streaming in, lighting up the dust motes in the air like fiery meteors burning in the atmosphere. Mortimer clasped his hands, looked up into the haunted eyes of Christ.

In that moment there was no sound. Time seemed to grind to a halt.

In the pure quiet, voices arose, perfect and clear. A hymn from nowhere, singing clear and sweet. Strange yet so very familiar. The song filled the room, filled Mortimer, lifted him up.

And then . . .

The figure of Christ moved. Mortimer gasped. The figure descended, floating down toward him. Mortimer's heart froze. He opened his mouth to scream.

"Look out down there," somebody yelled at him.

Mortimer closed his mouth, blinked, saw the men in the rafters, lowering the crucifix with thick rope.

"Stand aside, buddy."

Mortimer stood aside. The men grunted, lowered the heavy figure little by little.

Mortimer recognized the song now. "You Can't Always Get What You Want" by the Rolling Stones.

The foot of the big crucifix hit the stone floor with a loud *tunk*.

"Watch out for Jesus."

XXI

Mortimer sat hunched over a plate of baked beans, a slab of ham and a biscuit. In between bites, he slurped at a cool pewter mug of Freddy's Dishwater Lager. He might have claimed the meal tasted heaven-sent, except he wasn't sure he believed in religious experiences anymore. Anyway, the food was good and filled him.

A work crew had filled up the empty space in the church with chairs and tables. Mortimer glanced up from his plate. The crucifix had been replaced with a sign reading JOEY ARMAGEDDON'S SASSY A-GO-GO, lit up with garish pink light. The sound system worked well with the church's acoustics, and the Violent Femmes' "Blister in the Sun" came out of the speakers at a tolerable volume.

The twitchy, bug-eyed man sitting across from him squinted at the pink membership card again and began apologizing for the third time.

"You see, *officially* we're not even supposed to be open yet. It's just that it's so damned expensive getting everything up and running, and a little cash flow wouldn't hurt. You see what I mean, right? Serve a few meals, pour a few beers. I only have four girls and one's down with diarrhea."

Davis Shelby had been a syndicated film and television critic back when people had cared about such things. He was short and spindly and hawk-faced, with a thatch of Brillo-pad hair the color of dull copper. He made a habit of dabbing at his face constantly with a threadbare handkerchief. Somehow he'd come into a Joey's franchise, but in less than half an hour, Mortimer had formed the opinion that the whole operation might fall down around his ears any moment. Whatever qualities might be considered the exact opposite of leadership and organizational skills, Davis Shelby possessed them in spades.

"You're allowed a line of credit, of course," Shelby told him. "Normally up to five hundred dollars. That's just standard for Platinum members." He dabbed at his sweaty forehead with the handkerchief. "But we've just had the devil's worst time getting shipments. We were supposed to get a strongbox of currency a week ago, but there's been no sign of the wagon train up from Chattanooga. Without the currency, we can't buy goods to fill up the store, pay for booze deliveries. It's really been a pain in the ass."

"I'll take the five hundred in trade." Mortimer shoved another biscuit into his mouth, washed it down with lager. "Is there anything in the store at all? I need a gun, food and gear for a long hike. Socks. I want some socks."

"Of course," Shelby said. "We do have some things. We've been stocking since December. It really is never-ending. There's always something to do or something breaking, or you hire a fellow to tend bar and he's killed by Red Stripes or disease or some damn thing. I can't keep the place staffed for shit."

"Maybe owning a club isn't your thing."

"I thought it would be like Rick's in *Casablanca,* very romantic, and I could wear a white tuxedo jacket and there would be music and pretty girls."

"But without the Nazis."

"Right!" He wiped the back of his neck with his handkerchief. His body produced enough sweat for three men. "Instead it's like running a saloon in a spaghetti western. Men drink whiskey until they're ready for a whore, and if there isn't a whore available then they want to fight. And if they lose the fight, then somebody has to mop up the blood. And the guy who mops up the blood quit, so *I* have to mop up the fucking blood. Bogart never had to mop blood. A circus. It's like being ringmaster of some psycho circus."

Mortimer nodded at the pink light. "At least you have electricity."

"Six men for the bicycles in the basement. Got to have juice for music and lights and refrigeration."

Mortimer spooned in the last of the food, considered licking the plate. "I saw a place a few days ago that had electricity. One hundred percent solar."

"Men are easier to come by than solar panels," Shelby said.

Mortimer pushed away from the table and burped. "I'd like to get those supplies now. And a room for the night if you have one."

"Yes, sir. Absolutely."

Mortimer could get used to being a Platinum member.

The Joey's store was pitiful compared to the one in Spring City, but Mortimer was still able to purchase a number of useful items. He wished he had access to all of his supplies back in his cave.

He made an even trade for clothing. The suit and wingtips for jeans, a red flannel shirt, boxers and sweat socks. He bought a pair of black Timberland hiking boots with minimal scuffing and a khaki baseball cap with the word MAXFLI stitched on the front in navy blue. A gray overcoat with mismatched buttons.

The weapons selection was poor but nonetheless expensive. A .357 magnum revolver tempted him but was simply too expensive. He settled on a short double-barreled shotgun, twelve-gauge, and a half-dozen buckshot shells.

Assorted foodstuffs, a silver Zippo lighter with fluid, a compass that had clearly been a child's toy but worked, an extra pair of socks, a unopened bottle of Bayer aspirin, a bowie knife, a large terry cloth towel, fishing line and a small set of hooks, a tin cup, a pot and a fork. It all fit into a cheap Nike tote bag.

Total cost including a room for the night: 448 Armageddon dollars. He planned to use the rest of the credit for a big meal and many drinks in the bar that night. In the morning, he'd hit the road again.

He let Shelby lead him out of the Joey's store in the church basement.

"Come this way," Shelby said. "And I can show you where your room is, up a different set of stairs. We knocked through to the building next door. Don't mind the men on the bicycles."

A familiar sight, like the men in Spring City, leaning heavily on the handlebars, pumping legs and sweating and going nowhere. Mortimer wondered how many of them Bobby and Floyd had caught "trespassing." How long would they have to ride those stationary bikes until they'd worked off their sentences? Until replacements arrived? It all seemed too close to slavery. Had things really devolved to such a state? Maybe Mortimer was thinking about it all wrong. At least those men on the bikes had a place to sleep. Three square meals a day. Starving men can't pedal.

Mortimer couldn't quite convince himself.

"Mort!" A hoarse voice. "Mort, holy shit, it *is* you!" The voice growing stronger. "Over here! It's me!"

Mortimer looked up, met the eyes of the man on the far bicycle, the golden hair, the extravagant mustache. "Bill?" He rushed forward, a huge grin splitting his face. He patted the cowboy on the back, barely restraining an urge to hug him. "I thought the cannibals got you."

"They almost did," Bill said. "Listen, can you do me a big favor?"

"Sure. What?"

"Could you get me off this goddamn bicycle?"

XXII

Davis Shelby had grand plans for turning the Bank of Cleveland into a classy hotel.

Almost none of those plans had yet come to fruition.

But Shelby had made a valiant start. He'd knocked through the church basement into the bank basement, and steps up took him to the lobby. The lobby was undergoing a conversion into an informal lounge, with a heavy, ornate pool table and a dartboard and a foosball table that looked ready to crumble. Couches and plush chairs. The teller counter had been converted into a bar, self-service since Shelby couldn't staff it. There was a huge five-gallon jug of pink liquid labeled FREDDY'S TOOTHACHE MUSCADINE and a stack of mismatched cups.

They paused for a drink, and Mortimer understood the toothache part. The pink wine was like a thin, stinging cough syrup. So sweet it made him wince. He had a second cup.

The room was minimal but clean and warm. A single bed. A stand with a pitcher of clean water and a washbasin. A narrow couch along the far wall. No windows. Bathroom down the hall.

"Your pal can stay on the couch, I suppose." Shelby cast a sidelong glance at Buffalo Bill. He didn't have a handbook to tell him what to do when a valued Platinum customer asked for the release of one of his slave laborers. Shelby was loath to lose a bicycler but reluctantly decided he could use some goodwill with a Platinum member. Shelby even suggested that if Mortimer should happen to find himself at the home office he might put in a word about what a stand-up guy Shelby was.

Sure. A regular Conrad Hilton.

Shelby left them in the room, muttering about the chef.

Buffalo Bill fell onto the couch, sighed dramatically. "Jesus H. Christ, I'm glad you came along, old boy. I was thinking I had a long, tedious future riding a stationary bicycle into the sunset."

Mortimer flopped on the bed. "What the hell happened to you after the cannibal camp?"

"It is a long, hair-raising tale of woe and toil."

Mortimer shook his head. "Can't listen to a hair-raising tale dry. Better go downstairs and get the jug."

Bill grinned, left the room and returned thirty seconds later with the jug and two cups. He handed one to Mortimer and filled it with too-sweet wine.

Mortimer gulped, smacked his lips. "Okay, I'm ready."

Buffalo Bill had been scared shitless, running through the night forest, a raging gang of inhuman flesh-eaters on his heels. Sore from being tied up, he put the pain out of his mind and kept running. The thought of being cowboy stew had spurred him on. But even with the heart-pounding fear turning his mouth all cottony, Bill found himself circling back. Maybe with the entire tribe on the chase, the camp would be unguarded. Bill could not bring himself to leave his hat and six-shooters.

But they had left guards at the camp, and Bill was forced back into the woods, directionless, cold, unarmed, tired and alone.

Mortimer thought him foolish, to run back into the hellish maw of the cannibals for a hat and a pair of guns. But maybe

Bill was doing something more than that, something even more important than Bill himself realized. He wasn't going back for guns and a hat. He'd been going back for his identity. Even now, on the couch without his hat, without the gleaming pistols, Bill looked deflated, somehow less than he was. Mortimer remembered first seeing him on the road coming down the mountain, standing with his legs spread, six-shooters blazing, demanding Mortimer's release with wild confidence. He'd looked like a hero.

Now he looked like another dirty, ragged refugee. What could a man do if he couldn't even hang on to who he was?

Anyway, he was safe now, and drinking cheap wine. There were worse things.

"None of that explains how you ended up on a Joey's bicycle," Mortimer said.

Bill laughed, shook his head. "That's the most boring part of the whole story. I finally found a road, walked along until I found a barn and crawled in to sleep for the night. Guy kicks me awake the next morning, points a shotgun in my face and tells me I'm trespassing. Next thing you know, I'm pedaling my ass off."

"I'll drink to that." Mortimer lifted his glass.

"Screw you." But he laughed again and drank. "What about you?" Bill asked. "Any adventures on the way here?"

Mortimer's laughter trailed off. He took a long, slow drink. The image of Ruth's face made his gut twist, beautiful and innocent one second, terrified and mad the next. The memory of Mother Lola's grotesque nudity made him shudder. So much since the panicked flight from the cannibals. It seemed like a month ago.

"I'll tell you about it sometime."

"Sure." If Bill sensed anything awry with Mortimer's mood, he kept it to himself. "I'm gonna grab a shower."

"I'll be here."

Bill left Mortimer alone.

The bed was comfortable and warm, and Mortimer had a full belly. It was a welcome change not to be afraid and cold. *Stay,* a voice in his head told him. *Rest.* Sure, then what? *Go home.*

The cave? That didn't seem like home anymore, it couldn't be, not now that he knew there was a living, breathing world going on. A strange world, and a dangerous one, but it was the only thing going. No, Mortimer would keep looking for Anne. Maybe it was his version of going back for his hat and gun.

Surely nature must abhor stasis. There's something in a man that makes him go and go and go, and maybe the direction wasn't even important. He would find Anne, and it would be everything or it would be nothing, but it would be forward motion if nothing else.

Mortimer dozed.

He was nudged awake five minutes later by a freshly showered Buffalo Bill. "Come on and buy me a drink."

XXIII

The Cleveland Joey's lacked the party atmosphere and pure sexual energy of its sister establishment in Spring City. No girls dancing in cages. No smiling women working the crowd. But as a reasonably friendly neighborhood saloon it was passable. Men playing poker and drinking at various tables, an ancient toothless crone behind the bar, serving slow but eventual mugs of beer. The lighting was low but not too dark. The music was something by the Dixie Chicks. Mortimer recognized it because Anne had been a fan. Maybe she still was.

The old lady indicated they should take any open table, so they found one in a corner and sat. Shelby showed up ten seconds later, looking harried and put out.

"If you want a girl, I'd get on the waiting list now."

Mortimer shook his head. "Just food."

"And beer," added Bill.

"There's omelets and sausage. The eggs are fresh. I just got them."

Mortimer smiled. Looked like he'd have a chance to try some of Bobby's eggs after all. "Okay."

"You got anything else?" Bill asked.

"No. I'm cooking myself. No chef."

"He quit on you?"

"Hell if I know," Shelby said. "He never showed. At least if I was running a circus the fucking clowns would turn up for work, right? Anyway, I thought I heard some shooting, so maybe he's dead."

Mortimer frowned. "Shooting?"

"Way out on the edge of town. Like an hour ago, and it's been quiet since."

Mortimer and Bill exchanged glances. Mortimer asked, "Should we expect trouble?"

Shelby shrugged. "Town militia will handle it. Anyway, a thousand Red Stripes could ride in on Harley Davidsons for all I care as long as they brought me a chef and ten guys for the bikes. You want the omelets or not?"

"We'll take two plates," Mortimer said.

"And beer," Bill shouted after Shelby.

The old lady brought two mugs of the Dishwater Lager. They sipped. Mortimer realized he was comfortable. Warm. He'd been warm since coming here and figured maybe the church was old enough to have an oil-burning furnace. Maybe even coal-burning. He wondered if there was anyplace a nuclear power plant still functioned. That would be a lot of energy. A town could pretend nothing had happened with that kind of power, dishwashers and microwave ovens and televisions. Except there were no TV channels anymore. You could watch DVDs maybe.

"This sure don't compare to the Joey's in Spring City," Bill said.

"Nope."

"You want me to go put our names on the waiting list?"

"Nope."

"Oh."

The omelets arrived with long, thick links of sausage. Mortimer tasted the eggs. Fresh and good. The sausage was heavily spiced, perhaps to cover the taste of the meat itself. He remembered pigs and cows were scarce.

"What do you think this is?" Mortimer stuffed another big chunk of sausage in his mouth.

Bill shrugged. "If we're lucky, squirrel or raccoon or something. Best not to ask."

They ate. They drank. It was pleasant and quiet. They didn't ask.

Barely audible over the sad notes of a Kelly Clarkson song, the distant *pop pop pop* of small-arms fire froze everyone in the saloon. Mouths stopped chewing. Patrons held beer mugs halfway to lips. Everyone waited and listened. The seconds crept by, and everyone was about to breathe again when they heard another burst of fire. Maybe a little closer. Maybe a little farther away. It was hard to tell.

A tall man pushed away from a table across the room. He sighed and stood. He was thin; his face had deep lines and thin lips. He wore a state trooper's hat and a Georgia Tech sweatshirt, and had an automatic pistol on his belt. "Keep on with what you're doing, everyone. I'll take a look." He left through the front door.

"Who was that?" Bill asked.

An old man leaned over from the next table. "Officer in the town militia."

"Trouble?"

The old guy snorted. "Hell, there's always trouble. The world is sewn together with it."

Right.

They finished their meals, and Mortimer said he was heading

back to the room. He wanted an early start. Bill said he wanted to stay a while longer, have another beer and see if he could get some more news out of the locals.

Mortimer went next door. The bank lobby was empty. It might have been nice to shoot a game of pool. On the way upstairs, he noticed somebody looking at him through a cracked door to another room. The door closed quickly as he passed.

Mortimer entered his own room, sprawled on the bed. He stared at the ceiling a long time. Tired, bone weary, but sleep didn't come. The stucco patterns on the ceiling were random, but if a person looked at them long enough, they formed images. Even as a kid, Mortimer had seen that, the faces in the stucco, animals and battleships and the Empire State Building. The mind wanted to see things, wanted something to be there, needed there to be anything but nothing.

Mortimer looked at the ceiling and saw pigs and cows. Maybe it was the sausage playing tricks on him. He tried to see something else, a message, anything useful.

Pigs and cows and no sleep at all.

He almost didn't hear the knock at first, thought it was part of some obscure dream, but he'd never really gotten to sleep, had only been lying there letting his thoughts drift. He waited until he heard the knock again before saying, "Who is it?"

The door creaked open, a sliver of hallway light widening to put the small figure into silhouette. She turned, and Mortimer could see her figure wrapped in something thin and silky, small breasts turned up and firm, thin waist. She was short and young, although difficult to tell how young in the poor light.

"Who are you?" he asked.

She closed the door and went to the bed, sat on the side next to Mortimer. Her weight barely registered, sagging the mattress only a little.

"Did Shelby send you? I'm not paying for this." But there was little conviction in Mortimer's words. She smelled good. Soap.

"I saw you coming up the stairs." Her voice was light and sweet. She was very young. She put her hand on Mortimer's leg, ran it gently down to the knee. He winced slightly when she rubbed over the arrow wound but didn't say anything. An erection began working in his pants.

With her other hand, she reached toward the nightstand and switched on a lamp. It was a pink lamp with bunnies on the shade, a child's lamp. The twenty-five-watt bulb cast weak yellow light.

He could see her face now, heart shaped with full lips. She was sixteen or seventeen at most, but Mortimer wasn't sure that sort of thing mattered anymore. Her copper hair looked like a dye job, but it was clean and shiny and bobbed at her neck. Her skin was clear and smooth and white. She looked familiar, but maybe that was just something he wished, so he wouldn't be in bed with a stranger.

She started working on his belt, her feather touch unbuckling him with practiced ease. He opened his mouth to object again but couldn't make any words come out. Soon he was lifting his ass, letting her pull down his pants. She reached for his erection. It was so hard, it was almost painful. He gasped when she stroked it. She cupped his balls, held them a moment, then stood and dropped her robe. She was white. Pink nipples. A small, downy patch of brown hair between her legs.

There was something in her hands, a little package she ripped open. She grabbed the base of his erection, unrolled the condom over him.

She straddled Mortimer, lowered herself slowly onto him. He moaned. Mortimer had forgotten. It had been so long. How could he have forgotten?

She started to ride, bouncing with quickening rhythm.

Mortimer took her by the hips, held her. "Slow down." He wouldn't be able to hold back, and he didn't want it to be over so soon.

She slowed, rocked back and forth. He cupped a breast, and she leaned down so he could take it in his mouth. When she sat back up again, Mortimer looked at her face, took in the shape and the eyes.

"I know you."

She smiled and nodded.

"Sheila." She no longer looked like the squashed, terrified child who had been at the beck and call of the Beast, the man who had beaten and robbed him and cut off his pinkie finger.

"This is my way of saying I'm sorry, I guess." She nibbled her bottom lip, shrugged, looked almost coy. "I couldn't help you before, when Kyle was doing all those things."

The Beast's name had been Kyle. Not Bruno or Spike or Butch. Kyle.

Now he did let her ride. She picked up a good rhythm, made little circular motions as she slipped up and down. He thrust back into her, hands full of her backside, moaned from the throat raw and feral. She made whining little grunts every time she came down, tiny gasps as she went back up again.

He came so hard, he thought he might blast her into the ceiling. She yipped surprise and shuddered on top of him, then slid off with a little giggle, curling next to him, both of them breathing heavily, soaking the sheets with their sweat.

Sheila put a hand on him, idly stroked his chest hair. They lay for a while not saying anything. Mortimer mused that Sheila had been exactly what he'd needed. He felt like he could sleep now all the way to morning, although he found he was even more eager to find Anne.

When they heard the gunfire, it seemed much closer this time. And when they heard it again, it was right out in the street.

XXIV

Mortimer exited the room quickly. He'd already packed. He even had his shoes on. All he had to do was pull up his pants and buckle his belt. He ran out of the room with the double-barreled shotgun in one hand and the Nike tote bag in the other. Somewhere behind him, Sheila had jumped up and grabbed her robe. Mortimer didn't look back.

I accept your apology, little girl. Stay safe if you can.

He heard more gunfire and saw flashes in the window as he ran through the bank lobby. He went across to Joey's, where he saw men upending tables, facing the front door, rifles and pistols ready. He saw Bobby and Floyd crouched behind one of the tables, Bobby with his single-barreled shotgun and Floyd with a very-small-caliber revolver.

Mortimer knelt next to them. "What's happening?"

"Red Stripes overran the barricades," Bobby said. "A shitload of them. Just came out of nowhere."

"I thought you'd be home guarding the chickens."

Bobby snorted. "I should have been, but dumbass here needed to dip his wick. Dumb horny idiot."

Floyd flicked his brother the bird. "It was worth it. That Sheila can fuck like a demon."

Mortimer tried to pretend he hadn't heard that. "I'd love to stay and chat, but I'm looking for a pal. Seen a guy with blond hair and a big mustache?"

Bobby shook his head. "Ask Shelby. He's hiding behind the bar."

Mortimer hoisted himself over the bar where the church altar had once been. He found Shelby and Bill passing a bottle of Freddy's Bowel Explosion Bourbon between them.

"I'm selling this place," Shelby said. "I mean, seriously, I've fucking had it." He took a swig of bourbon.

"Don't bogart the bottle." Bill took it, drank.

Mortimer dropped between them. "I'd like to cancel the room for tonight, Shelby. Credit the difference to my account."

"No refunds."

Mortimer took the bottle from Bill. "You want to get out of here or not?"

Bill grabbed the bottle back. "How? They're shooting out there." He drank deep and fast, coughed, some of the bourbon splashing on his chin.

The front door burst open and somebody yelled to hold fire. The jagged racket of a gun battle came loud from the streets. Two men stumbled in, carrying a third between them. The man they carried bled from the belly. They kicked the door closed behind them.

"Fucking hell!" one of them said. It was the lanky militia officer Mortimer had seen earlier. "They're swarming out there like flies on a turd. Get one of them tables up."

A pair of men with deer rifles righted their table. The officer and his comrade dropped the wounded man on the table faceup. He groaned and clutched his belly, thick blood oozing red, pumping out like they'd struck oil. He was crying and moaning and asking for his momma.

"Is there a doctor?" the officer asked the room. "Somebody with medical experience?"

A flurry of gunshots and one of the front windows shattered, spraying glass. Everyone hit the deck. The door flew open, and two men rushed in. They were met immediately by a half-assed volley of rifle fire, but it was enough to put them down. More invaders crowded the door. Shots flying inside.

"Pick your targets," the officer yelled. "Don't waste ammo shooting wild." He drew his pistol and fired at a face that appeared in the shot-out front window. The wounded man was still groaning on the table. Shots shattered bottles behind the bar, and Mortimer ducked down again, throwing his arms over his head as glass and booze showered him.

Shelby began to laugh uncontrollably. "I paid for that fucking booze!"

Mortimer didn't want to stick his head back up to see what was happening. But he could hear. Shots and furniture scooting on the floor and men screaming and the gut-shot man on the table crying out for his mother.

Mortimer held the shotgun tight against his chest. Maybe he should be helping with the firefight. Or maybe he should have stayed in his room.

"Shelby, is there a back door to this place?"

"Through the kitchen. Opens to an alley. But the alley goes to the street and that's where all the shit is happening."

"At least we could make a run for it." With the bullets flying, Bill seemed a lot more willing to make a break for it.

"Your call," Shelby said. "Die in here or die in the alley."

Somebody leapt over the bar and landed three feet from Mortimer. He swung the shotgun, only just stopped himself from pulling the trigger and turning Sheila's face to hamburger.

She'd changed. Instead of a seductress, she now looked like a teen on her way to a high school campout. Jeans and a denim shirt and a black leather jacket. Reebok sneakers. A khaki Jansport backpack.

She looked at Mortimer, her face strangely calm and confident. "I'm getting out of here. You coming?"

"Let's go."

"Wait for me," Bill said.

They crawled behind the bar, following Sheila.

She paused in front of Shelby. "I quit."

"Me too."

They crawled all the way to the end of the bar, the firefight still flaring in spurts out front. Sheila stood and dashed for a side door. Bill and Mortimer followed. Mortimer paused, looked back. A handful of men lay dead behind the overturned tables. A pile of dead Red Stripes choked the doorway. Others fired in through the broken window.

Mortimer went through the door, found himself on the other side with Bill and Sheila in some kind of vestibule. They followed Sheila through another door, down a hall and then into the kitchen.

Bill said, "We can't go this way. Shelby says it just leads to an alley and the street."

"I know a way," Sheila said.

As they went past stoves and refrigerators, Sheila grabbed a string of uncooked linked sausages and hung them around her neck. They found the old crone sitting on a stool near the back door. The door was metal and barred. It shook with thuds, men on the other side trying to knock it down.

"Will you be okay, Edith?" Sheila asked.

The old woman patted the MAC-10 in her lap. "I have a full clip. And anyway, it'll take a bulldozer to knock down that door."

"We're leaving through the pantry. Can you close it behind us?"

The old woman nodded.

Sheila flung open the pantry door, motioned for Bill and Mortimer to follow. Inside, shelves were lined with various canned goods and foodstuffs. A canvas bag hung on a nail just inside the door. Sheila grabbed it, tossed it to Bill. "Fill it up."

Bill didn't hesitate, began scooping random items into the sack.

Sheila reached to the back of one of the middle shelves, knocking off cans. "Come on, come on. Where is it? Ah!"

An audible click, and the back of the pantry swung open. Stone stairs on the other side spiraled down. She lit a candle. "This way."

They went down the stairs. The door thudded closed behind them, and the little candle was the only light. The sound of the outside world had been cut off. The stairs ended at the mouth of a tunnel, which was dank and tomblike.

They followed Sheila into the tunnel. She picked her way carefully, watching her steps in the dim candlelight. The ground was uneven, the ceiling low enough in places that Mortimer had to hunch over.

"They used to smuggle slaves through here during the Civil War." Sheila's voice was barely above a whisper. "Edith said the pastor had been an abolitionist and part of the Underground Railroad. When she was a schoolteacher, they brought kids on field trips here."

They walked for a while, maybe twenty minutes, until they arrived at a wooden door made of heavy planks and iron hinges. Sheila grabbed an iron ring and pulled. "Help me."

Mortimer grabbed the ring too, pulled, his muscles straining. Finally the door swung open. They stepped into fresh air and darkness. Mortimer blinked, letting his eyes adjust. They'd come out under an unused railroad bridge, a small creek flowing in front of them.

"We can follow the tracks," Bill suggested.

"No," Sheila said. "If we go along the creek a mile or so, we'll cross a dirt road that takes us south. Nobody will see us. Come on." She didn't look back to see if they followed.

They hesitated only a moment before running after her.

The stars were brilliant in the night sky, the moon a crescent of glowing silver. The night was cold but not bitterly so. Mortimer slung the Nike tote over his shoulder, fixed the Maxfli cap firmly on his head.

"Where's she taking us?" Bill asked.

"Away."

Behind them, the scattered shots sounded like popcorn. Like a string of firecrackers on the Fourth of July.

HIKING AND CAMPING

XXV

Sheila led them farther and for longer than Mortimer would have hiked if it were up to him. The creek twisted past houses and into the forest. After a long time it hit a dirt road.

"The logging trucks used to come through here," Sheila said.

Mortimer expected her to stop and make camp, but she climbed up the embankment to the road and kept going.

Bill finally spoke up. "Any time you want to s-stop is f-fine with me. I wouldn't say no to a fire." He didn't have a coat and shivered.

"Not yet." She kept walking.

They marched by starlight and the wan glow of the moon. Another hour slid by. Bill marched with his head down, his back bent, carrying the sack of goods from the Joey's pantry. At last, Sheila halted, looked about, seemed to get her bearings. She dove into the woods, and Mortimer found himself on a narrow path.

The path soon opened into a clearing, and Mortimer made out the vague shape of a structure. As they approached, he saw it was some kind of picnic area.

To Bill Sheila said, "Get wood if you want a fire."

Bill dropped the sack, started picking up sticks.

"What is this place?" Mortimer asked.

Sheila relit the candle and held it up to a brown sign with yellow lettering. TVA STATE PRESERVE. PICNIC AREA E.

"We were here when it got the worst," Sheila said. Her voice was flat and cold. "A Brownie troop. Kyle was the husband of our den mother."

Mortimer was glad it was dark. He didn't want Sheila to see the look on his face.

Bill dropped an armload of wood next to the fire pit. "Let's get this f-fucking thing lit. I'm freezing my b-balls off."

They made a circle around the fire and ate chunks of brown bread taken from the Joey's pantry. Nobody had the energy to cook anything. Sheila pulled a tightly rolled, very thin sleeping bag out of her backpack. She unrolled it three feet from the fire and slipped inside. The sleeping bag was pink, with pictures of the Little Mermaid on the front.

Mortimer gave his thin blanket to Bill, who didn't have a coat. He used his tote bag as a pillow. The fire took the edge off the cold. Even Bill had stopped shivering.

In spite of a deep exhaustion, none of them could fall immediately to sleep. The buzz of the danger they'd left behind still coursed through Mortimer's veins, his mind tumbling and turning with a hundred thoughts. Maybe the others felt the same way. Mortimer glanced around the small camp and saw open eyes glinting in the firelight.

"Maybe we should count sheep," Mortimer said.

Bill yawned. "That'll just make me hungry for mutton."

"How did you end up at the Cleveland Joey's, Sheila?"

She didn't say anything for a while, like she was trying to figure out how to start. Finally, she said, "I sort of panicked after Kyle was killed. I know that probably sounds stupid, but you get used to someone telling you what to do all the time, when to eat and when to sleep, and, well, just everything. I went back to the firehouse at first."

Sheila sat up, wrapped the pink sleeping bag around her, stared into the fire. "After spending one night by myself, I knew I couldn't just stay there and do nothing, if only because the food would run out. But it wasn't that so much. I just felt I had to go, you know? I haven't really thought about it until now, not clearly, not asking myself what I was thinking or if I had any plans, because I didn't. I didn't have any plans except I had to go. But thinking back, I guess I knew that it was up to me. That I could go or stay or live or lie down and die and it was completely up to me and nobody else. It was scary that first day, not having anyone tell me what to do, but once I packed everything and left the firehouse, I didn't see how I'd ever lived before. I guess I hadn't lived, not actually. I was just this thing that Kyle used. When he died, I started living."

Mortimer propped himself up on one elbow. "What happened?"

She pulled her gaze away from the fire, met Mortimer's eyes. "What do you mean?"

"Well, to end up at Joey's. You were suddenly free, but then you ended up . . ." Mortimer couldn't bring himself to say *a whore*. "It seems like you went from serving one man to serving any old man who walked through Joey's front door."

Sheila cocked her head to one side, eyes squinting like she was trying to understand a duck that had suddenly started speaking French.

"It's different," she said. "You don't understand at all. Men come from miles around to see me. They need what *I* can do for them. Kyle made me think I needed him. And that was wrong. Men want *me*. Need me."

"Don't get upset," Mortimer said. "I didn't mean anything."

"I'm not upset. I just can't believe you don't understand. If you think being at Joey's is the same as being with Kyle, if you don't see how it's totally different, then I don't know how to explain it to you."

Now Mortimer sat up, made vague shushing motions. "Look, I know it's a lot safer at Joey's. They treat you well and feed you and it's like a million times better than what Kyle was doing. Of course it was a better situation."

"You still don't get it." She did appear angry now, her hard eyes flashing in the firelight. "I have worth. At Joey Armageddon's they recognize that worth. They showed me I have value. All those years, Kyle wasn't raping me. He was robbing me."

Sleep came eventually. Mortimer awoke the next morning to the smell of sausage and coffee and thought he'd weep for joy.

"Morning." Sheila tended the fire, cooked the mystery sausages in the pan Mortimer had purchased just yesterday. She didn't seem upset. The morning was bright. Birds sang. The air was crisp and sweet.

"Where's Bill?"

She said, "Off somewhere taking a shit, I think."

Right.

She pointed deeper into the forest. "If you go that way you'll find a nice, clear stream if you want to wash up. I got some water earlier, but I used it for the coffee." She handed him his tin cup.

The cup was hot, and Mortimer used the tail of his shirt to

hold it. The cold morning air drifted up his shirt and chilled him. He ignored it, held the coffee up to his nose. It smelled damn good. "Thanks."

Sheila poked at the sausages with a fork. "Breakfast soon."

"Okay. Guess I'll splash some water on my face."

He wandered off to find the stream, in no particular hurry. The forest was starting to fill in with green; still no underbrush, but pine needles were thick on every branch. It was pleasant. Mortimer could almost pretend he was on a camping trip. It was pretty here; maybe there was even good fishing in the stream. He had not been fly-fishing in a long time.

Anne had never cared for fishing, but she liked hiking and the outdoors in general. Their last real vacation had been to Las Vegas, and neither of them had enjoyed it; they had spent most of the time complaining that they should have gone to Yellowstone instead. Maybe if they'd gone to Yellowstone the next year it could have saved things. Maybe that would have been the start, gotten things back on track.

They never got around to it.

Mortimer found the stream, splashed water on his face. It was freezing, but even that was pleasant, the wet sting waking him up. And the coffee. That woke him up too, warmed his belly.

Mortimer sat on a rock and watched the stream go by and sipped coffee, and was quietly happy that not everything in the world was broken. There were still clear early mornings and hot cups of coffee.

Sheila's scream echoed through the forest. Mortimer dropped the tin cup and was already running before it hit the ground.

XXVI

Halfway back to camp, Mortimer made himself slow down. He wouldn't be able to help anyone if he ran straight into a trap. He moved as quickly as he could while remaining quiet.

At the edge of the camp, he crouched low. He saw bodies moving through the low-hanging pine boughs. He scooted around, trying to get a better look. Two men, no, three, standing near Sheila. One had her by the shirt lapel. She was trying to pull away. The men laughed.

"Doing some camping, sweetheart?" asked the one holding her.

"Fuck off."

That made him laugh more.

"Who's here with you?" asked one of the other ones.

"Just me, asshole."

"She's got a mouth on her," the third one said.

"She's got a sweet little caboose on her." The one who held her pulled her closer, dropped his rifle so he could grope.

Sheila aimed a kick at his groin. He turned and took it on the thigh, grunted.

The other two men laughed at him. Mortimer saw the arm-bands. Red Stripes. He tensed to spring out at them, but what could he do? All three carried rifles. Mortimer could see his shotgun leaning against his Nike bag on the other side of the camp-fire.

"Stupid cunt." He yanked at her shirt and it ripped, the but-tons popping halfway down. Sheila gasped, fear blooming in her eyes, no trace of defiance anymore. He yanked again and the shirt ripped open. She wasn't wearing a bra, and her breasts sprang out, immediately goose-pimpled in the cold air. He grabbed a fistful of her hair and pulled her head back, her mouth gaping open, a scream caught in her throat.

Three of them. Mortimer couldn't take three. Not bare-handed.

The bushes rustled on the other side of the camp, and Bill bumbled through, buckling his belt. "I thought I heard—oh, hell."

The third Red Stripe swung his rifle, aimed it at Bill. The tip of the barrel was a foot from Bill's nose. "Hey, man! Hold it right there."

Bill froze, eyes big.

Sheila dropped to one knee, grabbed the coffeepot off the campfire.

The guy holding her looked down to see what she was doing, and she splashed it all. The scalding coffee hit his eyes and he dropped her, screaming. Falling to the ground, pawing at the bright red flesh of his scorched face.

Mortimer was already out of his hiding place and running toward them. He threw himself on one Red Stripe, pinned his arms so the guy couldn't bring his rifle up. The one near Bill turned, aimed at Mortimer. Mortimer saw what was happen-ing and turned his captive toward the Red Stripe firing at him. The rifle barked, and Mortimer felt the man in his arms twitch and die, a bloody hole in his chest. He dropped him, turned toward the man with the coffee eyes, who was already on his feet again.

Bill jumped the Red Stripe near him. They wrestled, went down.

Mortimer advanced on coffee eyes, but the Red Stripe pulled a revolver from his belt, brought it up toward Mortimer, who flinched back.

An explosion, the echoing crack of pistol fire.

The Red Stripe's head exploded above the temple, hair and bone and blood flying up and away. His whole body vibrated like some obscene tuning fork before it collapsed.

Sheila stood a dozen feet away, holding an enormous automatic pistol in both hands, her open shirt flapping in the breeze, a look of wild animal rage on her face.

Bill had wrested the rifle away from the last Red Stripe. He stood over him, about to bring the rifle butt down on his head.

"Wait!" Mortimer shouted.

Bill took a step back, but still held the rifle ready to strike.

Mortimer bent and pried the pistol from the dead Red Stripe's hand. He took it to the Red Stripe near Bill, aimed at a spot between the Red Stripe's eyes. There was fear there, and he held his hands up feebly like he might ward off the bullet.

"Now," Mortimer said. "I'm going to need you to answer a few questions."

They used Sheila's ruined shirt to tie the captive's hands behind the trunk of a thin pine. He sat up against the bark, looking afraid.

Sheila put on her only spare shirt, a navy blue turtleneck, and joined Bill and Mortimer in staring down at the prisoner. They made a menacing trio. Mortimer held the .38 revolver he'd liberated from the head-shot Red Stripe, and Bill cradled one of the deer rifles in his arms. Sheila's automatic turned out to be a .50 Desert Eagle, and Mortimer marveled that the little girl had not been knocked back on her ass when she'd fired the thing.

The Red Stripe said his name was Paul.

Sheila said they couldn't give a shit and pointed the giant gun at his face.

"Just hold on." Mortimer took her by the elbow and pulled her back, felt her muscles tense. "I want some information."

"Look, I really don't know much," Paul said.

"We'll decide that."

"I didn't even want to be a Red Stripe."

Bill smirked. "You just in it for their generous medical benefits?"

"I got drafted," Paul said. "They found me down in Georgia. I was just minding my own business and scrounging for food, and they picked me up and said I could join up or they would put my head on a pike as a warning to everyone else."

"Like hell," Sheila said.

"I'm telling you true, man," Paul said. "Let me go, and I'll run in the opposite direction."

"If you didn't want to be a Red Stripe, then why didn't you three just run off now while you had the chance?" Bill asked.

"They always make sure there's at least three of us together. The guy with the pistol was our unit leader, and we can never know if the other two will gang up on us if we try to run away. They always rotate us around, so we can't ever trust anybody."

Mortimer recalled the three Red Stripes he'd killed up on the mountain. "Check the rifles, Bill. How many rounds?"

Bill looked in each rifle. "Only one bullet each."

Mortimer thought about it and nodded. "I think he's telling the truth."

Sheila snorted. "I think he's a lying sack of shit."

"I ran into three Red Stripes before," Mortimer told them. "They only had one bullet each."

"That's right," Paul said. "You see? They don't want us to mutiny."

"Why did you attack the Joey Armageddon's in Cleveland?"

"I don't know," Paul said. "They said attack, so we attacked."

"Who gives the orders?"

Paul said, "The company captains give the orders to the unit leaders. I just do what I'm told."

"I mean the head guy. Who's in charge of the whole deal?"

"Nobody knows."

"He's lying." Sheila thrust the gun back at him.

"I'm just a grunt." Paul cast a pleading look at Mortimer. "You got to keep her off me, man."

"Like you were staying off me a little while ago?" She spat at him, and it landed on his ear.

"That wasn't me, man. That was Brandon. He's, like, a fucking animal."

"You didn't try to stop him." Cold hatred in her eyes.

"I told you. I'm just a grunt."

"You must've heard rumors," Mortimer said. "Something about your leader."

"There's always talk around camp. Nobody knows what's true and what's bullshit."

"Talk."

"They say he's eight feet tall and has pointed teeth like a shark's."

"Do you want me to shoot your goddamn face off?" Sheila yelled.

"You asked, so I told you."

"Try us with something a little more credible," Mortimer suggested.

"Most stories agree his headquarters is down south," Paul said. "He sends out his spies to get information and deliver orders to the company captains. Sometimes people will just disappear, and everyone always says it's one of the Czar's spies doing an assassination."

"The Czar?"

"That's what everyone calls him."

"Why?"

Paul shrugged. "Hell if I know."

Sheila growled. "You're a useless asshole."

"Take it easy," Mortimer said.

"Fuck easy," Sheila said. "You don't think this guy would have taken his turn if you hadn't come back? Him and his buddies?"

Paul shook his head. "No way. I—"

"Shut your goddamn mouth." She put the barrel of the automatic against his forehead, pressed hard.

"Hey, man, get her off—"

"Sheila, let's not get excited, maybe just . . ." Mortimer took a step toward her.

"I should blow your fucking balls off, pig." She aimed the gun lower.

"Sheila, don't—"

"She's crazy, man. Get her away—"

Bang.

Paul howled.

Bill jumped back. "Fucking shit!"

Mortimer could only watch in horror.

Blood gushed from the ragged hole between Paul's legs. It came out fast, forming an ever-widening pool, like somebody had kicked over a five-gallon tub of raspberry syrup.

"Oh, God! Holy shit, man." Hot tears rolling down Paul's suddenly pale face. "You've got to help me. Oh, Jesus."

"In some places, they chop off a thief's hand," Sheila said. "This is what you get."

"Oh, Jesus God, help me, fucking shit, I'm going to die, oh, shit." The blood gushed out so fast, they could see him actually deflate, shrinking against the pine trunk.

Mortimer gulped. "Do we have a first-aid kit, something to staunch the blood?"

"Are you kidding?" Bill looked green. "He's like a damn blood geyser or something. How do we stop that?"

Paul's head flopped, and his chin hit his chest. The bloodflow had slowed to a dribble. The former Red Stripe sat in a pool of his blood so big and round, it seemed impossible that it had all fit inside him. Paul had drained and looked shriveled. A raisin that had once been a grape.

"I never seen anybody bleed out that quick before," Bill said. "Must be some kind of world record."

"Good." Sheila turned her back on the mess and began to pack.

Mortimer stood a little while, feeling vaguely sick. The copper smell of blood mixed with coffee and pine.

They finished gathering their gear and followed Sheila back to the road. They walked a long way in silence.

XXVII

They walked for two days toward Chattanooga, looking for human settlements but finding none. There was only the long broken highway and the occasional dead automobile. They saw people in twos and threes once or twice in the distance but paid them the courtesy of leaving them be. Once, a line of Red Stripes sent them into a ditch, where they watched and waited as the column marched past.

They said little to one another. An uneasy pall hung over the trio. To Mortimer, Sheila now seemed like something alien and dangerous. Equally disturbing was how Bill took the episode in stride, almost as if a young girl hadn't blown a stranger's testicles into hamburger at all.

Mortimer realized his problem had nothing to do with Bill or Sheila. They knew how to conduct themselves in this shattered world. Mortimer didn't. But he was learning. *Violence is the way now. It gets you what you want. Solves your problems. What could we have done with the guy anyway? Let him go? No. Squeeze a trigger and the problem goes away.*

Mortimer considered his brief interrogation of the Red Stripe. Somewhere a ghostly, mysterious leader pulled the strings of a reluctant army. This too must be part of the natural order. It was too much to hope that the world might be left to heal on its own.

Society had always been defined by its antagonists. The Greeks fought the Romans and the Romans battled the barbarians. Now the desperate and bedraggled refugees of a broken civilization had the Red Stripes to deal with. It depressed Mortimer to think that conflict was the natural state of the universe. It all started with a Big Bang, and it would just bang and bang and bang until it banged itself out.

No wonder Nietzsche said people would need to invent God if He didn't exist.

Stupid Kraut.

Who decided to invent Nietzsche?

One of Anne's books. She had so many egghead books, wanted to go to the University of Memphis to study philosophy, but Mortimer had talked her out of it. He had talked her out of so much. Talked her out of living. Oh, God. No wonder she'd left him.

Nine years to figure that out.

Jesus.

That night they made camp in the middle of Interstate 75, the husks of old cars on three sides of them providing shelter from the wind. Over a modest campfire, Bill fried the last of the suspicious sausages Sheila had liberated from the Joey's pantry.

"I should have asked him if anyone else made it out," Sheila said.

Mortimer looked up. He'd been nodding off. "What?"

"The Red Stripe. Whatshisname."

"Paul," Bill said.

"I should have asked Paul if any of the other girls made it out. I tried to find them before we left, but I guess they were with clients. I hope they're okay."

"I'm sure they're fine." Mortimer didn't believe it for a second.

"Sure."

For a moment, she seemed to want to say more, but maybe she didn't know how. She rolled over and went to sleep. After a while a sound like soft crying came from her side of the campfire, but it was difficult to tell over the howl of wind through the busted-out car windows.

They next morning they started walking again, every muscle in Mortimer's body groaning from sleeping on the ground.

By midday he spotted the remains of Chattanooga's insignificant skyline, humping up from the horizon like the yellowed bones of some long-lost skeleton rising from the dead.

XXVIII

Sheila told Mortimer this: The Chattanooga Joey Armageddon's (*the* Joey Armageddon's, the first, the prototype, the home office) was at the top of Lookout Mountain.

This is what Mortimer knew about Lookout Mountain:

When he was ten years old, his father had taken him. There was a legitimate Civil War memorial at the top, a historical landmark, flags, cannons, etc. Additionally there were a few cheesy tourist destinations in the area. Ruby Falls, a long cave with an underground waterfall at the end. The proprietors shone a red spotlight on the rushing water to give it the "ruby" effect. At certain times of the year, the underground river that fed the falls slowed to a sad trickle. But nobody wanted to go to a tourist attraction called Ruby Trickle. Another place: Rock City was a collection of unique rock formations connected by flimsy bridges and walkways. Ceramic gnomes had been placed strategically to heighten the cheese factor. To a ten-year-old Mortimer it had all seemed like a magical land of wonder and enchantment.

As an adult, these wonders were much less wondrous. One Labor Day weekend, a year after his wedding, Mortimer had taken Anne to see the sights. He'd talked her out of attending a Shakespeare festival.

Anne had not been amused. It was a blisteringly hot day, and she was dirty and sweat-stained by the time they'd finished touring Rock City. Even Mortimer wondered why he'd thought the trip would be a good idea. Looking around he'd seen only families. Moms and dads with two or three kids on the loose. The realization had hit him palpably in the gut that a hot summer day among ceramic gnomes might not have been his father's idea of a good time. The things parents did for their kids.

Not knowing what else to do, Mortimer had pressed on, taking Anne to Ruby Falls. At least the caves would be cooler. The gift shops were filled with the bright debris of future spring cleanings.

At the end of Anne and Mortimer's long cave tour, the music swelled, and suddenly, in the total darkness, the red spotlight had blazed forth to illuminate a pathetic trickle of water. A recorded voice boomed *Behold Ruby Falls!*

In the indifferent silence that followed, while the bored tour group shuffled and looked over their shoulders for the exit, Anne suddenly burst out laughing. It had all been so ridiculous, the big buildup, all for a little dribble into a puddle. Mortimer had started laughing too, and kitsch value had saved the weekend, at least a little. They adjourned to a Mexican café and got slightly drunk on watery margaritas. They'd had fun, but Mortimer had always been aware that in some important way, on some important level, he and Anne weren't fully connected. Perhaps she would have thought the same about him if they'd ended up at the Shakespeare festival.

One last memory struck Mortimer with wry amusement.

The Incline was a trolley-style railroad car that climbed Lookout Mountain to the Civil War park on top. As a ten-year-old, Mortimer had ridden with his dad down the Incline to St. Elmo Station, where tourist shops and ice-cream parlors and arcades and frolicking fun in every form clustered around the foot of the mountain.

When Mortimer had returned with Anne, he'd been shocked to find the area had fallen on hard times. The streets were deserted and most of the shops had been boarded up. The once bustling tourist zone around St. Elmo Station had become a ghost town.

It was the only place Mortimer thought might actually be better off for the fall of civilization.

They still had a long walk ahead of them.

Lookout Mountain was south of the city. They hiked I-75 until it intersected with I-24, then headed west on 24. They found out quickly enough which exit to take. A large wooden sign had been erected, featuring the vivid illustration of a thrashing, large-breasted woman against a pink mushroom cloud. An arrow underneath with neatly painted lettering read THIS WAY TO JOEY ARMAGEDDON'S SASSY A-GO-GO.

Their moods picked up at the sight of the sign, and they all three exchanged sheepish smiles. It wasn't quite like coming home, but it beat the hell out of camping on the interstate. They picked up the pace as they hit the exit ramp. They wanted a bed and a meal and a drink. Many drinks. And loud music and all the extravagant good times for which Joey Armageddon's was famous. It was why people came from miles and miles. To lose themselves in indulgence and forget the daily horror of simply waking up every morning and *living*. Respite, haven, sanctuary, and yet much more than that. Something that reminded you on a primal level that it was good to be alive.

Five minutes later, a dozen men pointed automatic rifles at them.

XXIX

"*Good evening, sir. My name* is James. I'd like to direct you and your party through our checkpoint, at which time you'll need to check your weapons with our clerk. He'll be happy to give you a receipt, and you're free to reclaim your weapons upon departure."

The man who'd uttered this well-rehearsed speech was young, with neatly cut blond hair and a smile full of straight, white teeth. He wore impeccable black trousers, black wingtips, a starched white shirt with black tie and black blazer. He held an M16 automatic rifle on Mortimer and his companions. The men behind James were dressed and equipped in the exact same manner.

Bill clutched one of the deer rifles to his chest like he was being asked to give up his firstborn. "Like hell."

The smile never wavered from James's face. "I'm afraid you will be denied entrance if we are unable to secure your firearms. For the safety of our drunken, irresponsible patrons, we must forbid all unauthorized weapons. Joey Armageddon thanks you for your cooperation."

Mortimer admired the young man's professionalism. Mortimer was confident James would remain polite and friendly the whole time he and his chums were shredding Mortimer and his companions with a lethal rain of automatic gunfire.

He edged closer to Bill, nudged him in the ribs. "Just pretend it's Dodge City and you're giving up your guns to Wyatt Earp."

Bill frowned. "Ha-fucking-ha-ha."

"Come on," Sheila said. "I just want to go in."

"Okay," Mortimer said to the guards. "We'll check the hardware."

James seemed genuinely delighted. "We appreciate your cooperation. Please follow the path through the gate. The clerk is on the other side."

The gate wasn't some half-assed blockade of dead cars like he'd seen in the small towns to the north. They'd put a cinder-block wall across the road. It was eight feet high with sporadic guard platforms on the other side, crisp men in starched shirts staring down over the sights of their M16 rifles. An iron gate swung open on well-oiled hinges, and Mortimer followed Sheila and Bill through to the other side.

It took a moment for the little village to snap into focus. Mortimer wasn't sure what he was seeing at first, but recognition dawned in ten seconds. They were on St. Elmo Avenue, and Mortimer could see St. Elmo Station a block and a half away.

Mortimer took another few seconds to realize why everything looked so strange. It looked like an actual town, a place where people lived and worked and hadn't endured nearly a decade of doom. If there had been cars on the road, Mortimer might have believed he'd finally awakened from a long, detailed nightmare. The village around St. Elmo Station bustled with commerce. The goods and services from various shops spilled out onto the streets, giving the place an open-air-market feel. Everything was clean and organized, the streets and buildings in good repair.

And light. With the oncoming darkness, a man walked the

street lighting oil lamps set high on thin iron poles. They did not fear the dark here. There was no starvation or danger. Even the men with machine guns were courteous.

"Sir? Excuse me, sir?"

Mortimer blinked out of his stupor, turned to see a squat, round gentleman with a sweaty red face watching him expectantly.

"Sir, my name is Reginald, and I'm the master gun clerk. Please step to the kiosk."

The gun kiosk was some kind of converted ticket booth with a kid barely out of his teens at the window. Behind the kid hung all manner of rifles and pistols. Even a sword or two. Sheila and Bill were already folding receipts and putting them into pants pockets.

Reginald said, "If you please, sir, hand your weaponry through the window to Steven. He'll tag it for you and make out a receipt."

He handed the kid the shotgun, then the pistol he'd taken off the Red Stripe. He felt oddly naked without the guns. They'd become an important part of his personal inventory. The kid handed him back a receipt, which Mortimer shoved down the front pocket of his jeans.

"What if I need to defend myself?"

Reginald smiled with practiced patience. "You need only defend yourself from quality service and premium female companionship. I'd surrender."

Good suggestion.

Mortimer, Bill and Sheila made their way toward St. Elmo Station, walking in no particular hurry, craning their necks and gawking at the village. At one point, Sheila uttered a muted squeal and skipped toward a shop with dazzling women's clothing hanging in the window. She pressed her face against the glass like a five-year-old gazing longingly at a candy store display.

Mortimer came up behind her. "Buying a dress for the ball?"

She sighed. "Not likely without money." She brightened slightly. "But I'll get a job as a Joey Girl again. Then I'll get clothes even better than these."

"I don't doubt it."

"What gets me about these clothes is that some of them are only pretty," she said. "Not made to keep you warm or dry. Just to be pretty. Can you believe they'd make clothes just for that? I guess they used to all the time."

Anne had always wanted the most impractical clothing and loathed Mortimer for pointing that out. "Every girl should have at least one dress just to be pretty."

Mortimer didn't know if he quite believed that, but it was the right thing to say. A smile flickered across Sheila's face, and for an instant the hardness fell away and she wasn't a teenage whore and killer. She was just a young girl looking at pretty dresses in a shop window.

They realized they'd lost Bill. It was bound to happen, so many things to catch the eye and turn the head. Soon Sheila was off looking into another store window. Without vehicular traffic, the middle of the avenue had become a sort of town square. A man played a banjo while a small monkey performed acrobatic feats. Mortimer was glad the monkey hadn't been eaten. How many escaped zoo animals roamed the countryside? A few yards down, another performer juggled flaming batons. Someone else dealt three-card monty. He smelled cotton candy and some kind of meat on a stick.

He realized he didn't have any money but hoped he could get the same credit here he'd gotten at the Joey's in Cleveland. He really wanted to sleep indoors tonight. It would be a great gift to Bill and Sheila to buy them both a big dinner, a few bottles of wine. Hell, maybe he'd even get Sheila a new dress for the occasion. Mortimer admitted to himself he was thinking about everything except why he'd come all this way in the first place.

Somewhere at the top of Lookout Mountain his wife, Anne, waited.

Now that he was here, the idea of marching up to her and saying, "Hi, honey, it's me, your husband. Long time no see," seemed ludicrous. A juvenile part of him did relish the surprised look he hoped to see on her face, but mostly he didn't know how she would react, and that made him nervous.

But Mortimer owed her something. He couldn't articulate what that might be, not exactly, but he needed to see her, and he honestly believed she'd want to see him. Sure she would. They were married after all.

He was stalling. Was it possible Mortimer no longer wanted—or needed—to see Anne? He'd come down the mountain alone. It might only be natural for him to seek out his wife. To connect again with the world via the only person he could think of who might want to see him. But Mortimer wasn't alone anymore. He counted Bill as a friend. Sheila . . . well, he didn't know what to think of Sheila and her "apology." She was more than an acquaintance but not quite anything else, yet Mortimer still felt he wanted to call Sheila friend. Even if she was a scary, ferocious demon child.

So what did he want from Anne? What did he think she might want from him? He stood in the town square, eyes going unfocused as he thought hard about it, jugglers and monkeys and cardsharps plying their trades around him. He blotted them out. Something was coming to him, some significant thought coalescing from all the loose ends knocking around in his head.

Sheila emerged from the crowd to stand next to him, tentatively touched his arm. "Are you okay?"

"Shhhhh. Don't talk," Mortimer said. "I'm having an epiphany."

He had come all this way, fueled by the misguided notion that he still loved Anne, that he needed to find her again, win her back somehow. What he really wanted was to stem his abject loneliness, the hollow ache that had clawed and gnawed his gut for nine years, until finally he had to fill that burning hole with . . . something. His desperate mind grabbed for something familiar and had latched on to the memory of Anne. Mortimer had not wanted to march into the gray unknown of a shattered world without a destination, without hope of the familiar, so he'd fabricated the myth of Anne and their possible reunion.

But Mortimer found that he wasn't alone. He had Bill and Sheila and a Joey Armageddon's Platinum card. He was doing all right. He was reinventing himself in a new context. This different, surprising, shocking world might disgust him, confound him, bruise and terrify him, but so far it had not knocked him down, not so badly that he couldn't find his feet again. Mortimer Tate could stand up. He did not need his ex-wife.

He thought maybe that he loved her still but wasn't *in* love with her. Is that what women meant when they said that bullshit? Yes, Mortimer understood now. His mind had broadened to understand this simple truth. All it took was the end of the world.

He blinked himself out of his daydream, clapped his hands and rubbed them together. "Okay, figured that out. Now let's go get something to eat."

XXX

They found Bill and headed for St. Elmo Station and the Incline Railway. The trolley car's tracks climbed the steep slope of Lookout Mountain, terminating at Point Park, the Civil War historical site at the top. From the side, the trolley looked peculiar, slanted at a severe angle, but since it traveled up such a steep slope, it meant the passengers could sit in level comfort. The trolley was packed, 80 percent of the passengers male. There was an electric vibe in the trolley car, a spark of eager expectation as they headed to Joey Armageddon's at the summit.

In some places, the grade was more than 70 percent, and as a kid, Mortimer remembered hearing that the Incline held the world record for steepest railway. He also remembered spectacular views toward the top of the mountain, but night had fallen now and all he could see were flickering pinpricks of light along the mountain and in the valley, scattered campfires and lanterns. He leaned out one of the windows, looked up ahead toward the end of the line.

Shimmering colored light crowned the top of Lookout Mountain, orange and yellow and a crazy purple shot through with searchlight stabs into the heavens. As they inched closer, the music grew louder, some sort of symphonic cymbal-crashing music. If the combined effect had been designed to heighten anticipation, it was working beautifully. Mortimer couldn't wait to get to the top.

Mortimer no longer felt he was on a quest. The desperate urgency had drained from him. He still wanted to see Anne, still felt some sort of closure would be beneficial, but he had no expectations. *What will be, will be.* The future was his to shape. Perhaps he would find a house nearby, set up shop. The thought of further travel wearied him. No, he would not think beyond tonight.

He was a Platinum member.

Let the good times roll.

The top of Lookout Mountain hummed and buzzed and bustled with activity. Large stereo speakers hanging in the trees boomed the classical music, which Mortimer now recognized as the theme from *Star Wars.* More armed but ever-friendly guards in clean black suits watched over the crowd. The passengers spilled out of the trolley car into the throng. The crowd headed for a set of gates that took them on a circular path to the front entrance. Mortimer, Bill and Sheila fell into the slowly moving mass of people. It reminded Mortimer of the few times he'd been to a Tennessee Titans game, the expectant crowds drifting en masse through the turnstiles into the stadium.

Above them, music filled the sky, spotlights danced among the trees; it was the circus and the Super Bowl and a Hollywood premiere all rolled into one. Mortimer was simultaneously awed and giddy.

After five minutes of edging forward in the line, Mortimer saw a small gate in a white wooden fence off to the side. A discreet sign in small lettering read VIP ENTRANCE. He reached in his pocket, came out with the pink Platinum membership card. He grabbed Sheila by the hand, met Bill's eye. "Come on!" He fast-walked toward the gate, pulling Sheila behind him.

"We'll lose our place in line," Bill said, but he followed.

Mortimer went straight up to the iron gate and then backed away immediately when a hand stretched through the bars holding a snub-nosed nickel revolver. The man on the other side of the pistol wore the standard black suit and gleaming white shirt, but a well-crafted, pink pin shaped like a mushroom cloud on his lapel possibly denoted some kind of rank.

He cocked the revolver with a thumb. "Good evening, sir. I'm the V.I.P. host on duty, and my name is Lars. I'm sorry for any inconvenience, but this entrance is reserved for special guests of Joey Armageddon. We thank you for your cooperation in avoiding unnecessary bloodshed and ask you to please step back in line."

"Uh . . ." Mortimer took a half step forward, holding the pink membership card in front of him. He readied himself to jump back if need be. He didn't quite have faith in the card's ability to stop bullets, no matter how well it was laminated.

Lars reached through the bars with his other hand and took the card, read it, smiled at Mortimer. "Very sorry for the misunderstanding, Mr. Tate." Lars made the revolver disappear into a shoulder holster and swung the gate open. "If you and your party could step this way."

They walked through the gate, and Lars closed it behind them.

The other side was gardenlike, well manicured, with tall hedges bordering a path that paralleled the slow-moving line on the other side. Discreet lanterns lit the flagstone path.

Mortimer gestured down the path. "That way?" He hoped. It would be a hell of a lot faster than waiting in the huge line on the other side of the hedge.

"You need not walk, sir. I can arrange transportation if you like."

Mortimer exchanged bemused glances with Bill. "Uh . . . sure."

Lars picked up an old-fashioned phone from a pedestal near the gate and dialed three digits. "Yes, I need a sky chariot for a Platinum member and his two guests. How long? Fine." He hung up.

To Mortimer he said, "It will only be a few minutes. You're not scared of heights, are you?"

THE GREATEST SHOW ON EARTH

XXXI

Mortimer had not known what to expect when Lars had ordered a sky chariot. He'd stood for a moment, openly curious, when he'd heard a whoosh and the creak of gears and pulleys. He'd looked up, seen the hot-pink gondola fly overhead, suspended from a thick cable. It had probably been looted from some nearby amusement park. It angled down and landed at a port forty feet away. They crowded in. Lars joined them, explaining first-time Platinum visitors were escorted personally for better service. The open-air gondola (sky bucket, Lars called it informally) was just big enough for the four of them.

So they floated, music wafting up to them, lights playing across the sky. Mortimer began to laugh, deep and throaty, holding his belly. Sheila smiled too, but looked at him curiously.

Bill raised an eyebrow. "What's funny?"

"I don't know." Mortimer kept laughing.

Lars smiled knowingly. "You've had a hard journey to get here?"

Mortimer wiped his eyes. "Like you wouldn't believe."

Lars said, "First-time visitors often feel a distinct and sudden euphoria that manifests itself sometimes in an uncontrolled burst of laughter. Upon realizing you have miraculously come through certain death and horror, the relief stimulates an endorphin release in the brain, which facilitates the process. Typical after prolonged exposure to stress and trauma."

"Whoa," Bill said. "Were you a psychologist or something?"

"Tax auditor for the IRS."

Mortimer leaned out of the sky bucket for a better look. They passed over a well-lit section of ground, roughly the size of a football field. Rows and rows of men pedaled stationary bicycles. They all wore black shorts and pink T-shirts, and a thick, steamy heat rose from the area.

The sight of the slave riders put a minor dent in Mortimer's endorphin production, and his euphoria deflated. Mortimer wasn't any kind of a historian, but he could think of no era in which the haves hadn't benefited from the labor of the have-nots. Was there something about the fall of civilization that nudged a man toward socialism? Or were the concepts of "fair" and "unfair" simply less abstract when one observed hundreds of bike-pedaling slaves from the safety and comfort of a soaring sky bucket?

Still, and Mortimer hated admitting it to himself, a small part of him thought, *Better them than me.*

"We can take you directly into the club for seating," Lars said. "But if I might make a suggestion, you and your party might like to check in to the hotel and clean up first."

"Sounds good."

Sheila said, "I won't need a room. I'm here to sign on as a Joey Girl."

The slightest possible twitch of anxiety passed across Lars's face, but he hid it immediately, smiling instead. "Of course, madam. I'd be happy to drive you back to Human Resources."

"I don't have any money," Mortimer said. "I was given membership in Spring City and was hoping to talk to somebody about credit. I probably need some new clothes."

"I can attend to every detail," Lars said.

Lars turned out to be a whirlwind of service and efficiency. He met Mortimer and Bill in their hotel suite after the two had showered, bringing with him Armageddon dollars from Mortimer's account and fresh suits of clothing for both men.

"Lars, you've done a hell of a job," Mortimer said. "Is tipping still in vogue this day and age?"

"Of course, sir. We're civilized people here after all."

Mortimer counted out twenty of the coins and dropped them into Lars's palm. Lars tried to keep his face neutral, but it was clear he was having some kind of interior argument with himself.

"I feel it's my duty to inform you, sir, that this amount is, in fact, equal to a month's salary. And I'm considered senior staff."

Mortimer tossed back a glass of wine, considered. "I appreciate your telling me the truth. I've been out of touch, and I still haven't got the hang of the new economy. Let's just say you keep that. And if there are any special favors we need but are too stupid to ask for, you can help us out, okay?"

Lars bowed slightly, had already slipped the coins into his jacket pocket. "It is my utmost delight to make your stay here at Joey Armageddon's as comfortable as possible, and I assure you that your needs will be in my every thought."

"Great. Now, if possible, my friend and I would like to see naked girls and get shit-faced."

"Absolutely, sir. And may I say it will be our pleasure to clean up your vomit should you overindulge."

XXXII

Lars escorted them via golf cart through a VIP side entrance. He'd had the foresight to reserve them a table down front, less than ten feet from the stage. Mortimer couldn't help the dopey grin on his face.

The place was marvelous.

It was set up like a big, indoor band shell, the room opening wider and taller as it went from the stage back to the front entrance. The stage jutted out in a semicircle, edged with small tables, another identical row of tables behind Mortimer. Above that another tier of tables and behind that the club proper with scattered tables, bars along each wall and sequined women in miniskirts hovering from table to table, delivering drinks and flirting with patrons.

Smash Mouth blasted from the sound system, segued into a brassy big-band instrumental with a new pop flavor.

Above, girls in bikinis hung from trapezes, waving and blowing kisses. Once in a while, a spotlight would land on one of the girls, who would then spin around or perform some other minor trapeze trick, prompting enthusiastic applause.

Mortimer's grin wilted as he thought of Anne. Had she performed on the trapeze? Who were these women? Wives and sisters and daughters. Mortimer didn't want to think about it. Thinking about it would ruin it.

A stunning, thin brunette with aquiline features handed Bill and Mortimer a drinks menu.

"I don't see any of that Freddy's crap," Bill said.

"Good." Mortimer pointed to the Jack Daniel's on the menu. "It's only six dollars a bottle. Do you think that's a misprint?"

"Must be fake stuff they're just calling Jack Daniel's," Bill said. "I'm game if you are."

They ordered a bottle of Jack Daniel's, and the waitress said she'd return with food menus.

Bill looked at Mortimer for a long second, then said, "You haven't mentioned your wife."

"She'll keep." Mortimer smiled. "I had an epiphany."

"Well, I don't know anything about that, but you're not puking so much."

Mortimer cocked an eyebrow. "What?"

"When we first met," Bill said. "Seemed like you were puking all the time."

"Give me a break."

The waitress arrived with a bottle of Jack and two tumblers. They declined ice, and she poured three fingers of Jack into each glass.

"Are you ready to order?"

"It says steaks on the menu," Mortimer said.

The waitress nodded.

Mortimer asked, "Real steak? Not rat steak or steak made from couch cushions or Soylent Green or something? Steaks from actual cows?"

"Rib eyes."

"Two steaks, potatoes and whatever vegetable is most fresh," Mortimer said.

She wrote it down and went away.

"Real steaks." Bill whistled. "Do I want to know how much that's going to cost? An arm and a leg, I bet."

"Two arms and three legs," Mortimer said. "But I don't care."

They drank. Their eyes got big and they looked at the glasses and at the bottle.

"Is it just me," Bill said, "or is this Jack Daniel's fucking fantastic?"

"It's not just you. Do you think it's real?"

Bill shook his head. "It's too damn cheap. Maybe we're just used to that Freddy's stuff."

They both laughed.

"I don't know." Mortimer grinned. "That Dishwater Lager grows on you."

"One time I had something called Freddy's Dung-Brown Tequila." Bill made a gagging face. "It seriously tasted like ass. I mean it. Sweaty ass."

They both drank the Jack Daniel's again. It was just as good the second time.

Mortimer felt pleasantly warm. It started in his belly and spread through his limbs, lightened his head. He looked up, smiled at one of the trapeze girls. He tapped his foot to a song called "I Touch Myself" and tried to remember the group.

The waitress dropped by for a visit, put a soft hand on Mortimer's shoulder. "The chef will put your steaks on the grill soon. Everything okay here?"

Mortimer said, "Maybe you can help me. I'm looking for Anne Tate. I'm told she works here."

A light came on in the waitress's eyes. "Oh, yeah. I think I know her." A slight frown. "But it's been a while since I've seen her. They employ so many people here. I can ask."

"I'd appreciate that. I'm sort of . . . an old friend."

"No problem."

"Hey!" Bill held up his tumbler, swirled the amber liquid. "What is this stuff?"

The waitress looked at him like maybe it was a trick question. "Jack Daniel's."

"I know. I mean who makes it? It practically tastes like the real thing."

"It *is* the real thing," she said. "The distillery never closed. You can read about it here." She turned the bottle around so the back label faced Bill.

"I'll be damned," Bill said. "They still make the stuff." He squinted at the label's small print.

"Read it," Mortimer said.

XXXIII

Jack Daniel's: The Tradition Survives

*M*uch blood has been spilled to preserve the smooth-sipping Tennessee whiskey you've enjoyed through good times and bad. Governments might rise and fall, but the recipe for your favorite adult beverage has remained unchanged even when the world as we know it has been through the wringer. You can count on our seasoned and indestructible distillers to continue bringing you the finest whiskey in what's left of the known world.

A mere three months after the Fall, humanity quickly discovered it did not want to endure the end of all civilization sober, so raiding parties at the Jack Daniel's distillery were frequent and disruptive. The owners soon gathered the remaining distillery employees into a fighting militia known as the Jack Squad. With the help of some intrepid local NRA enthusiasts, Fort Lynchburg was built and defended. The fort almost fell to a band of wild Civil War reenactors who had replaced their muzzle-loaders with army-surplus M1 rifles. At last, General Ira "Stonewall" Weinstein surrendered his sword before being hung from a Kentucky Fried Chicken sign, where his bones still hang today as a reminder for those who'd fuck with the producers of the finest, smoothest liquor ever made by true Americans.

So challenges may come and go, but Jack Daniel's pledges to keep using only the best, purest ingredients available. Unlike those responsible for the short-lived resurgence of Sam Adams beer, Jack Daniel's *promises to use pure spring water, free of radioactive or other toxic materials.*

So whether you're fleeing violent rape gangs, remembering those lost loved ones, or daydreaming of a future where wild dogs no longer roam the streets, we hope you'll keep making Jack Daniel's your preferred beverage.

XXXIV

"Pour me another one."

"Right." Bill grabbed the bottle, splashed more Jack into each glass. "I have to admit, things have been interesting since I hooked up with you."

"'May you live in interesting times,'" Mortimer said. "That's an ancient Chinese curse."

"Yeah, I guess. Some of it's been a curse," Bill admitted. "Like almost getting eaten and losing my guns and my hat. Stuff like that. But a lot of it's good too. I like drinking well and eating well and sleeping indoors with flush toilets and electricity. I like Joey's. But it's expensive."

Damn right.

"I'm sort of painfully aware that you've been floating me this whole time, and I don't like feeling that I'm not contributing my fair share."

"Don't forget you saved my life," Mortimer said. "That's your fair share and then some. When you found me I was on a leash."

"Yeah, but you saved my life too," Bill reminded him. "I expect a couple of fellows pal around long enough they'll save each other pretty regular. No, I need to pull my weight . . . although I sure as hell won't say no to that steak when it arrives."

Mortimer grinned. "Okay, so starting right after you finish your steak, what do you propose?"

"You've got the capital and I have the knowledge," Bill said. "I'm a hell of a good shot when I have my pistols, and I know my way around the country. You sold that stuff to the Spring City Joey's store for a bundle, and you're sitting on a pile of cash. But even so much money will run out eventually. You're going to need to figure some way to earn a living, and I'm tired of not always knowing where my next meal's coming from. I have a few ideas where we might be able to make a good haul. You outfit us for the trip, and I'll lead the way. We split fifty-fifty."

"What kind of haul?"

"Fair question." Bill tossed back the rest of his Jack and eyed the bottle, which they were consuming at a surprising rate. "What do people want? Guns, food, booze, clothing, a safe place to live."

"Right."

"But things are getting better, and I think if we put our heads together we can figure out the next level of things people will need."

Mortimer slurped Jack Daniel's. "Next level?"

"Like . . . hell, I don't know. Like if everyone is dying for a Pepsi Cola and willing to pay big money for a Pepsi Cola, and then they finally start getting Pepsi Cola on a regular basis, then the next thing is they want *ice* for their Pepsi Cola."

Mortimer nodded. "I see. So we corner the market on ice. Or whatever the next thing is."

"Exactly. Like I said, I might have a few ideas, but—"

"Give me that goddamn bottle!" Sheila's sudden appearance at the table startled Mortimer. She grabbed the Jack Daniel's bottle, upended it into her mouth. She coughed, sputtered. It splashed down her chin.

"Don't waste it," Bill said.

"Fuck off." She coughed, wiped her mouth with the back of her hand, then took another drink. She winced but kept it down this time.

"You want to sit down?" Mortimer asked.

"Okay."

Mortimer flagged down a busboy, who brought another chair for Sheila.

"What happened?"

"They don't want me," Sheila said. "Oh, they were sort of polite about it, I guess. They said they needed more kitchen help, or I could get on the list to ship out to one of the new Joey locations."

"Well, I can't say I'm surprised," Bill said. "This place must get women from all over looking for work." He gestured to the trapeze girls. "And they're all incredibly hot too."

Mortimer frowned. "Could you be a little more sensitive, please?"

Sheila sighed. "No, he's right. That's more or less what they told me. Shit, now what am I going to do?"

Mortimer felt suddenly, crushingly sorry for the girl. She had been so confident, and now it had all been so easily taken away. Maybe it was the booze sneaking up on him. He could get sloppy and sentimental sometimes. He could smell her sitting there next to him. Not so bad, not really, but like campfire smoke and road sweat. She hadn't even had a chance to clean up.

"You can eat at least," he said. "And maybe another drink?"

She nodded, wiped at her eyes and looked embarrassed. She cleared her throat. "Sure. Okay. But not this stuff." She meant the Jack Daniel's. "It's making me ill."

Mortimer called the waitress over and ordered three draft

beers and another bottle of Jack for the boys. "Did you ask about Anne?"

"Uh . . ." The waitress wouldn't meet his eyes. "No. Not yet."

Mortimer sensed some kind of hesitation he didn't understand. He was getting too drunk, maybe. The beer arrived with the steak. They all fell to eating like condemned prisoners. The steak in his mouth tasted like salt-and-garlic heaven. The meat so soft, as if the cow had been bludgeoned to death before grilling.

Mortimer felt pleasantly stuffed, sipped beer. The waitress cleared away the dishes just as the show started, spotlights washing the stage in hot-pink light, the curtain going up as four women took the stage, waving to the audience amid scorching applause.

Mortimer raised an eyebrow at Bill.

"Beats me," he said.

"Wait," said Sheila. "These are the Glam Van Dammes. I heard about them in Cleveland."

The girl band picked up their instruments. A blonde in black leather on guitar and a short, striking Asian woman on bass. The bass player really seemed to be working the Asian angle, her hair in a tight bun pinned with chopsticks. She wore a Chinese dress with a floral print and a high collar. The combat boots seemed out of place but *worked* because they were out of place. The drummer was a black girl with a bright red buzz cut and the athletic build of a beach volleyball player. She wore a dark green tank top, cutoff denim shorts and high-top sneakers. She had a big gold hoop in her nose and way too much makeup.

The singer was something else. A powder-blue prom dress coming off the shoulder, platinum hair in little-girl pigtails. Barefoot. She snapped her fingers four times quickly and shouted into the microphone, "One two three four!"

The band jerked into motion, and the singer belted out R.E.M.'s "It's The End of the World as We Know It," not quite screaming, but definitely toward the punk end of the spectrum.

Mortimer found himself tapping his foot. They were *good*.

They segued into a Bangles song. When they hit the chorus, the band suddenly stopped and the lead singer pointed at the audience. The entire place shook with hundreds of voices singing "Walk Like an Egyptian."

The evening began to get fuzzy around the edges. Mortimer kept sucking down Jack Daniel's, pausing occasionally to sip cold beer. The band played two more songs Mortimer didn't recognize and then this really crappy song called "Total Eclipse of the Heart," which made him so nostalgic for his youth in the eighties that his eyes went a little misty.

He began to drift but had wits enough to lay off the whiskey. The place felt hot and crowded suddenly, and there was a thin layer of sweat on his forehead. He leaned toward Sheila's ear to tell her he was going to the restroom, but the words came out, "Gonnagothereshroom."

She frowned. "What?"

"Piss."

He left the table, wormed his way through the crowd and found the men's room, relieved himself in a urinal. He ripped off a handful of paper towels, wiped his forehead and the back of his neck. He should probably drink some water. The steak lay in his gut like a poorly chewed medicine ball.

His waitress intercepted him on the way back to his table. "This way," she whispered in his ear.

"What?"

She was already walking away. Mortimer followed. She turned

down a hall away from the music and revelry. The Glam Van Dammes sounded muffled and distant. She opened a door, paused to motion him on.

Mortimer hesitated. "What's this about?"

"You want to see your wife, don't you?"

"Anne?" He went inside.

It was a large storage room, kitchen utensils and foodstuffs.

There was a clanging sound, and the darkness whirled around and around. His knees unlocked and the floor came up to catch him. Part of him wondered distantly what had struck the back of his head.

Some sort of skillet, he was pretty sure.

XXXV

The light came through the barred window of the tiny cell. Cement walls and floor. Mortimer lay in the narrow, hard bunk, his head pounding some sort of rumba. His tongue tasted like a water buffalo had used it to wipe its ass. There was a hard crust around his eyes, which he wiped away with a thumb. Somebody stood over him.

Mortimer blinked. It was Lars.

"Good morning, sir." Lars poured a slim test tube of white powder into a glass of water. It bubbled and foamed. Lars handed it to Mortimer. "I anticipated your condition. This isn't quite the same formula as the old plop, plop, fizz, fizz we grew up with, but our pharmacists are quite talented."

Mortimer gulped it down. For a moment, it threatened to come back up, but Mortimer held it down and belched. The concoction took the edge off his torment. He was now merely miserable. "Where am I?"

"Jail."

"What's the charge?"

"I'm really not at liberty to discuss it," Lars said. "But if you can stand now, I need to escort you."

"Where?"

"That will be made evident."

Lars led him out of the small building, a cement bunker where Mortimer guessed they kept troublemakers out of the way of the better-behaved patrons. The bunker sat alone in the woods, a golf cart waiting for them on the narrow gravel path. In the backseat of the cart sat James, who'd let them through the gate the day before. He held his M16 across his lap and nodded a polite hello to Mortimer. Lars sat behind the wheel and gestured for Mortimer to sit next to him. They were soon zooming along the path, the gravel crunching beneath the tiny cart tires.

Shortly, they passed through an area Mortimer recognized, the sky bucket floating past overhead. Then Lars turned into new territory, a winding path along the edge of the mountain. It led them down the mountain in a gentle slope. Lars stopped the cart, frowned down into the valley, where a column of black smoke rose from distant buildings.

Mortimer shielded his eyes with his hand, craned his neck to see. "What's that?"

"Hard to say," Lars admitted. "We're trying to keep control of the region, but gangs still roam the city. Not so bad as a few years ago."

The trail ducked into the woods and came out again in a small clearing. A large L-shaped house sat on a level outcropping and commanded a breathtaking view of the valley. Three levels, constructed of wood and native stone, a wraparound porch and a balcony above. It looked old but well kept.

"That's Cravens House," Lars said.

"Who's Craven?"

"Made his money in cotton and iron before the Civil War. Or maybe after. I'm no historian."

Lars parked the cart. James climbed out of the backseat, stretched and lit a cigar.

"Where'd he get that?"

"We get tobacco shipped from Virginia," Lars explained. "Now I must ask you to go inside, sir."

"In there?" Mortimer jerked a thumb at Cravens House.

"Those are my instructions, sir. James and I are to wait here."

"Thanks for the ride."

He entered the house, stood in the foyer and waited, but nobody immediately appeared to tell him what to do. On either side of the doorway were Civil War uniforms in glass cases. Part of some tourist display, Mortimer assumed. There was a Confederate officer's uniform and one from the Union as well.

The house smelled like roses. A bench with coat pegs, polished wooden floors. Down the hall he saw some sort of sitting area, wide windows letting in the sunlight.

He cleared his throat. "Hello?"

He heard something move in one of the rooms down the hall, rustling papers, a chair sliding back, footsteps.

A head stuck out from one of the doorways. "Oh, you're here already. That was fast. Tate, right?"

"Right. I hope I'm not . . . uh . . . catching you at a bad time."

"Not at all, not at all. I just assumed you might need some more time to pull yourself together. Never mind. Come in, come in." He ushered Mortimer into the little office.

He was short but not significantly so, and Mortimer thought he might have been chubby before the Fall but was now sort of baggy skinned, although he had a bright complexion and seemed in very good health. Bald. Large blue eyes and full lips. Small ears. He motioned for Mortimer to have a seat.

The office was done in French country style, and Mortimer sat on the other side of a simple desk of white wood. The office was clean, well lit, and airy; a vase filled with fresh yellow flowers sat in the corner.

"How's your head?" the man asked.

Mortimer's hand automatically went to the back of his head. "Oh, uh, better, I guess."

"Nasty business, but it's turned out okay, I suppose."

"Sure."

"Can I get you anything?" the stranger asked. "It's a bit early for a good stiff drink, but we have tea and coffee. Some water?"

Mortimer sat forward. "Listen, no offense, but who the hell are you?"

"Oh, my, but of course, we haven't been introduced." The man offered his hand. "I'm Joey Armageddon."

Mortimer gulped as he took the hand. "Ah. Then, yes, I guess I'd better have some coffee."

XXXVI

A matronly woman in a blue pantsuit brought the coffee. It was excellent and strong.

"Thank you," Mortimer said. "This is wonderful."

"Don't get used to it." Joey Armageddon looked apologetic. "Coffee is almost nonexistent in the continental United States. Nothing's come up from South America for years, not through Florida anyway. I've ordered all coffee stores to my personal stash."

"I'll buy some from you," Mortimer said.

"Don't be ridiculous."

Right.

"I understand you have cigars," Mortimer said, changing the subject.

"Hand-rolled by Cubans."

"You have Cuban cigars?"

"No," Joey Armageddon said. "I have Cubans. Refugees. They hand-roll the tobacco we get from Virginia. You can get a box from the tobacconist near St. Elmo Station."

"Mr. Armageddon, am I under arrest?"

"That's what everyone thinks, but not really, no. Mr. Tate— may I call you Mortimer?"

"Please."

"Mortimer, I think we're in a position to help one another."

"I can't think what I can possibly do for you." Mortimer had not imagined the seemingly simple man before him. He'd pictured a warlord on a throne of skulls with slave girls in dog collars. Not a polite gentleman in a modest, tasteful office. Still, this was Joey Armageddon. What favor could Mortimer Tate do for a man like that?

"You'd be surprised," said Armageddon. "What is it you think I do here, Mortimer? Just run a fancy saloon? Humor me."

"More than one saloon," Mortimer said. "And more than just a saloon. A store. An eatery." He scratched his chin, thought about it. "But more than that too. A rallying point. A place everyone knows."

"Good," said Armageddon. "*Very* good. You're a thinking man. I like that."

"Thanks. I went to college."

"Stay with me while I elaborate. I hope you'll see that we're doing some important work here."

Mortimer sipped more coffee, nodded.

Armageddon put a serious look on his face. "We are doing nothing less than rebuilding civilization. I know that sounds high and mighty, but it really is just that simple. In the dark ages, the Catholic Church was the single institution to stand against illiteracy and barbarism. One institution, preserving language and knowledge. Well, this is America, Mortimer, and there are too many different churches with too many different truths. It would have to be a different institution this time. It would have to be us."

Naked ladies and hooch. Sure. Mortimer said nothing.

Armageddon chuckled. "I can read your mind. I know how it

sounds, and I know what you're thinking. But have a look at the big map, and I think I can convince you."

Armageddon stood, pulled down the blind covering the window behind him. It turned out to be a map of the southeastern United States, pink flags stuck in different cities across the surface.

"Each of these flags is a Joey Armageddon's Sassy A-Go-Go. Nashville, Louisville, Oxford, Wilmington, twenty-one locations in all. Not all are doing well. I can't deny it. The lack of leadership in some of the franchises has set us back. You probably remember what it was like in Cleveland."

"You know I've been through Cleveland?"

Armageddon nodded. "Shelby made it out. We've been keeping track of your progress, Mortimer, and we know your situation. Part of the reason we think you can help us. But more about that later."

He turned back to the map. "You saw the village when you came in."

"The village?"

"The collection of merchants clustered around the St. Elmo Incline station at the bottom of the hill," Armageddon explained. "You outfitted yourself at the Joey's store in Spring City. Up until a year ago, that was the model for all the clubs. But we started something here and also at the Joey's in Wilmington. We turned the Joey's store into a sort of brokerage, and instead of selling goods directly to the consumer, we've become wholesalers. An example: We bought several tons of cotton from a grower in Mississippi. We've been selling to tailors who have in turn opened clothing stores in the village. We paid the cotton grower in Armageddon dollars, most of which he spent to resupply himself down in the village, so the cash went right back into the local economy."

He tapped Lookout Mountain on the map and traced an outward spiral with his finger. "What started as a single economic location—Joey Armageddon's—has now widened into an economic zone. If similar zones expand around the other Joey's locations, the ever-increasing circles will eventually meet and overlap. A working, growing civilized economy.

"In Europe during the Middle Ages, a single institution stood against ignorance and barbarism—the Roman Catholic Church, as I've already told you. In our time, we also have an institution that has come to our rescue: the franchise."

Armageddon sat back at the desk, sipped his own coffee. "It all has to be gradual, of course. We still own half the merchants in the village and subsidize others. But there are merchants who have opened shops on the edge of the village, and I have no idea where they came from. They simply showed up one day to join the economy. People aren't waiting to be led anymore. They're taking initiative."

Mortimer thought about it, absorbed what he'd heard. Impressive. Still, it seemed odd, hard to swallow, that civilization could be reborn through a franchise of nudie bars. "It's great . . . really . . . but . . ." He trailed off with an embarrassed smile.

"I want you to speak freely," Armageddon said. "I'm not a dictator, and I'm not perfect. I want to hear if you have concerns."

"I don't understand why a go-go club," Mortimer said. "If you're setting out to save civilization, or build some kind of new civilization, then why not . . . well . . . anything but a titty bar?"

Armageddon cracked up laughing, genuinely amused. "Hell, man, you think I started all this to save the world? Hell, no. It was an accident. And it's not a titty bar. It's a go-go club. It might not make any difference to you, but it's an important distinction to me."

"I'm sorry." *Don't poke the bear.*

"We try to strike a certain tone. But I was going to tell you how it started. It's still early but I think I could use a drink after all. Join me?"

"Anything but Jack Daniel's."

They went out to the porch, a table and chairs overlooking the valley. Mild, only a chill in the air but not cold. Mortimer definitely anticipated an early spring.

They smoked cigars, and Armageddon drank Jack Daniel's over ice. Mortimer almost could not stand the smell of it, but a cold draft beer helped take the edge off his hangover. The cigar smelled good.

"It was never part of any grand scheme," Armageddon began. "Like so many people back then, I found myself running for my life. Talk to anyone who lived through those first years, listen to their stories. They'll always be stories of running."

Mortimer wondered if he would forever be separated from the rest of humanity by this lack of experience. He'd hidden during those times. He'd been lonely, but he hadn't been hunted.

"I was just coming out of a looted Ruby Tuesday's in Birmingham when they spotted me." Armageddon cradled his drink, a faraway look coming into his eyes as if he were trying to picture the episode, recall each detail precisely. "I'd been scavenging for food, hadn't found any and was on my way out when I saw the three of them. They had that raider look about them.

You learned the type fast enough if you wanted to live. You saw them coming, and you found a hiding place. Fast. But they saw me a second later, and I dashed back into the Ruby Tuesday's. I ducked behind the bar, knowing that wasn't good enough. So I'm looking around for something, anything, an idea of how I'm going to get out of this, but knowing I am truly fucked. And my eyes land on a bottle. I can't believe it. In the midst of destruction is one unopened bottle of Captain Morgan spiced rum. I take out my pocket handkerchief and wipe the dust out of three shot glasses, just as I hear boots crunching through the rubble on the floor, and I know they're creeping through the place looking for me. They're coming slowly because maybe I have a gun, or who knows?"

Armageddon sipped his Jack and shook his head like he couldn't believe what he was going to say next. "So I popped up, started wiping the bar with the handkerchief and said, 'Gentlemen, how are you doing today?' And I lined up the shot glasses and put the bottle on the bar. I was about to wet myself, and my legs felt like noodles. But you couldn't guess it. On the outside, I was steady as a rock.

"The three of them looked at each other like they weren't sure what was going on. Two of them had knives and one had a huge wooden baseball bat with nails sticking out of it. I didn't look at the weapons, just smiled. There was this long, silent ten seconds. And they came over to the bar. Just came right over and nodded at the shot glasses. I kept filling the glasses and made small talk. Yes, it was a hot day. No, I hadn't thought to cook rats that way. And I kept smiling and kept pouring and let myself believe I might actually bluff my way through this.

"And then the booze ran out. I figured that was it, but I smiled and said, 'Thanks for coming in, gentlemen. I hope you stop back again soon.'"

Mortimer found he was hanging on Armageddon's every word. "What happened?"

"They left. I shit you not, they waved good-bye and were on their way. They didn't offer to pay, and I didn't ask, but I thought about it a lot over the next few days. I think I reached something in them, triggered by the familiar sight of a neighborhood saloon. I realized that the most comforting thing a person could see was a place open for business, even if it was just pretend."

They sat in silence, sipped drinks and smoked cigars. Mortimer thought he could understand. More than anything, people were desperate for normalcy. The comfort of routine and familiarity.

"So you see," Armageddon said, "I didn't plan anything. It all evolved. And try to imagine if I had set out with the sole intention of helping my fellow man. Maybe I should have given away food to all who needed it. But where would the food have come from? How would it be replaced? Never give to the needy. They take and take and use and use and never put back. I could give it all away and feel like a hero for a day, but then we'd be right back at square one."

Mortimer frowned, tried to hide it by sticking the cigar in his mouth.

"You don't seem convinced."

"It's just hard to believe the best way to help people is not to help people."

"What political persuasion were you?" Armageddon asked. "Back when such things mattered, I mean."

"I was a registered independent. My wife was a Democrat."

"Ah, one of the independents." Armageddon grinned. "The

luxury of blaming everyone but taking no responsibility. Forgive my little jibe. The point is that none of that matters now. Nobody's pandering for anyone's vote anymore. There is only what works and what doesn't work, and the difference is life and death."

"I'll take your word for it," Mortimer said. "This is all still new to me."

"Well, it's a beautiful day," Armageddon said. "Let's drink our drinks and smoke our cigars and I promise not to bore you with any more of my amateur babble on politics and economics."

"It's not boring," Mortimer said. "But you are keeping me in suspense. You said we might be useful to each other."

"You've heard of this Red Czar, I'm sure," Armageddon said.

"Leader of the Red Stripes. I saw some of his handiwork in Cleveland."

"That's the man," Armageddon said. "Little is known about him. What we'd like you to do is infiltrate his organization, find out what he's planning." Armageddon took a long, slow drink of his iced Jack, smacked his lips. "And if you can get close enough, we'd like you to kill him."

XXXVII

Mortimer sat in stunned silence for nearly a full minute before saying, "Is that all? Anything else? Would you like the moon a little bit to the left?"

"I'm serious," Armageddon said. "You're uniquely qualified for the task."

"First, no way," Mortimer said flatly. "Second, how the hell do you figure I'm uniquely qualified? And third, no fucking way."

"Don't be hasty. Let's consider this from all angles."

"Don't you have people for this?" Mortimer asked.

"We've already lost six good men," came a deep voice from behind them.

Mortimer started, turned his head to look at the newcomer. A tall, broad-shouldered black man in his middle forties, fit, but with patches of gray in his close-cropped hair, hard features and piercing alert eyes of light brown. He wore an olive-green dress army uniform, but of what army Mortimer could only guess. He wore a star on each shoulder, but the pink Joey's mushroom cloud on each lapel.

"We've sent spies and assassins," the black man said. "None have returned. One was a navy SEAL and another a former FBI agent."

"Ah. Malcolm, just in time," Armageddon said. "Please join us."

Malcolm approached the table, bent suddenly and kissed Armageddon on the lips. "Sorry I'm late."

"Don't give it a second thought." Armageddon gave Malcolm's arm a gentle squeeze. "We're having a drink if you want something."

Malcolm shook his head and pulled up a chair. "It's a bit early, isn't it?"

"Don't start."

Malcolm turned his attention back to Mortimer. "I briefed those men myself and sent them into enemy territory. I feel responsible for them. We only found out later that there are spies among us, men sending the details of our every move back to the Czar."

Mortimer sat up, cleared his throat and tried to look apologetic. "Look, I'm flattered you thought of me, but if trained men couldn't—"

Armageddon held up a placating hand. "Let General Malcolm explain. Then you'll understand."

"For months now, we've had reason to believe the Czar is brewing something pretty big," Malcolm said. "And we've been brewing our own little rebuttal. We received word that a refinery has begun production again just outside the malaria zone of New Orleans. Think about what I'm saying."

"Gasoline." Mortimer remembered all the dead cars along the interstate, the uncomfortable ride in the mule wagon. A plentiful supply of gasoline would change the world. Again.

"With a steady supply of gasoline, the sky's the limit for what the Czar can throw at us."

"And it's not just what he can do to us in a military way," put in Armageddon. "Shipping will change, the flow of goods and services."

Mortimer said, "That would be good, wouldn't it?"

"If he would play along, it would be *very* good," Armageddon said. "I would gladly pay Armageddon dollars for gasoline. Others would trade too. If he were smart that's what he'd do. But tyrants never think like that. No, his Red Stripes have already shown they'd rather take what they need than trade for it. Fueled with unlimited gasoline, they'll plow through here like locusts and leave nothing, destroying everything we've worked so hard to build."

"Why would he do that? It doesn't make sense."

Armageddon shrugged. "How can one understand the twisted mind of the megalomaniac? He is the Napoleon of our time, the Hitler, the Stalin. Every so many years, these men come along and ruin it for the rest of us."

"That still doesn't explain why you think I'm the man for the job."

"Allow me to give you a quick bullet-point list of why we want you involved," Malcolm said. "One: you've proven resourceful, having come through a number of unique dangers just to get here. Two: as a Platinum member, it's in your best interest to protect Joey Armageddon's, not destroy it. Three: since you've only just arrived, you're an outsider."

"Why is that a plus?"

"As I said," continued Malcolm, "we have spies among us. Even if I picked one of my most trusted men, I don't think we can prevent word getting out. The Red Stripes would be waiting for him, and I'm not losing another man if I can help it. We've already fabricated a story for your arrest. We plan to stage your escape. Then the Czar and his men won't suspect we've sent you. We have strong evidence that one of our guards is on the Czar's payroll, and I'll arrange for him to be on duty when you break out. He'll report to the Czar that you're not one of my soldiers."

Mortimer shook his head. "No, I don't think so. Just because I'm not one of your soldiers doesn't mean the Red Stripes are going to throw me a welcome party. Why should they care if I got drunk and thrown in jail?"

"We've thought of that," Armageddon said. "Tell him, Malcolm."

"We're going to let it leak that you've stolen our defense plans," Malcolm said. "The Czar won't be able to resist that." To Armageddon he said, "I'll have one of my people leak it to the kitchen staff. That'll be like broadcasting it on the radio."

"Naturally, we'll supply you with everything you need," Armageddon assured him.

"And what's my motivation to say yes to this suicide mission?" Mortimer asked.

"Beyond defending our tenuous grasp on civilization from the marauding forces of darkness?"

"Way beyond that."

"We would compensate you, of course. Say twenty thousand Armageddon dollars."

"No amount of money will—how much?"

"Twenty thousand," said Joey Armageddon.

"It doesn't make sense." Mortimer rubbed his eyes. His hangover was coming back double. "It still doesn't have to be me. You could bribe anyone."

"We thought you'd want to undertake the mission, considering certain personal reasons," Malcolm said.

"There are no personal reasons," Mortimer said. "There are personal reasons *not* to do it. To keep my person from getting killed, for example."

"I'm afraid there *are* personal reasons. Reasons that you might find compelling," said Armageddon. "The Czar has Anne. Your wife."

XXXVIII

What kind of man would leave his wife in the evil clutches of somebody called the Red Czar?

I would, damn it. I had an epiphany. Doesn't anyone respect my goddamn epiphany?

Nobody respected his epiphany.

Joey Armageddon and his gay general were right. They had Mortimer's number. He had to try to help Anne. Mortimer waffled. But eventually he agreed to do it. He'd see this thing through to the end. He would find Anne. For better or for worse.

"If I'm going to do this," Mortimer said, "then I'm going to do it my way. And I'm going to need some things. Get a pen and paper."

Mortimer told them what he needed, and the general briefed him on how it would work.

"We'll arrange a contact who will guide you when you get there. He's trustworthy."

"How will I know him?" Mortimer asked.

"Don't worry," Malcolm told him. "He'll know you."

Armageddon took Mortimer's hand, shook it firmly, looked him straight in the eye. "I know you're not crazy about this, probably even feel somewhat coerced, but you're going to do some good. Frankly, you'll be a hero."

Mortimer returned the handshake, could only nod and smile weakly. *Hooray for me.*

"We can't take him back to his cell like this," Malcolm said. "He looks too good."

"You're right," Armageddon said. "We're supposed to have interrogated him to get our defense plans back."

"What?" Mortimer didn't like where this was headed.

Malcolm came up behind him. "I'll hold his arms. Work over his face a bit."

Back in his cell, Mortimer prodded at his puffy eye with his fingertips.

They enjoyed that. Assholes.

A black eye and a swollen lip. He could live with it. He'd had worse. Mortimer rubbed the stump where the Beast had taken his little finger. It seemed an eternity since he'd come down the mountain. Events had swept him along, pushed him forward. Fate was a terrified horse dragging him over rocky ground.

Take it easy, man. It'll be okay. All you have to do is bust out of Armageddon's prison, meet up with the mysterious guide, foil the Red Czar, assassinate him if possible while fighting off hordes of Red Stripes (no problem, since they seem to have only one bullet each). Oh, yeah, find your wife and tell her where the hell you ran off to nine years ago.

Child's play.

Mortimer waited patiently until finally the expected controlled explosion blew back the cell door, ripping it partway off the hinges. Smoke filled the cell and the hallway beyond. Shouting. Confusion.

Buffalo Bill leapt through the smoke and landed in the cell. "Come on, man. They're waiting for us."

Mortimer followed him out of the cell, down the smoky hall. They burst out of the bunker, where Mortimer spotted Sheila behind the wheel of a golf cart. That surprised him. Mortimer had told Armageddon he wasn't going anywhere without his partner, Bill, but he hadn't said a thing about the girl. No time to wonder about it now. They hopped into the cart, the sound of machine-gun fire cracking behind them.

"Drive!" shouted Mortimer.

Sheila stomped the accelerator, and they shot down the narrow path, twisted in and out of the trees until the bunker was well behind them.

"Do you know where we're going?" Mortimer asked.

"Sort of," Sheila said.

"We were told where to drive the cart," Bill said. "After that we don't have a fucking clue. I was hoping you'd fill us in. We were instructed to bust you out of jail, and the rest is a mystery."

"I got us a gig," Mortimer said.

"Say what?"

"You said we should be partners, right? I'll tell you all about it when we're in the clear."

Sheila turned off the road and headed into the forest. They soon came to a ring of stones, some kind of long-unused camping area. Sheila parked the cart. They held their breath and listened. A moment later, they heard footsteps through dry leaves. Lars stepped into view. He'd been hiding behind a stand of trees and wore a camouflage poncho over his black suit.

"This way," Lars said. "It's all here."

They crowded around and Lars directed them to a pile of

luggage hidden among the shrubs, six backpacks. They were mismatched but all of good quality and stuffed with supplies.

"We'll need to put on a bit of a show as if we're looking for you," Lars told them. "But the pursuit won't make it this way for a while, and they won't look for you very hard. Still, I would advise you not to linger." He handed Mortimer a folded map. "We've marked the best route on here, but you might have to improvise as events dictate." He shook Mortimer's hand. "I wish you luck, sir."

"Thanks, Lars. It's been grand."

Mortimer, Bill and Sheila slung the backpacks over their shoulders, headed south into the woods.

"Back on the road again. I'm going to miss that soft bed," Bill said. "Where we headed anyway?"

THE LOST CITY OF ATLANTA

XXXIX

It was already a notorious place of legend and peril throughout the new world.

Atlanta.

Just the name of the place sent shivers through some of the old-timers. Mothers frightened naughty children by threatening to send them south to Atlanta. Stories became more colorful in the telling and retelling. The Headless Zombies of Buckhead was a favorite tale for those who enjoyed loose talk in saloons, as was the myth of the entire Braves baseball team turning cannibal and roaming the city in search of people to deep-fry in hot canola oil. It was generally understood that the ghosts of Delta flight attendants haunted the airport, and that anyone spending the night in or near the airport experienced vivid, disturbing dreams often resembling footage from *Airport 1975*. It was commonly known that various gangs, almost like tribes, ruled sections of the city. This was not uncommon for many metropolitan areas where food shortages were sudden and devastating, a situation that encouraged the strong and ruthless to prey upon the weak. No citrus had come up from Florida for years, nor anything else from merchants traveling in or too close to the forbidden city.

Other stories, while unconfirmed, were widely believed nevertheless. The most popular rumor claimed Atlanta was the headquarters of the Red Czar. Furthermore, the Czar himself was credited with killing all the gang chiefs in the city one by one, by challenging them to duels, beheading them with a fireman's axe and putting their heads on spikes as a warning to any who might defy him.

"And that's what you've gotten us into," Bill said.

"How the hell was I supposed to know?" Mortimer pushed aside a tree branch, followed the narrow game trail. "It's not like anyone pulled me aside and said oh, by the way, the city of Atlanta is now instant death, so don't go there, whatever you do. Next you'll tell me they don't make Coke anymore."

"Ha ha. I'm serious about this, man."

"I heard there's a rapist grizzly bear," Sheila said. "He escaped from the zoo, and he catches people camping and rapes them from behind."

"Oh, now, come on!" Another branch slapped Mortimer in the face. *Fucking bullshit map. Where the hell's the road?*

"I don't know about no rapist bear," Bill said. "But I know people who go there don't come back."

"And how do you know that?"

"A friend of a guy of somebody I talked to in Nashville."

"A friend of a guy of somebody you talked to, huh?" Mortimer squinted at the map, hoped he hadn't gotten them lost.

"I'm just saying it would have been nice if you consulted me first is all," Bill said.

"Me too," Sheila said.

"I couldn't very well consult you from my prison cell." To Sheila Mortimer said, "And what are *you* even doing here? I thought you were going to try to talk them into letting you be a Joey Girl."

Sheila made a disgusted sound. "I had a change of heart about that. I don't want any sweaty men climbing on me unless I say so. A whore is a whore no matter how fancy. I want to kick ass and explore like you guys."

"Did you hear that, Mort?" Bill asked. "We kick ass and explore. I think we should put that on our business cards."

Sheila stuck out her tongue.

Mortimer stopped, sat down on a log, dropped his gear. They each carried two backpacks stuffed with supplies, and Mortimer wiped sweat from his forehead with the back of his hand. Spring had definitely come early. "Take five."

Sheila and Bill dropped their backpacks too, sat on the ground, visibly relieved.

"When do we find the road?" Sheila asked.

"Not much farther." *I hope.* Mortimer swigged water from his canteen. "Okay, let's redistribute some of this stuff." He clapped his hands. "Gather 'round, kids. Christmas time."

He opened three backpacks before he found what he was looking for, a slightly dented Union cavalryman's hat, blue with gold trim. He handed it to Bill. "Not quite like the one you lost, but it's the best I could do on short notice."

"Whoa." Bill took the hat, tried it on. It fit well. "Hell, now I *do* look like George Custer. Where'd you find it?"

"Museum display. But wait, there's more. Armageddon said he'd get whatever I needed for the journey, so I put in an order for these." Mortimer went into the backpack and came out with a pair of pistols with belt and holsters, handed them to Bill.

"Oh, my," Bill said, taking the pistols. "Oh, my goodness."

Mortimer wasn't sure, but he thought he saw the cowboy's eyes go watery.

Bill cleared his throat. "These are beautiful." The .45-caliber

Colt Peacemakers were handsomely made, well oiled, the finish a deep blue. He strapped them on, performed a couple of experimental quick-draws, a wide grin splitting his face.

"I hope these are to your liking," Mortimer said. "Of course, I didn't have time to *consult* you . . ."

"Oh, hell." Bill looked mildly embarrassed. "You know I'm not going to let you run off into danger all by yourself."

The backpacks also contained three .45 MAC-10 machine pistols with shoulder straps and extra magazines and two .45 automatics with shoulder holsters. He handed the weapons around, and they spent a few minutes strapping them on and getting the feel.

They continued to search the backpacks until they found food, and Mortimer was delighted to discover a pound of ground coffee and a small supply of cigars. When Armageddon paid them the twenty thousand, Mortimer would damn well lay in a supply of coffee, whatever the cost.

They ate, drank more water from the canteens.

"Okay," Mortimer said. "Let's get moving."

The road was only another ten minutes' march. They checked the map again and set off. They were armed, fed and headed to Atlanta.

In the time before chaos and destruction, one could streak down I-75 from Chattanooga to Atlanta in under two hours. Now the world was again an enormous place, and from Lookout Mountain, via the zigzag "safe" route Lars had outlined on the map, the forbidden city of Atlanta was a good week's hard hike.

The fourth day, it began to rain and didn't stop. They shivered in the bone-numbing cold. Staying dry was an impossible task. They tried to stay positive. Mortimer and his companions trudged on undaunted, spirits refusing to be dampened.

XL

"My spirits are fucking dampened," Sheila said. "And I hate you."

Mortimer wiped rain from his eyes with a dirty hand, left a smear of mud across his face. "Try to remember that nobody invited you."

Even with the camouflage rain ponchos, they were all cold, soaked and miserable. Sheila especially had been vocal about her discomfort. They'd slogged the old, muddy Forestry Service road that roughly paralleled Highway 78 until they'd hit a little-known entrance into Stone Mountain Park. They lay under a dripping hedgerow and watched the Stone Mountain Inn through a pair of small binoculars.

"Maybe this is a bad idea," Bill said.

"We're already past today's rendezvous time for our contact, and I'm not sleeping in the rain one more night." Mortimer scanned the plantation-style hotel, broken windows, thick vines growing up the brick. "And it looks deserted to me." They hadn't seen a single person for two days, not even at a distance.

"I suppose I would like to dry out," Bill admitted. "See the chimneys? Some of those rooms have fireplaces."

"Somebody will see the smoke," Sheila said.

Mortimer made one more quick scan with the binoculars. "It'll be dark in an hour, hour and a half at most. Nobody will see the smoke then, and we'll cover the windows."

"I'm sold," Bill said.

"Me too," said Sheila, "and I want my own room away from you dickheads."

Bill snorted. "I second that emotion."

"You snore!"

"Okay, shut up," Mortimer said. "We'll take one last look and listen, then dart across the open area and hit that door fast." The front door was off the hinges, only darkness beyond.

They dashed across the overgrown parking lot and into the door without incident. The place smelled old and mildewed, vines creeping into the open doorway. Debris, old cans, torn drapes, broken bits of furniture. Upstairs and away from the entrance, Mortimer lit a small kerosene lantern. Flashlights were easy to come by. Batteries weren't.

The first half-dozen rooms they investigated were too demolished to occupy. In one room, they found a relatively undamaged queen-size mattress, which Mortimer and Bill carried to a nearby suite while Sheila held the lantern. Broken glass and crushed beer cans littered the fair-sized fireplace. They cleaned it out and built a fire of busted furniture. They had to search five more rooms before finding another serviceable mattress.

"I think two is enough," Mortimer said. "Two can sleep while the third is on watch."

"Right," Bill said.

Sheila nodded. In spite of her earlier claims, she wanted to stay close to the group. They were far from friendly territory. Bill strung up a thin rope across the room, and they all changed into dry clothes, hanging the wet ones on the line.

They ate a cold meal of sausage and stale bread. They didn't talk. Fatigue had sapped them of the will to socialize, and they'd heard all of one another's conversation by now anyway.

Bill picked up the lantern, stretched, his joints popping. "I'll scout the rest of the hotel, make sure we don't have any surprise roommates. Then I'll take first watch if that's okay."

"Sure," Mortimer said. "Wake me when it's time."

When Bill left with the lantern, only the orange coals from the fire lit the room, making everything look like a vague monochrome dream. He sprawled on the mattress, weary.

He was almost asleep when he felt the mattress shift, Sheila's warm body sliding in next to him. She wore only dry panties and a clean white T-shirt. She smelled like girl sweat and sausage.

"Is this okay?"

"Yeah."

Her hand went to his crotch. "I can do things. If you want me to."

Yes please. "You don't have to."

Her hand slid up to his chest, and she nestled her head into his armpit. "I'm scared."

"Me too."

"I mean all the time, even out in the forest with nobody around. I'm afraid something could happen. I don't know what."

"You don't have to come with us," Mortimer said. "We'll give you some of the food. You could head back. Or wait here. The hotel seems safe enough." Although he could not promise he'd be able to come back for her.

"No, that's worse. I tried that at the firehouse. At least this is my choice. I can't just be nowhere doing nothing, right? A person has to be about something. I'm more afraid of not being about something than I am of anything else. No, I'm going with you. I can help. You'll see."

Soon he felt her breathing become steady and deep. The rhythm of it put Mortimer to sleep too.

A gentle nudge on the shoulder woke him. Sheila still lay with an arm across his chest.

Bill squatted next to him, whispered, "Sorry to disturb . . . uh . . . whatever it was you were doing." He spared a glance for Sheila. "Your watch."

"Okay."

Bill flopped onto the other mattress as Mortimer pulled on his shoes and strapped on the .45. He looked down at Sheila one last time, so innocent and adolescent in sleep. She was neither, and Mortimer needed to remember that. *What am I going to do with you?*

Sheila was right about one thing. You had to be about something. Mortimer had come down the mountain because he couldn't hide in his cave any longer. He needed the world. Needed to see it, be part of it again. And it occurred to him he couldn't hide atop Lookout Mountain either, drowning himself in Armageddon's decadence, because eventually the world would come looking. Better to march out and meet it halfway.

The night passed without trouble. The next day, they climbed Stone Mountain.

XLI

They made a wide circle around the front of the mountain where the huge stone-carved likenesses of Jefferson Davis, Robert E. Lee and Stonewall Jackson kept watch over the park. East of the mountain, they found the hiking trail that wound its way over a mile up the mountain, a much gentler slope than the sheer face with the three Confederates.

They climbed, stopping occasionally for canteen breaks, pausing to listen to suspicious woodland sounds before moving on again. Gray clouds hovered and roiled, but the downpour had finally abated.

Mortimer's instructions were clear. Stay on the path and your guide will find you. He's a little odd but trustworthy, Lars had told them. Sure.

They were two-thirds of the way up the mountain when Bill stopped and frowned. "Did you hear that?"

Mortimer shook his head. "Nope."

"I did," Sheila said. "An owl."

"It was *supposed* to be an owl," Bill said. "Sounded more like a five-year-old pretending."

The hoot came louder from the path ahead of them, and Mortimer heard it this time. Bill was right. It was the worst owl imitation Mortimer had ever heard. He thumbed off the machine pistol's safety.

"Let's go back." Sheila moved close to Mortimer, whispered, "Somebody's fucking with us."

"This is where we're supposed to be," Mortimer said. "Come on. Take it slow."

They eased up the mountain path, machine pistols held in front of them. Every few seconds they heard the phony hoot. Finally Mortimer saw him and held up his hand for the others to halt. He pointed at the shrubs, and Bill nodded, lifted his machine pistol.

Hoot. Hoot.

The stooped man behind the shrubs apparently thought he was hiding. A giraffe behind a potted fern had a better chance of concealing itself. He was old, with white hair and wearing a black overcoat unbuttoned, ratty polo shirt and khakis underneath. Scuffed loafers. He held two leaves up to his eyes and crouched lower.

Hoot. Hoot.

"Come out of there," Mortimer called.

Hoot. Hoot. "Where's it coming from?" shouted the old man. "Behind you? In front? Above in the tall trees? We move like the cat, like the Indian, like a ghost." *Hoot.* "We have you surrounded. Throw down your arms."

Mortimer glanced to either side. They were in no way surrounded.

"Shoot him," Sheila said.

Mortimer ignored her. "Come out, please. Let's talk."

Hoot.

"Look, we can see you, okay? You're, like, thirty feet away behind that bush. And it's not a very big bush."

The old man paused, then stood straight. He was tall, broad

shoulders, snow-white hair and moustache. As he came closer, Mortimer saw the slight gap between his front teeth, piercing blue eyes that Mortimer found a bit unnerving.

"Ah, you have earned my respect," said the old man. "There's not many who can outfox old Ted. Yes, you have mighty skills and keen senses. I can see why Armageddon chose you for this mission."

"You're our guide?"

"I am indeed."

Mortimer barely heard Bill mutter, "Jesus."

"Yes, let Ted be your guide," the old man said grandly. "Mr. Atlanta, they called me. I know the way and I know the town. Old Ted knows all, the way of the wasp and the willow, the minds of all the creepy crawlies. The song of the pigeon. I see and I hear."

"Are you going to talk like this the whole time?"

"We must get off the path," Ted told them. "Others use it besides us. Come. I know a place."

He darted into the woods.

Sheila grabbed Mortimer's arm. Tight. "He is a fucking loon. We're not really going to let him guide us, are we?"

"I'm with Miss Sassy Pants here," Bill said.

"I don't have any other ideas," said Mortimer. "Just follow him."

A half mile away they sat in a circle of large boulders, which concealed them well enough. "We'll wait here awhile," Ted told them.

Ted gratefully accepted their offer of dried fruit and chunks of salami. The old man had apparently been living on rat jerky the last few days. Ted insisted that with enough seasoning it was a little like buffalo. He claimed to have a big farm out west with a giant herd of buffalo, but naturally they'd probably all been poached by now, the majestic creature vanishing from the old west a second time. Ted peppered them with relentless, fragmented stories of how he'd been "a big man" in the old days.

"I'll be back on top again." Ted cackled. "Slay the Czar, put a knife in his gizzard. Then old Ted will be duke of Atlanta. Emperor of Georgia!"

"You said other people use the path," Mortimer prompted.

Ted nodded vigorously as he chewed and swallowed a slice of dried apple. "Indeed. The Stone Mountain Goats. We're in their territory."

"I don't suppose that's some sort of benign bluegrass band."

"A gang, of course. I took one of their crossbow bolts in the ass last year," Ted said. "Want to see the scar?"

"No!" Mortimer, Bill and Sheila said together.

"Crossbow? They renaissance fair geeks or something?" Bill asked.

"The Red Czar's men control the inner city," Ted explained. "He subsumed most of the gangs into his outfit and killed the rest. But he lets some gangs patrol the outlying areas for him, like subcontractors, I guess. The Stone Mountain Goats here, the Kennesaw Blades to the west. The Czar's kinda paranoid. He lets the gangs rule themselves as long as they don't have guns. I think he's afraid they might band together and turn on him." He cackled again. "Fat chance. Those motherfuckers are so disorganized, they're like a circle jerk that doesn't know where to aim."

"What's the problem, then?" Bill slapped the machine pistol

hanging at his side. "If all they got is medieval bullshit weapons, we can walk right through them."

"No, no, no. You listen to old Ted. That's not a good idea, no, sir. They're not so well armed but they're ruthless cocksuckers and there's a *lot* of them. Quantity has a quality all its own, as Joe Stalin said. And they're usually so hepped up, they don't feel the first few bullets anyway."

Sheila raised an eyebrow. "Hepped up?"

"Sure. The Czar gives them all the crank and cocaine they want. That's how he bribes for their loyalty. Hell, I seen a Stone Mountain Goat charge a rabid wolf with nothing but a Swiss Army knife. I mean, the wolf shredded the shit out of him, of course, but still . . ."

"Okay," Mortimer said. "So we'll avoid those guys."

Ted looked at his watch, and Mortimer was surprised to see it was a battered Rolex.

"Okay, they should've changed shifts by now. Let's go."

They made their way back to the path and continued up the mountain.

"Why are we going up here anyway?" Mortimer asked.

"The Goats have a ham radio, and we need to use it."

"The *Goats* have a radio?"

"Well, I don't have one," Ted snapped. "You think I carry around a big-ass ham radio in my back pocket? Now, hike faster."

They hiked faster. After five minutes, Mortimer noticed Ted hanging back, glancing over his shoulder. The old man climbed atop a boulder, squatted there, looking back down the trail. Mortimer went back, asked what was happening.

"Old Ted has the eyes of an eagle, he does. The nose of a wolf. The sharp hearing of a rhinoceros."

"Do you see something back—a rhinoceros?"

"Shit!" Ted leaned forward, squinted his eyes. "Shit shit shit!"

"What is it?"

"Stone Mountain Goats," Ted said. "Twenty-five. No, more like thirty of them. Coming up behind us. I can see them rounding the bend on the path below. Hell and damnation."

"I thought you said the path was clear." Mortimer stood on tiptoes, tried to see the approaching gang.

"Well excuuuuuse me. They probably saw you from one of their watch posts." He hopped down from the boulder, ran back up the path. "Come on. We've got to double-time it. We're almost there anyway."

"To the top? Won't that trap us up there?"

"Am I the guide or not? Now, come on!"

They ran.

Uphill.

Each carrying two backpacks, except for Ted, who bounded ahead of them.

Mortimer's heart pounded, breath coming hard, lungs burning, the heavy gear strapped to his back pulling him toward the ground. Sweat in every crease. Dripping into his eyes.

The path opened suddenly into a clearing, trees falling away on either side. The ground was solid stone spreading in every direction, sprawling views of Georgia expanding to every horizon. Directly in front of them sat a small, low building, wide windows in the front, some kind of concession stand at one time, a large antenna twenty feet high on the roof. A guy came out the front, sandwich in his hand, leather jacket covered in silver studs and a machete hanging from his belt. He saw Mortimer and his team running straight for him and dropped the sandwich, ducked back inside the building and came out with a crossbow, desperately trying to cock it, fumbling with the bolt.

Ted pointed. "Somebody shoot that guy!"

One of Bill's six-shooters flew into his hand. He fanned the hammer twice, shooting from the hip. The shots cracked, echoed along the mountain for miles. Red splotches erupted in the guy's chest, and he dropped the crossbow, twitched and fell, a dying noise gargling in his throat.

Mortimer glanced over his shoulder. The Stone Mountain Goats were visible now behind them, a screaming mob waving blades in the air as they ran. They didn't carry heavy backpacks and gained fast.

"Into the building," Mortimer shouted.

They piled in through the front door, Mortimer and Sheila collapsing on the floor, both heaving for breath. Bill slumped against a wall, breathing hard too but also watching the Goats come at full speed. "No time to rest, folks."

The snack bar was similar to a Waffle House. Booths lined wide-open windows in front; a counter with stools spanned almost the entire length of the restaurant, grills, refrigerators and food prep on the other side. Where the cash register had once been sat a ham radio, all blinking lights and knobs, static leaking out of it at low volume. Wires came from the back of the radio, went up to the roof, connecting, Mortimer assumed, to the big antenna.

A crossbow bolt streaked through the glassless window, struck with a loud *thock* into one of Mortimer's backpacks. Something spilled from the hole rent in the backpack.

"They got the coffee," Bill said.

Mortimer looked at the brown granules hitting the floor and felt the blood surge in his veins, a white-noise buzz of rage in his ears. "Cocksuckers!"

Mortimer stood, brought up the machine pistol and squeezed the trigger at the onrushing mob. The little gun hissed fire, spent shells ejecting and hitting the tile floor with a tambourine tinkle. Another sound roared in Mortimer's ears, and he realized it was his own voice raised in an improvised war cry.

The first four Stone Mountain Goats exploded across their chests in a spray of blood. They continued forward another half-dozen steps, not realizing they'd been killed, only to fall into a heap of dead meat just outside the snack bar's front windows. The next three behind them howled and came on undeterred. Mortimer cut one more down before the machine pistol clicked empty.

Mortimer fumbled for another magazine.

The other two climbed onto the window ledge, one with a hatchet raised high, the other leading the way with an improvised spear fashioned from a shovel. Drool flowed down their chins, eyes afire with narcotic insanity.

The room shuddered with the report of Bill's Peacemakers. The first Goat fell back, shot in the chest. The other's head exploded, brain and blood landing wetly on the tile and wall.

Three more crossbow bolts flew into the open window, one an inch from Mortimer's left ear. They bounced and rattled behind the counter.

"We're too exposed out here," Mortimer yelled.

"Behind the counter." Bill dove across.

Sheila and Mortimer followed. Ted was already there, fiddling with the radio.

Sheila was the first to bounce back up, spraying lead through the open front window with her MAC-10. She didn't hit anything but sent the rest of the Goats into hiding behind rocks and trees forty yards away. The open stone ground in between was red and slick with blood and quivering bodies.

Mortimer looked at Bill and the six-shooter in each of his hands. "You don't like the machine guns?"

"Can't aim those fuckers."

"Give it here."

He slammed a fresh magazine home into his own MAC-10, held Bill's in the other hand. *Two-fisted death. That's me.*

Ted kept twisting radio knobs, the hiss of static growing louder, then waning. "Blowfish, this is Big Ted. Come in, Blowfish. Damn it, I can't get the frequency."

"Do you think he's really calling for anybody or just pretending?" Bill asked.

"Part of me hopes he is pretending." Mortimer popped up, squeezed off a quick burst, sending the Goats diving for cover. Mortimer ducked back behind the counter as another bolt bounced off the back wall. "What are they waiting for?"

"They don't want another face full of MAC-10," Bill said.

"They can sit out there forever, until the rest of the Goats get here. Every minute we wait it gets worse."

"Let's run for it," Sheila said.

Bill snorted. "You want a bolt in the ass?"

"Blowfish, where the hell are you?" Ted smacked the side of the radio with an open palm. "Douchebags!"

"What the hell are you doing?" Mortimer yelled at the old man.

"I'm calling a cab. Now shut up and let old Ted work."

"This is really—wait." Mortimer edged up, peeked over the counter, eyes darting. "They're doing something. Sheila, look out that side window."

She crouch-walked to the window, keeping her head below the counter. She popped up, looked out the small side window, then ducked again quickly. "They're out there. Right by the wall." She popped up and down again for another quick look. "They're piling up dead branches."

"Shit," muttered Bill. "Bonfire."

The radio crackled, a voice coming through the static. "Big Ted, this is Blowfish. We are a mile out. Repeat, we're one mile out."

"Hot damn!" Ted yelled.

"They're lighting the branches out here." A hint of panic in Sheila's voice. "I'm serious, guys. This fire's getting big." The smell of smoke grew stronger.

"Here they come," Bill shouted.

A half-dozen Goats screamed toward the snack bar, weapons in one hand, flaming brands in the other. The one out front carried a bucket instead of a brand, some kind of liquid slopping over the sides. Mortimer stood straight, fired two quick bursts from each machine pistol. Three Goats stumbled and went down, including the one with the bucket, but he heaved it as he went down. It flew, landed against the front windowsill with a watery metallic *clung*. The liquid splashed half in through the window and half down the front of the snack bar. The pungent odor hit Mortimer immediately, unmistakable.

Gasoline.

Ohhhhhh . . . shit.

Mortimer blazed away at the other three running Goats coming fast with the fire, the machine pistols bucking and smoking.

He put two down fast, but only caught the third with a grazing hit in the shoulder, a light mist of blood flying. The slobbering, crazy-eyed Goat didn't even flinch, leapt through the front window, ignited the fire, flames spreading up the outside of the snack bar and over two booths within.

The Goat caught himself on fire too, stood there in the middle of the sudden blaze, his pants and sleeves burning. He screamed and danced.

Bill put him down with a shot from the Peacemaker.

Smoke filled the interior of the snack bar, and Mortimer felt the heat wash over him. He slammed home two new magazines, cocked the machine pistols and fired at the vague figures barely visible through the thick smoke, not knowing if he hit anything or not.

"Be advised, Blowfish," Ted yelled into the radio mike. "Zone is hot. Repeat, zone is hot."

"We see your smoke," came the voice of Blowfish through the static. "We're inbound now. Be prepared to board."

A helicopter, thought Mortimer. *Holy crap, the old wizard arranged a chopper.* Mortimer could hear something coming, the high-pitched buzz of some engine. It was coming.

"Time to go," Mortimer shouted.

Sheila coughed, wiped her red eyes. "You think?"

"I'm ready," Bill said.

The flames licked higher, but the doorway was still clear. Mortimer emptied the machine pistols to clear the way, then slapped in the last two magazines.

"Now!"

They climbed over the counter, shrinking from the flames, snot running, eyes watering. They hit the door, out into the open.

The cool air hit Mortimer, clean and fresh. He filled his lungs but didn't have time to enjoy it. Crossbow bolts flew past his head. He blasted back at the Goats with the machine pistols, sent them scurrying for cover. They popped their heads up again, yelled obscenities, and Mortimer emptied the MAC-10s. He dropped the spent weapons clattering on the stone ground.

"There it is!" cried Ted. He pointed into the sky behind them. "Blowfish! Blowfish!"

Mortimer turned to look at the helicopter.

It wasn't a helicopter.

The blimp floated through the smoke of the burning snack bar. Filling the sky suddenly, the hornet buzz of its tiny motor and rear propeller was a bizarre contrast to its silent, looming mass. One would almost be tempted to call it majestic.

And one would be mistaken.

The aircraft had probably been used for advertising, providing aerial coverage for golf tournaments and college football games. It was a ragged affair now, patched with mismatched material, netting thrown over the whole thing to help attach the thick ropes that held the open-air gondola underneath, sandbags hanging over the sides.

As crossbow bolts bounced off the stone around his ankles, Mortimer's disappointment at seeing the inflated monstrosity instead of a rescue chopper was the most profound of his life.

"You must be fucking kidding me."

The blimp lumbered and bobbed, its descent excruciatingly slow. Figures appeared in the gondola. A top hat and a very long white scarf caught Mortimer's attention. *More lunatics.* The blimp passed over them.

And kept going.

Ted jumped into the air, waved his arms. "Where you going? You're overshooting. Dumb sons of bitches, you're overshooting!"

The blimp listed, nose dipping as it sailed past, disappearing over the other side of the mountain, down into the tourist area of the park.

Mortimer grabbed Ted by the elbow. "Is it coming back for us?"

Ted jerked his arm away. "It ain't a goddamn sports car. Blowfish is awkward. A steamship could turn around faster."

"Decide fast," Bill said. "We got company."

The remaining Stone Mountain Goats had worked themselves into a frenzy, jumping up and down, brandishing weapons, grunting like apes. *Probably just snorted a few more lines of courage.* The Goats must have used up the crossbow bolts, because no more flew. The Goat leader howled bloody murder, and the mob charged.

"Follow me if you want to get off this rock alive." Ted ran across the stone surface of the mountain toward some kind of small installation two hundred yards away.

Mortimer, Sheila and Bill followed immediately. Mortimer pulled the .45 from his shoulder holster, racked it and thumbed off the safety. Soon Ted had pulled ahead of them, and Mortimer's breath came short again. The Goats were gaining.

"Drop the backpacks," Mortimer shouted.

They dropped the gear and picked up speed. Mortimer turned slightly, fired behind him with the .45 without aiming.

Thirty yards out, Mortimer saw they were heading for a Swiss cable car system, a tourist ride, similar to the sky buckets back at Lookout Mountain but with a much larger enclosed gondola. The cable ran down to the tourist area at a steep angle. Ted flung open the door to the cable car and climbed in, turned and waved them on. "Hurry!"

They rushed into the cable car. Mortimer was the last in, turned and emptied the .45 at the oncoming Goats. Two clutched their guts and pitched forward. The rest kept charging, bellowing their rage.

"Does this thing even have power?"

"Nope," Ted said. "But gravity still works."

Ted grabbed a sledgehammer from a hook on the interior of the cable car, swung it sideways at a pin in the floor keeping a loop of cable in place. He knocked the pin out, and the cable flew out through the floor like a kid sucking up a strand of spaghetti. The car shook, slid down the cable, picking up speed.

Mortimer looked back through the open door. The Goats stood on the edge of the mountain, shaking fists and screeching incomprehensible curses. They dwindled rapidly behind as the cable car flew faster.

And faster.

"Brace yourself, kids," Ted said. "This E-ticket ride is gonna go splat."

Nobody enjoyed the crash.

XLII

When Mortimer had been in the insurance business, he hadn't sold anything too glamorous. Residential, auto, the occasional policy on a bass boat. As he pushed himself up from the pile of bodies in the forward section of the cable car, he wondered how amusement parks and tourist attractions had ever been able to afford liability coverage. The premiums must have been murder.

In the last sixty feet of their lightning descent, Ted had thrown the hydraulic brake, had leaned his entire body weight into the lever. A clamp grabbed the cable above, sparks flew against the hideous screech of metal on metal. They slowed, but not enough. The cable car crashed into the station, pitching them all forward into one another. They stood up now, stretched and rubbed bruises.

"Everyone okay?" Mortimer asked.

Bill groaned, picked up his Union officer's hat and snugged it on his head. "Nothing broken."

"I'm fine," Sheila said, but she rubbed her shoulder, winced.

"Old Ted has the hide of an armadillo, the bones of—"

"Don't start," snapped Mortimer.

They climbed out of the cable car and looked around. Mortimer reloaded the .45, ready to fend off another band of savages.

"There." Sheila pointed.

Just past a budget motel, in the middle of the street, the Blow-fish bobbed six feet over the asphalt, straining against a thick line tethered to a mailbox. A figure awkwardly lowered himself down a rope ladder, the man with the ridiculous scarf and top hat. He saw Mortimer and the rest, waved them on, frantic, harried.

"That's Reverend Jake," Ted said. "Come on."

They ran to the blimp, and the man in the top hat—Reverend Jake—clapped Ted on the shoulder. "Thank Jehovah you've made it. Sorry to overshoot the landing zone."

"Dumbass." But Ted grabbed the reverend in a tight hug.

Jake looked past Ted at the others. "These are the ones Armageddon sent?"

"I'm Mortimer." He introduced Bill and Sheila.

"Let's get better acquainted in the air," Jake advised. "We saw more Stone Mountain Goats and they have one of those big arrow shooters. Probably only a half-mile away by now, maybe closer, and coming fast."

They all climbed the rope ladder, threw legs over the side of the heavy wicker gondola and dropped inside.

Another old man waited for them, wiry and short, barely over five feet. A full white Santa Claus beard and more white hair leaking from under a blue US Navy cap. He wore a leather bomber jacket and jeans and dirty deck shoes.

"This is Chief Larry," Ted said. "Our intrepid pilot, sky master, he smells the ebb and flow of the air currents, knows the mind of the hummingbird—"

"We're sinking." Sheila had her hands on the rail, was looking over the side at the ground slowly coming up to get them.

"Overweight," Jake shouted.

He and Chief Larry ran around the gondola, yanking on ropes

and sending sandbags dropping to the pavement below. The blimp ceased its descent, but it didn't quite rise either, hovered in place, a slight breeze pushing it in a circle.

"Hell." Larry grabbed a burlap sack, chucked it over. "There goes dinner."

Ted and Jake were already pulling at wicker chairs attached with thin rope. They tossed them over, looked around for more items to discard.

Mortimer stood at the rail with Sheila, looked toward the end of the long road where something rolled into view at the other end of the park. He heard a revving sound, the squeal of tires.

Reverend Jake lifted his hands to the heavens. "Dear Jesus, take this flying contraption in your almighty hands and gather us to your bosom. Hear us, Lord, and deliver us from the savages below."

A truck! Mortimer rubbed his eyes. It was a truck, a pickup, and coming toward them fast. He had not seen a working automobile in years. He gazed at it in wonder, forgetting the truck was bringing a gang of Stone Mountain Goats to kill him. *It's true. The Red Czar's getting gasoline. Somebody's producing again.*

Larry picked up the heavy ham radio.

"We need that, damn you!" Ted shouted.

"We're too damn heavy," the little pilot yelled back. "I didn't know you were bringing three people."

Ted lunged for the radio. Too late. Larry heaved it, and it smashed into a thousand pieces on the road below.

The truck was only a hundred yards away. Mortimer saw three Goats across the bench seat inside the cab, another half-dozen clinging in back, waving spears and ad-libbing war cries.

Something else in the back of the truck. A giant spool of cable or thin rope, and next to it a huge crossbow mounted in the bed of the truck.

Mortimer cleared his throat. "Guys, I think we need to get organized."

Even as he said it, the blimp began to rise.

"That's it. Out of the way, Ted." Larry skipped to the aft end of the gondola, picked up what looked like a big weed-whacker, a gas engine at the end of a long shaft. He yanked on the cord three times before the engine sputtered to life. The other end of the shaft went out the rear of the gondola to a propeller, which now turned faster and faster as Larry gave it gas. He held the weed-whacker like it was a tiller on some old Viking warship, leaned into it, and the blimp slowly started turning away from the approaching Goats.

Mortimer estimated they were maybe twenty-five feet up and slowly climbing. Not enough to feel safe. "Higher!"

Larry shook his head. "The propeller is only for steering and forward motion. Lift is all according to weight, and we've already tossed everything out. Unless you'd like to jump. That would really help us out."

The truck screeched to a halt forty yards away, and all the Goats piled out, a flurry of activity. One stood behind the over-sized crossbow, used a hand crank to cock it and loaded a five-foot bolt the size of a spear.

Reverend Jake appeared at Mortimer's elbow, squinted at the truck. "They call it a ballista."

"I call it trouble." Bill drew the six-shooters and opened fire, slugs bouncing off asphalt near the truck, one shot puncturing the passenger door. The Goats crouched lower but continued loading and aiming the ballista.

Bill holstered the pistols. "These aren't built for long range."

They were forty feet up, with the Goats a hundred yards behind them, when the ballista operator let fly. The spear flew fast and straight, a thin line trailing behind like the wriggling tail of a sperm. It hit the gondola low and aft, punched through the wicker with ease, and caught Larry in the upper thigh, the pyramid-shaped head coming through with a gout of blood and shredded flesh.

Larry screamed, high pitched, fell, letting go of the tiller. He writhed like a spiked trout against the bolt, howling and going a pale green almost instantly. The Blowfish drifted.

Sheila screamed, backed away at the sight of the gushing blood. Mortimer and Jake crowded forward, tried to stanch the wound with their hands, the blood pulsing through their fingers and covering their hands to the wrists in seconds.

Larry sobbed, howled, grunted inhumanly as he gasped for oxygen, convulsed once and threw up on Jake.

Something jerked the Blowfish taut. They were going down.

Mortimer stood, looked back at the truck. Men were cranking the spool of line, pulling it tight and reeling the blimp in like a game fish. Mortimer watched them crank. It was a slow process; there must have been some kind of glitch in the winch, because every fifth or sixth crank, the line would go slack again and the Goats would scramble to fix it. They started again, and this time it came loose after the third crank.

"Cut the line!" Ted shouted.

Mortimer pulled the bowie knife from his boot sheath, bent over the side of the gondola, stretched his hand. The bolt had punctured too far down. Mortimer couldn't reach it. The line was tied to the end of the bolt, and the bolt was made of some light metal that would take him twenty minutes to get through with a hacksaw.

And he didn't have a hacksaw.

The Goats kept cranking them in, the blimp edging lower a foot at a time.

"Reload, Bill."

"I'm on it." He was already thumbing fresh shells into the Peacemakers.

The rumble of engines. Three more pickup trucks rolled into view, each filled with more bloodthirsty Goats.

He knelt again next to the screaming pilot. "Is he going to make it?"

Jake was covered in the little man's blood. He met Mortimer's eyes, shook his head.

"Sorry about this." Mortimer set his jaw, dug his hands in around the wound, trying to get a grip behind the bolt head.

Larry writhed. "No, please—oh, God."

Mortimer waited. He needed to time this just right. He felt the pull on the bolt ease and yanked. A wet tearing sound inside Larry's leg. The little man screamed louder, if that was possible. Mortimer kept pulling. The bolt shaft came all the way through, but the knot caught on the other side of the leg. Mortimer braced himself, heaved, put his back into it. He had to get it through before the Goats started cranking again. *Pull.* The knot came through in a splash of blood and flesh.

Larry passed out.

Mortimer sawed at the thin rope with the knife. It frayed, came apart, and shot out of his hands, back through the leg wound and the gondola. The blimp bobbed, tilted and suddenly released. Ted grabbed the weed-whacker tiller, aimed them away from the Goats.

"They're reloading," Bill said.

Mortimer lifted Larry, dead weight, arms flopping, and let him fall over the side. Mortimer turned away. He couldn't bear to see the little man land.

Without the weight of the corpse, they lifted much higher, much faster.

XLIII

Blowfish could not feel urgency, did not know panic or recognize the need to put itself beyond the range of the ballista. Nothing would hurry its steady rise to a hundred feet, then two hundred feet and more. The next ballista shot never came, and the blimp's five passengers shivered in the blood-soaked gondola as the temperature dropped with the increased altitude.

Mortimer welcomed the wind in his face as it helped dry the panic sweat and wash away the smell of blood.

"Hell, I sure hate to lose a man." Ted still held the tiller, heading them toward downtown Atlanta.

Reverend Jake took off his top hat. "May the Lord guide his soul to Heaven."

"You better tell him to guide our sorry asses back to the ground," Ted said. "Larry was the pilot. I kinda sorta know how to steer this thing. Maybe."

"And the radio," Jake reminded them.

"Problems?" Mortimer didn't need these guys crapping out on him now.

"A moment please while I confer with my colleague." The reverend went aft, leaned in to converse with Ted in hushed whispers.

Bill plopped down in the bow of the gondola. "What now, boss?"

Mortimer shrugged. "Let's see what they come up with."

Bill frowned, pulled the Union hat down over his eyes for a quick nap, arms crossed tight against the cold.

Sheila was back at the rail again, standing close to Mortimer, looking down. "I've never seen it like this. I mean, I've been up on a mountain, seen what things look like far away, but not like this, with nothing underneath us at all."

"Afraid of heights?"

"No. I like it up here. We're disconnected." Houses, trees, roads, shopping centers, fields, all passed silently below, too distant to detect the destruction and decay. "You could almost believe everything was okay down there."

Dorothy coming back from Oz, thought Mortimer, *floating in the wizard's balloon. There's no place like home. Except this time when Dorothy lands, sees Kansas up close, she'll see it was torn apart by a twister.*

Reverend Jake returned from his conference with Ted, cleared his throat. "We think it might be best to put down in one of the nearby open spaces, a field or parking lot maybe. Ted's dubious ability to steer Blowfish might become hazardous if we were to venture among the taller buildings and narrow avenues downtown."

"And then what?" Mortimer asked.

"And then we walk," Jake said.

Landing involved a controlled deflation of the blimp. There was much pulling of lines and opening of valves. Nothing seemed to happen at first, so lines were pulled further and valves opened wider.

Then suddenly they were dropping rapidly.

"Shit almighty, too much," Ted yelled. "Close the valve. Close it."

They were not plummeting, but neither had they achieved the gentle descent they'd intended. The ground grew big beneath them, and Ted jerked frantically on the tiller, attempting to guide them toward an overgrown suburban baseball diamond.

"Brace yourselves," he shouted.

They set down hard but without incident and climbed out.

Mortimer pointed to a set of bleachers. "Bill, get as high as you can, look around."

"Right." Bill jogged toward the stands.

Mortimer looked at Ted. "I need to talk to you."

"Talk."

"Is there a plan B?"

Ted cackled, shook his head. "There was barely a plan A."

"Tell me."

Ted explained. He was part of a ragtag, underground army whose goal was to wrest power from the Red Czar. Here's how Mortimer would help. He would get close to the Czar and find out his evil plans, specifically when the Czar planned to attack Armageddon. Warned ahead of time, Armageddon would be able to organize a surprise counterstrike. It had been Ted's plan to take Mortimer all the way to downtown Atlanta via Blowfish, landing under cover of darkness on one of the tall buildings. Using the ham radio (now smashed on the road back in Stone Mountain Park), Ted would have coordinated with their "man on the inside," one of the Czar's trusted men, to capture Mortimer and take him to the Czar. By then it was hoped the Czar's spies would have reported that Mortimer had recently busted out of Armageddon's prison with secret knowledge of Armageddon's defenses, his military strength, etc.

"The Czar won't be able to resist. Once you get close to him, you find out his plans, kill him if you can."

Mortimer sighed, looked up, taking in the blue sky and puffy white clouds, scratched his chin. "That's a pretty feeble plan."

"Well, it's a fucked-up plan now," Ted said. "We'll have to improvise. First, we need to get Blowfish out of sight. The Goats will spread the word and the whole metro area will be on the lookout for it."

They deflated the blimp, the compartments going flaccid as it collapsed in on itself. They shoved the thing into one of the Little League dugouts. All of them together pushed the gondola into a small circle of trees, covered it over with branches.

They walked, Reverend Jake on point a hundred yards ahead of them, ready to signal them into hiding if necessary. They zigged and zagged through a residential neighborhood, finally finding an abandoned house with a fireplace just after sundown. They were all exhausted and slept like rocks.

They yawned and stretched awake at the first crack of sunlight, Mortimer spewing a string of curses after remembering they'd lost the coffee the day before. "I wish we'd been able to hang on to our gear."

Bill hid a yawn behind the back of his hand. "I still have a few of the cigars in my shirt pocket if you want one."

"Later. You sleep okay?"

"Could have been better. I was right next to Ted. Guy has bad dreams and talks in his sleep. Man, he sure hates Jane Fonda."

"We have a long march ahead of us," Reverend Jake told them. "Let's start the morning right with a quick prayer. O Lord, hear us in our time of need as we march into the bowels of Satan's stronghold, to wrest a once-prosperous city from his evil clutches. And if it is Your will for us to be gutted and beheaded and our heads put on pikes for the crows to eat our eye sockets hollow and the black flies to plant maggots in our ears, then so be it, although, naturally, we'd prefer that not to happen."

"Amen," Mortimer said.

XLIV

The five of them marched steadily, either Reverend Jake or Ted scouting ahead, finding the open path. They passed the debris of an extinct nation, hollow Exxon stations, Subway sandwich shops, Dollar General, Cracker Barrel, check-cashing places, pawnshops, banks and a Laundromat with a yellow Hummer crashed through the front window. On the back of the Hummer was a bumper sticker that said I BRAKE FOR GARAGE SALES.

They passed through another residential neighborhood and crossed into a park on the other side: swings, slides, trees, benches. The grass was long and brown.

"Break for lunch here," Ted told them. "I need to scout around, get my bearings."

Ted left them in the park.

"Benches over by that odd-looking tree." Mortimer pointed. "We can take a load off."

They walked toward it and realized it wasn't a tree at all but something fabricated of metal and wires, meant to look like a small weeping willow. When they were standing right in front of it, Mortimer saw that the trunk of the tree had been fashioned from several car bumpers welded and bent. The limbs were car antennas. Headphones and iPods and electrical charge cords hung from the limbs, draped nearly to the ground.

Sheila knelt, ran her hand over a wooden plaque, letters burned neatly into the surface:

NEW WORLD WILLOW
—ANONYMOUS

"L'art pour l'art," Reverend Jake said.

Mortimer looked at him. "What?"

"Nothing. Let's eat."

They sat on the benches. Lunch was meager. Jerky and stale bread, what some of them happened to have in pockets. Most of the food had gone over the side in the mad rush to lighten the blimp.

Mortimer munched jerky without enthusiasm, considered the willow again. Somebody had decided to do that, had decided to stop in the shadow of a dangerous city, had paused in the necessary ongoing routine of gathering sustenance and finding shelter, had simply put it all aside to make this thing. To make art.

Mortimer couldn't decide if that was dedication or stupidity. Maybe the harder you fought to live, the more obligated you felt to live for something.

He looked at the dangling wires, headphones, MP3 players, computer gadgets. Many were corroded, covered in bird poop. The new world willow had been here awhile. Maybe years. Maybe the artist was dead now. The willow might have been the last thing he ever did.

"I used to have an iPod," Bill said around a tough chunk of jerky. "I used to love to download songs from the Internet. Man, I loved Christina Aguilera. And Moby. I wish they still had music."

"They do still have music," Sheila said.

"I mean like on CDs and digital and all that," Bill said. "You go into Joey's and the band plays and that's fine and everything, but it's not like going through ten thousand songs on Napster and picking and choosing whatever you want."

"Electricity's coming back," Mortimer said. "People are going to start using things again, microwave ovens and CD players. Maybe even the Internet."

"It's not the same," Bill said. "Not like being connected with everything while it's happening. You can scavenge old CDs and a player and make it work, but it's always going to be leftovers. It'll never be now."

"We'll make a new now," Jake said. "It'll be tough, but we'll fight and hang on and make things new again. Here comes Ted."

Ted had found the path. He led them until nightfall, and they camped within spitting distance of the ruined Atlanta skyline.

XLV

Mortimer tossed another stick on the fire. "It's decision time."

The others looked up from their places around the camp, eyes wide and curious. They hadn't realized an announcement was coming.

"This is up to me now," Mortimer said. "We're about to get neck-deep in Red Stripe territory. I have a personal stake in this. As you know, I'm looking for my wife. I need to see her. Anyway, it's enough to say that in addition to putting the brakes on this Czar asshole, I have my own motivations, which are nobody else's problem but mine."

Sheila frowned, broke eye contact.

"You can shove your hero speech up your ass," Bill said. "If you think I'm the kind to cut out on a partner, then I guess you don't know me very well at all."

Mortimer smiled. *Damn, he's a good pal. I'm going to miss him when I get my dumb ass killed.* "I appreciate that, Bill. More than you know. But it's a one-man job, and there's just no sense in risking everyone."

"You're stupid." The venom in Sheila's voice startled them. "We live in a time when the most valuable thing a person can have is somebody to look out for you and that you can look out for," she said. "And you treat that like it's not anything. *We* are here for you. Did your fucking wife come looking for *you*? Fuck no. Fuck you."

Mortimer's mouth fell open. He shut it again. He was simultaneously touched and offended.

"I ..." Mortimer shook his head. So tired. "Okay. Thanks, guys. Sorry. Should have known better than to try that hero bullshit."

Sheila turned away, curled up with her back to the fire.

"Damn right," Bill said. "We'll figure it out as we go. You'll see."

"Sure."

Mortimer shot Ted a look across the campfire. The old man offered a slight nod in return.

The orange-pink smear of dawn was just hinting over the horizon when Mortimer clapped Ted on the shoulder and motioned him to follow. He waited until they were a quarter-mile away before speaking in a low voice.

"Thanks for taking last watch. Makes it easier."

"Your friends are going to be pissed," Ted said.

"It's for their own good. What about the reverend?"

Ted shrugged. "He's a practical man. He'll understand, and he can show your people a safe route away from the city."

"Let's make tracks."

They traveled quickly toward downtown, the buildings growing taller around them with each mile. Ted cautioned that they were well within the Czar's patrol radius and would need to keep their eyes and ears open.

Yeah, thought Mortimer, *like I've been on a Sunday stroll until now.*

They passed a number of rotting heads on tall pikes. The entire city had a haunted feel about it.

Near Peachtree Plaza, Ted abruptly pulled Mortimer into the shadows of a doorway. They watched in silence as six Red Stripes marched in loose formation on a cross street in front of them. The patrol did not appear to be particularly alert.

Mortimer and Ted scampered from hiding place to hiding place all day like that, dodging four more patrols, making their way closer to the Czar's headquarters.

Twice, Mortimer heard engines in the distance, and once he saw a Buick speeding across downtown with two Red Stripes inside. The Buick sported a flag on the antenna, white with a red stripe across the middle.

"If he's getting gas, why do the Red Stripes still patrol on foot?" Mortimer asked. "Seems like he could put them all in pickup trucks."

"Various reasons," Ted said. "First of all, they're saving up the fuel for some kind of big push. The Czar has some kind of surprise in mind, but none of my operatives can find out what it might be. Even old Ted can't sniff it out. Also, the Czar's not able to hang on to all of his gas shipments. Somebody's been raiding his supply line. Heck, we do that ourselves on a small scale. It's how we get gas for Blowfish's little motor."

"Who's making the raids?"

"Search me," Ted said.

They continued on, finally entering the back door of a building, walking the hallways all the way to the other side, ducking below a window that faced a street on the next block.

"That's the Czar's stronghold," Ted said.

Mortimer raised his head for a brief glance and ducked down again. "The Omni/CNN Center?"

"Can you believe that shit?" Ted's face went red. "Pisses me right off!"

Mortimer chanced another look, saw a dozen guards or so standing on either side of the entrance.

"That's the Czar's castle," Ted said. "He hatches all his schemes in there, and his men come and go all day and night carrying out his orders."

"What's the Czar look like?"

"Haven't you heard? Eight feet tall with fangs like a shark."

Mortimer's eyes grew big until he caught the old man's smile. He laughed. "I heard ten feet tall."

"What now?" Ted asked.

"This is as far as you go."

"Don't have to tell me twice. I'm not quite as concerned about your hide as your friends are, but I do wish you luck. You going to bluff your way?"

"Yup."

They shook hands.

Ted said, "I'm going to try to get in touch with my people. Who knows? Maybe we can come up with something to help."

"Thanks."

"Try not to die, Mortimer Tate." And then he was gone. Atlanta's old, gray ghost.

Mortimer watched and waited for an hour. He told himself he was trying to get the lay of the land first, familiarize himself with troop movements before going in. Who was he fooling? He was trying to get up the courage.

Mortimer took a deep breath, walked out the front door and crossed the street.

XLVI

When there had been such a thing as television, Mortimer had watched a show called *Cops*. In this show, police officers habitually wrestled perpetrators to the ground, where they would hit face-first—often on cement—and then have their arms pinned painfully behind their backs in preparation for a pair of handcuffs.

Mortimer knew *exactly* what that felt like now.

When Mortimer had crossed the street and casually announced he wanted to see the head honcho, the guards on duty had been momentarily frozen by his audacity. They recovered quickly and gang-piled him, leaving his bottom lip swollen and bloody, various bruises along the length of his body.

His hands were tied behind his back.

He was searched.

He was disarmed.

He was taken to a very small room just inside the CNN entrance and put in an uncomfortable chair, a guard standing in front of him, stone-faced, arms crossed, a pistol in a shoulder holster.

Mortimer waited for half an hour before another man entered the room. He stood medium height, medium weight, brown hair of a medium shade, but his eyes were blue and active, giving Mortimer a quick appraisal. He wore a well-cut black suit with a black tie. The red armband the only splash of color. An eel-skin briefcase in his grip.

"Hello." Too cheerful.

"Hi," croaked Mortimer.

"Throat a bit raw? Want some water?"

"Please."

The man left, came back thirty seconds later with a glass, tilted it to Mortimer's lips. Mortimer drank.

"Thanks."

"No problem. I'm Terry Frankowski. We're going to be spending some time together, so I hope you'll call me Terry."

"Okay."

"So let's have your story, Mortimer. I hope I can call you Mortimer. Mort?"

"Mortimer is fine. How do you know my name?"

"We found your Joey Armageddon's Platinum membership card among your belongings," Terry said. "Now, let's get down to business. Ready?"

"Sure."

Terry cleared his throat. "I'm a member of the Czar's intelligence organization, but, to be perfectly honest, my specialty is analyzing data. I'm not usually involved with interrogations, but I was the only one around, and, well, beggars can't be choosers. Am I right?"

"I'll try to go easy on you."

"Ha. That's the spirit," Terry said. "We're going to get along. I can tell."

Terrific.

"Now, I've got a list of questions and procedures here, so that should help things along." He produced a pencil and a clipboard from his briefcase. "First question: are you here to kill the Czar?"

"Actually," Mortimer said, "I think I can save us some time. If I can just talk to the Czar—"

Terry tsked, sucked air through his teeth. "Yeah, the thing is, I just have this list of questions, and I'd feel better if we just got through them. I'm a rules kind of guy, and, look, I'm going to be square with you, okay? I'm a little out of my comfort zone, so I really think I should stick with the format."

Mortimer said nothing.

"Let's skip ahead," Terry said. "Are you here to steal gasoline or sabotage Red Stripe gasoline supplies?"

"No."

"Super. Now let's—" Terry consulted the clipboard. "Oh, wait. It says here not to believe you and in parentheses it says *slap face*." Terry tsked again. "I guess we can skip that. Things are going well enough, don't you think?"

The stone-faced guard cleared his throat, shook his head.

"Oh." Terry seemed disappointed. "Rules are rules."

Terry leaned forward, swung his hand in a wide arc and caught Mortimer's face with a loud, stinging slap. Lights danced in front of Mortimer's eyes. He tasted blood, his cheek having caught on some teeth.

Terry flipped a page on the clipboard, then another page, reading ahead. "Oh, dear. Looks like we're in for a long day."

Mortimer assumed the dungeon had not been installed as part of the CNN Center's original design. He hung from a damp stone wall, held there with manacles and heavy chains.

Terry hadn't enjoyed a moment of the interrogation, but he was very conscientious about his job, had even taken twenty minutes to find a hand-rolled cigarette among the troops so he could burn Mortimer's forearm as the clipboard instructed. There had been more slaps and punches in between predictable questions.

Mortimer told him everything he could without giving away the show, sticking as close to the truth as possible. Yes, he was a Platinum member. Yes, he'd recently been to the Armageddon's on Lookout Mountain. Yes, he'd busted out of jail and escaped south. Had he been part of the recent disturbance at Stone Mountain? Huh? Who? What are you talking about?

Mortimer answered question after question, many seemingly irrelevant. But Mortimer had his chance too, made sure Terry knew that Mortimer had valuable information and was looking to trade. He'd talk only to the Red Czar himself.

So they'd put him in the dungeon.

He hung there, shoulders aching.

Waited.

He was half asleep, in a daze, when he heard the dungeon door creak open. He didn't open his eyes right away. If they were coming to dump more punishment on him, maybe they'd leave him alone if they thought he'd passed out.

He heard movement, somebody close to him. He felt a soft hand on his face, a cool, wet rag dabbing at the corners of his mouth. He felt something being applied to the cigarette burns on his forearm, a salve of some kind. Instant relief.

Mortimer chanced opening one eye, looked down at the top of a woman's head, rich brown hair with three thin strips of gray radiating from her part down the center. She stooped over a bucket, wrung out a rag in clean water.

He was so thirsty.

"Who are you?" His voice so hoarse and dry.

"How disappointing. You don't recognize your own wife," Anne said. "It's only been nine years."

XLVII

"Anne?" Mortimer blinked, looked into her pale blue eyes. She smiled. The gray in her hair told the years, a few more laugh lines at the eyes. But her tan face glowed smooth and young like on their wedding day, lips full, posture firm and athletic. She wore a heavy brown robe, looked like a medieval monk. She was okay. She looked good and she was okay. He'd come so far. She was okay.

He started to cry.

Anne's smile fell. "What are you doing? Don't do that."

The tears came hot and fast, sobs wracking his body, rattling the chains. He tried to talk, tried to tell her everything he felt upon seeing her, the love and regret and fear and so many things mixed together that not even he understood fully. He couldn't speak, could only gulp for breath between great heaving sobs, snot running over his lips.

Anne wiped at a tear in the corner of her own eye, wiped the snot off Mortimer's face with the rag. "You were always a sentimental jerk."

"S-sorry."

"What are you doing here anyway?"

She really didn't know? "I came for you."

"Me? Are you crazy?"

"You're my wife."

"That was *nine years* ago." Disbelief in her eyes. "I'm not your wife anymore."

"I never signed the divorce papers."

She snorted laughter. "Really? Divorce papers? Filed in what court? Do you think legal paperwork matters anymore? Do you think our mortgage matters, our life insurance policy? Where do you think you're going to cash the savings bonds your uncle gave us?"

"I never agreed."

"You don't have to agree. I agreed for both of us." She shook her head, went on, her voice softer. "This isn't really about our marriage, is it? It's been so long. You haven't really been thinking of me as your wife. Not after all this time."

No. Not really. He couldn't imagine anything could really be between them, not anymore, after so much had happened. "I had to see you. Just to know. After the way we left it. I felt I owed you. I wanted . . . I wanted to feel right about it."

"You did sort of leave me high and dry," Anne said. She continued to wipe his face as she spoke. "I didn't care for your little prank, and I wasn't going to stomp around the pocket wilderness with the divorce papers in one hand and a ballpoint pen in the other, calling your name. I'd hoped you'd come to your senses, come home and act like an adult."

She shook her head, let out a long sigh. She lifted a cup to Mortimer's lips. "Drink. Slowly."

He drank. Relief on his raw throat.

"And I would have waited you out," she continued, "but Mother called from Chattanooga. She was scared. You know she lives—lived—in kind of an iffy neighborhood. So I was caught there when all the shit really hit the fan. We actually made it through the first year okay, but she died that winter. I made my way back to Spring City."

"Looking for me?"

"I'm sorry, Mortimer, but no. Oh, I wondered if I'd see you, but no. I wanted to go home. That simple. So stupid. My house wasn't mine anymore.

"I took up wandering. Learned to kill to survive. I traded myself for food. Don't look at me like that. You know things are different now. I got tough fast. Sometimes, I thought I wanted to die, but it was never true. I wanted to *live*. And if you want to live, you have to understand the way things are and adjust."

"I'm going to get you out of here," Mortimer said. "Maybe that won't make up for everything, but it's a start. I'll figure it out."

"How did getting chained to the dungeon wall fit into the rescue plan?"

"I don't suppose you could get me down."

She shook her head. "No way. They let me come in to clean you up and give you some water. I think they want me to tell you to cooperate. Maybe they think seeing me will soften you up. They knew I was your wife. Did you tell them you were here for me?"

"I told them I was here for another reason. It's a long story."

"Here's my advice: Look out for yourself. If you can get loose, don't worry about me. I suggest telling them whatever they want to know. They can make things bad for you if they want to, a lot worse than chaining you up."

"I'm not leaving without you."

Anne frowned, made a disgusted noise. "Knock off the hero crap. I absolve you, okay? You're forgiven, so don't feel you owe me anything. Besides, when I was captured, they got some of my girls too, a dozen of them. I was taking them to Little Rock to open a new Joey Armageddon's. I'm responsible for them, and I'm not leaving them. So you see, I can't run off with you just so you can feel like a good guy."

"Don't be ridiculous," Mortimer said. "I've come a long way—"

"You're not the only one who's come a long way and been through a lot. So have I. So have my girls. Get over yourself."

She lifted the cup to his lips again. "Drink more. I'll probably have to go soon."

He gulped, emptied the cup.

"At least tell me why you're wearing that robe."

"This?" She stood back, opened it. Underneath she wore a hot-pink bikini. She was thinner than he remembered, stomach muscles well defined, long legs. It was the wrong place and the wrong time, but Mortimer felt the stirrings of arousal. He remembered those early days of the marriage, her legs wrapped around him, making love all night in a sweaty pile. He wanted to cry again.

She closed the robe, sighed. "The Czar keeps us all like a harem. We all have to wear bathing suits and underwear like it's the fucking Playboy Mansion or something."

"Does he make you . . . do things?"

"No. We never see him. I wonder if he even exists."

Mortimer managed a weak smile. "Eight feet tall with shark teeth."

She laughed. "Yeah."

A knock on the door, a deep voice on the other side. "Time's up."

"Okay." She put a gentle hand on Mortimer's face, kissed his nose. "Thanks for coming, but get out of here, escape or whatever, but don't worry about me."

He started to say something, but it caught in his throat.

She gave him one last sad look and was out the door.

Mortimer Tate hung his head. If he died right then and there, that would be just fine.

XLVIII

Had it been an hour or a day? Mortimer lost track of time, hanging there, feeling useless and defeated. His arms hurt.

Someone came for him at last.

The dungeon door creaked open. The newcomer took a step inside, stopped with his hands behind his back. An older man, maybe early sixties, dressed the same as Terry Frankowski had been, black suit with the red armband. He was gaunt, tall but slightly stooped, white hair and moustache, weak chin. He looked around the dungeon with clear brown eyes.

"I always thought this was a bit too theatrical." A smoker's voice, but kindly, like somebody's tough, lovable grandfather.

"It's nice," Mortimer said. "I'm thinking of doing my summer home all medieval. So who the hell are you?"

"Name's Ford. Jim Ford. I'm Terry Frankowski's boss. I'd have been the one to deal with you instead of Terry but I was off taking care of some things."

"You here for round two?"

Ford shook his head. "I'm just here to fetch you. Somebody wants a quick chat. But don't get complacent. I was an Atlanta cop for twenty-two years, and I know how to get information out of a suspect. And there's none of that Miranda bullshit keeping me from bringing in the thumbscrews. I figure I'll have my crack at you sooner or later."

"Thanks. I like you too."

"Keep it up, smartass."

Ford fished a ring of keys out of his pocket and approached Mortimer. Behind him two more thugs with pistols appeared in the doorway. Mortimer's shoulders were sore as hell. He didn't like the odds, but maybe after Ford got him out of the manacles, he could surprise them, get hold of one of the pistols . . . No. He was dreaming. They'd stomp him flat. All Mortimer could do was bide his time and see what they had in store for him.

Ford unlocked him, and Mortimer collapsed to the floor. He could hardly lift his arms.

"Take a minute," Ford said. "Try to work the circulation back in."

Mortimer moved his arms, slowly at first, rubbed the shoulders. The hot tingling flooding back into his limbs was sudden, excruciating murder.

"Feels nice, don't it?" Ford said. "On your feet, man. Time to go."

Mortimer didn't see much of the CNN Center. They walked down a short hall and stepped directly into an elevator. Up.

They have power. I wonder what the source is. Solar? But if they can get gasoline, maybe they can run the generators.

The elevator opened at last.

"This is your stop," Ford said.

Mortimer hesitated, then stepped off the elevator. Ford and his thugs didn't get off. The doors closed, and Mortimer was alone in a small foyer, only a single door across from the elevator.

He walked through the door into a large office area that had been transformed into the burlesque of a throne room. Four Red Stripes stood on either side of the room in straight lines, holding their rifles at attention. On the far side of the room was an enormous chair covered in red velvet, trimmed in gold. A large flag behind the throne, white with a red stripe.

The man sitting in the throne stood to face Mortimer. He wasn't ten feet tall, not even eight. But he was seven feet if he was an inch, and when he smiled, Mortimer saw the man's teeth had been filed to points. He wore a leather vest, no shirt, muscles rippling like Conan. He had a square, Frankenstein face, greasy hair. He carried a wooden club like a caveman's. He wore a necklace of human ears and noses.

Mortimer gulped.

"Who dares come to see the Red Czar?" His voice was thunder.

"Uh . . . Mortimer Tate."

"Oh, right through there, then." The giant pointed at a door off to the right.

Mortimer hesitated. "What?"

"You want to see the Czar?"

Mortimer nodded.

"Right through that door. Off you go."

Mortimer's eyes shifted to the door, back to the giant. He edged toward the door. Nobody stopped him. He walked through, shut the door behind him.

At first, Mortimer thought he was in some kind of enormous kitchen, long countertops, sinks, refrigerators, bubbling vats. A second look, and it seemed more like a laboratory, with beakers and test tubes. Mortimer also noticed a shortwave radio hissing in the corner. It was tempting to run to it and call for help. Bunsen burners heated some of the larger beakers. A chemical smell, yeasty and pungent but vaguely familiar. Many of the vats were labeled.

FREDDY'S DISHWATER LAGER.

FREDDY'S PISS YELLOW.

FREDDY'S TOOTHACHE MUSCADINE.

FREDDY'S DRY-HEAVE BRANDY.

Mortimer scratched his head.

"Welcome to my little playroom, Mr. Tate," said a voice behind him.

Mortimer spun, startled. A small man stood before him, a head shorter than Mortimer, bland, pale face, hair a mouse brown. Lips a bit too pink, smile way too happy.

"I'm the Red Czar," he said. "But please call me Freddy."

XLIX

When Mortimer recovered, he said the following: "You're shitting me."

"I shit you not," the little man said.

"But you're the guy who makes all the booze and beer and everything," Mortimer insisted. "You can't be the Czar. That's . . . that's . . . you *can't* be the Czar."

Freddy frowned. "What did you expect?"

"Ten feet tall with shark teeth."

Freddy chuckled. "Oh, you mean Horace out there in the throne room. Yes, it's good to perpetuate a certain image. The fear has been a useful tool, and just between you and me, I have a weak spot for that sort of thing. The dungeon too. I used to play a lot of Dungeons & Dragons."

"How . . . why . . . ?" Mortimer shook his head, gathered himself. "So what are you? A brewer who has taken up conquest as a hobby, or a warmonger who just likes to make shitty alcohol on the side?"

"It's a long, astounding tale of amazement and wonder." Freddy looked at his watch. "But since I'm launching an offensive tomorrow to smash Joey Armageddon out of existence, I don't really have the time to do the story justice."

"But why would you want to destroy Armageddon? He sells all of your booze in his clubs."

Freddy's face hardened. "He sells it because my Red Stripes control the supply routes. Any of his precious microbrew he tries to deliver gets captured by my men. Then only Freddy's beer and liquor get through. Stupid Marx thought the means of production was the key. He was a fool. It's always been about distribution. Only I am able to mass-produce enough product to keep his growing franchise supplied. Well, it's not good enough. I want the whole thing, soup to nuts. I'll take over his clubs and I'll run it all." There was a gleam in Freddy's eyes as he spoke of his intended conquest. An evil gleam.

Mortimer noticed a particularly long test tube on the counter close to him. He remembered Armageddon's instructions. Kill the Czar if possible. He edged toward the test tube. If he could break it off, maybe he could take out Freddy with the jagged end.

"Besides," Freddy said. "You think Joey Armageddon is such a good guy? Those club owners sitting like kings while the whole town bows down to them. Armageddon like an emperor on top of his mountain. It's positively feudal. He has everyone hypnotized with tits and ass."

Another two feet and he could make a grab for the test tube. If he jammed it right in Freddy's throat . . .

But Freddy was watching him. Mortimer had to keep up his end of the conversation. "So what am I doing here?"

"We know you escaped from Armageddon's jail," Freddy said. "My people say you might have useful information."

"That's why I'm here," Mortimer said. "I thought I might be able to trade the information."

"For what?"

"Maybe I want to move up in the world. Maybe I want to be

on the winning side. And maybe I thought I could trade the information for my wife."

"From what I hear, she's not exactly poised to fly back into your arms."

Mortimer shrugged. "I'm flexible."

"I'm not," Freddy stated. "I launch my assault tomorrow. Armageddon will be crushed, and his ridiculous clubs and all of their resources will belong to me. Once I control the region, the rest of the continent will kneel before me. There's nothing you can do about it."

We'll see about that.

Mortimer reached for the test tube. Froze. Slowly pulled his hand back.

The automatic pistol in Freddy's hand was pointed directly at Mortimer's stomach.

Freddy smiled. "I seem harmless, don't I? I didn't just fall off the turnip truck, you know."

"Let's work something out," said Mortimer. "I can tell you about Armageddon's defenses."

"Hmmmmmmm, no, I don't think so," Freddy said.

"You know I can. You have spies who can confirm it."

"I have many spies that tell me many things." Freddy looked past Mortimer. "Isn't that right, Lars?"

Mortimer turned. His mouth fell open.

"My apologies, Mr. Tate," Lars said. He also trained an automatic pistol on Mortimer's midsection. "Yes, I'm afraid I've been in the Czar's employ the entire time."

"An IRS auditor." Mortimer spat. "I should have known."

"I wanted to talk to you face-to-face," Freddy said. "There was a chance you really did have some useful information, but now it's obvious you were merely a pawn in one of Armageddon's feeble schemes. He must be desperate and weak, so I'm launching my attack immediately to take advantage."

Mortimer said nothing, exhaled slowly. *For nothing. I came all this way, was beaten and burned, all for nothing. My wife doesn't want my help, and I can't do a damn thing against the Czar.*

But he had to try. "I have information. Stuff Armageddon didn't know about. You've got to listen to me."

"You've grown tiresome, Mr. Tate," Freddy said. "Lars, please escort Mr. Tate to the elevator, where Jim Ford is waiting to take him to the dog pit."

"Now, hold on," Mortimer said. "I think you'd better—wait. Dog pit?"

Lars lifted his pistol. "This way if you please, Mr. Tate."

Lars took Mortimer back to the elevator. Jim Ford, Terry Frankowski and a brace of goons waited for him. Lars motioned him aboard the elevator, offered him only a slight nod of the head as the doors closed and the elevator began its long descent.

"So I hear you're for the dog pit," Ford said. "Good. The boys can use a little entertainment."

Mortimer said, "I don't suppose the dog pit is your colorful name for the local sports bar."

They all laughed at that.

"No, it's an actual pit," Terry said. "About twenty feet deep."

"With dogs," added Ford. "Rottweilers. Usually a half-dozen or so."

Terry's hand shot out, poked a finger at the button for the third floor.

Ford said, "We're supposed to head straight for the dog pit. What the hell are you doing?"

"I forgot something in my office," Terry said. "It won't take but a second."

"The hell with that," Ford said. "Get whatever it is later."

Terry sighed. "I've already pressed the button."

"Just let the doors open and close again, and we'll be on our way," Ford said.

The lights on the display counted down, seventh floor, sixth floor, fifth floor . . .

When the button lit up for the fourth floor, Terry grabbed Mortimer's wrist. When the light blinked for the third floor, Terry dropped, pulled Mortimer down with him right as the elevator doors slid open.

Jim Ford had just enough time to say, "Aw, hell—"

Ted and Reverend Jake on the other side of the door let loose with a pair of machine pistols, spraying the interior of the elevator at chest level. The blaze of slugs shredded meat, and the Red Stripes convulsed in place as the bullets hit. Blood rained down on Mortimer's head and back. Bodies fell on top of him.

He shoved them off. "What the fuck?"

Ted and the reverend each got an arm and pulled him up. Reverend Jake looked down at the bodies. "God have mercy on your black-hearted souls."

"Terry is our man on the inside," Ted explained. "He helped organize your escape."

"Sorry I had to burn you with the cigarette," Terry said. "I had to keep up appearances."

"No problem." Mortimer kneed him in the balls.

Terry whuffed air, bent in half, groaned. "Okay. That's cool. I deserve that."

"Did you get close to him?" Ted's eyes were wild with hope and anticipation. "He sent for you, right? Did you kill him?"

"I never had a chance," Mortimer said. "The Czar's been one step ahead the whole time. He knew who I was. He knew everything."

"Shit. You didn't find out anything?"

"He didn't spare me a lot of time," Mortimer said. "He's too busy getting ready for his big attack tomorrow."

"Tomorrow?" Ted and the reverend said together.

"Spawn of Satan," the reverend said. "He barely has enough gasoline. We thought for sure he'd wait another week, maybe even two."

"We've got to get word to Armageddon," Ted said. "And we've been standing here too long anyway."

They shoved the dead Red Stripes into the hallway and took the elevator. Ted pressed the button for the roof.

"Wait," Mortimer said. "My wife! The Czar has my wife and a bunch of other women held captive. We can't leave them."

"No time," Ted said.

"I'm not leaving without them," Mortimer insisted.

"They're all the way at the top of the other tower," Terry said. "We'd never make it."

"It's not negotiable." Mortimer reached for the Stop button.

Mortimer felt sudden fire explode against his ribs. His limbs stiffened, then went loose, his brain going to fuzz, little lights in front of his eyes.

Mortimer tried to talk. "You f-fuckers . . . what . . . the . . . ?" Drool down his chin. His eyes lifted, barely registered the buzzing stun gun in Ted's hand. *Again? Those fucking things hurt.*

"Sorry," Ted said. "But your pals said you might be stubborn."

The door opened, and they half-dragged, half-carried Mortimer across the roof.

Mortimer's fried brain registered night. He'd been hanging in the dungeon longer than he'd guessed. The second thing he noticed was the Blowfish on the far side of the roof, bobbing in the gentle breeze.

As they lifted him into the gondola, Sheila appeared, looking horrified.

"What did you do to him?"

"He made a fuss," Ted said. "Don't worry. He'll be fine."

Mortimer lay flat on his back in the gondola. "Where's . . . B-Bill?"

"Too much weight," Ted said. "He was mighty pissed about being left behind. We needed somebody to guard the blimp while me and the reverend came for you, and your little girl here don't weigh a thing."

Frantic movement, men pulling lines, tossing over sandbags. Mortimer felt the Blowfish lift. Subtle movement. They were letting the Blowfish drift on the wind, probably didn't want to risk the angry whine of the little engine.

Sometime later, Mortimer heard Ted say, "Okay, we're out far enough."

He heard the engine crank, and they pointed the Blowfish north.

Mortimer got to his feet, leaned over the side of the gondola, felt the cold air on his face. His whole body throbbed.

"Are you going to be okay?" Sheila asked.

"Yeah."

"When you feel better, remind me to kick your ass."

Mortimer nodded. "Right."

They'd replaced the blimp's ham radio, and Reverend Jake turned knobs and shouted into the microphone. "Blowfish to Joey One. Come in, Joey One."

Through the static came, "Joey One here. Go ahead, Blowfish."

"Black Bart plans to stampede the cattle in the morning. Repeat, it's on for tomorrow morning. You've got to mobilize right now."

"We hear you, Blowfish."

Mortimer watched the dark, dead city slide by beneath them. Somewhere down there, he'd abandoned his wife.

L

They eventually put down in a secure field north of Kennesaw just before dawn. Ted's underground comrades were there to light the landing zone and provide food. Mortimer sat in a big tent, a blanket around his shoulders, spooning pea soup into his face. He felt like a disaster victim getting Red Cross relief.

Ted perched on the picnic bench next to him, slurped soup. "Beats the hell out of rat jerky."

"All these people to land a blimp?" Mortimer said. "You've set up a whole camp."

"This is rendezvous point Alpha," Ted told him. "We've been gathering and stockpiling supplies and keeping them hidden for months. That way Armageddon's forces can mobilize quickly. We'll supply them when they breeze through here right before hitting the Czar."

Good, thought Mortimer. *Because if they're heading back to Atlanta, I'm hitching a ride.*

"Well, well, well, if it isn't the son-of-a-bitch, one-man-army superhero."

Mortimer looked up, saw Bill scowling down at him, the Union officer's hat back on his head.

"I know, I know," Mortimer said. "I already got an earful from Sheila."

"This partnership isn't going to work if you keep running off all by yourself and hogging all the fun."

Mortimer lifted his right hand. "It won't happen again."

"Okay, then. Follow me. I'll show you something."

Mortimer followed Bill out of the camp. He still clutched the blanket around him. They'd taken his jacket back at the CNN Center. Bill led him up a steep embankment, and they found themselves overlooking Interstate 75, twelve empty lanes that had often been bumper-to-bumper back in the day.

Bill pointed south toward Atlanta. "Watch for it."

Nothing at first, then Mortimer saw it, a flash of light, then another, a rapid-fire series of orange-white bursts. Every fourth or fifth flash, a faint *pop* reached them.

"Ted's underground folks," Bill said. "They're trying to fuck things up a little, maybe throw off the Czar's timetable. Ted said a team was going to try for the gasoline, maybe blow up their supply, but he doesn't think it'll work. Too well guarded. There's a lot of people dying tonight."

"It's a real live war, isn't it?" Mortimer said. "Not like a rumble between two street gangs. It's a war."

Bill nodded. "Yup. And I don't think we can sit this one out. He's the bad guy, and he needs to be stopped. It's that simple."

"Yeah." Mortimer wasn't so sure it was that simple, but Anne was back there, and that was enough. Whatever his wife—former wife—might have said, Mortimer simply wasn't going to leave her to rot.

Bill handed something wrapped in cloth to Mortimer. "Here, take this while I'm thinking of it. Managed to scrounge it up. Wouldn't want you running around naked."

Mortimer unfolded the cloth. A .38-caliber revolver, very

similar to the police special he'd been so fond of. And a clip-on holster for his belt. "Thanks."

"Can't have you guarding my back with nothing but witty rejoinders," Bill said.

Mortimer checked the load, clipped the revolver to his belt. "I guess we're committed to fighting for Armageddon. If he loses the war, we don't get our twenty thousand dollars."

They waited, the flashes above the city fading and finally stopping altogether. Dawn erupted red over the horizon like a bloody prophecy. The morning was damp, and a thick fog rolled in, gathered around Mortimer and Bill, sucked them in, cutting visibility to fifty feet in every direction.

"Does this help us or hurt us?" Mortimer asked.

"Hell if I know," Bill said.

A long way off, Bill heard it first. "You hear that?"

"No . . . wait. Yes," Mortimer said. "Engines?"

"I think so."

"Damn, which direction? Is it coming from the city?" If the Red Stripes were coming, Mortimer needed to warn Ted and his men.

"I can't tell," Bill said. "Damn fog's too thick."

"It's getting louder."

Bill drew his six-shooters. "Get ready to haul ass."

From the north, Mortimer saw them, like bright demon eyes in the fog, a single pair at first, then another, then ten, then a wall of headlights coming down the interstate. Vague blurs emerged from the fog, took shape. Cars.

Mortimer spotted a familiar figure in the lead car. The roof had been cut from the vehicle, a machine gun mounted in the backseat. The man stood in the passenger seat, head and shoulders above the windshield, resplendent in a crisp uniform and pink beret.

"General Malcolm!" Mortimer shouted.

The black man's head yanked around, spotted Mortimer. He picked up a headset, shouted something into the microphone, and all the cars slowed to a halt.

"Is that you, Tate?"

"Yeah."

Mortimer and Bill climbed the guardrail, jogged to the general's car. "What is this?"

"It's a Toyota Prius," Malcolm said. "We knew fuel would be an issue, so we only scavenged automobiles that would make the gasoline stretch. We have sixty-one total cars in the attack group. Fifty-one hybrids and ten MINI Coopers. We're the most eco-friendly assault force in history. Are you here with the underground?"

"Yeah. We've been waiting for you."

Even as Mortimer spoke to General Malcolm, members of the underground emerged from the fog with gas cans, ammunition and food, beginning the resupply of the attack force.

Ted appeared at Mortimer's side. "It's all going just like you wanted, General."

"Many thanks," Malcolm said. "Tell your people to hurry. The closer we can get under cover of this fog the better."

"Right." Ted rushed away to orchestrate the resupply.

Malcolm turned his hard gaze on Mortimer. "You'd better be right about the Czar's attack today, Tate. We've committed all our forces. It might be crippling to us if you're wrong."

"Can you use a couple more hands?" Bill asked.

"The MINI Coopers are short on gunners. They're in the rear.

But you'd better hurry. I'm not waiting one more second as soon as we're gassed up and ready to go."

"Understood."

They jogged toward the rear of the column. The sight of fifty-one hybrids in a row with heavy machine guns mounted in the backseats was not something Mortimer had ever expected to see. It was nice to know he could still be surprised.

"You dickheads!" screamed a voice behind them.

Mortimer looked over his shoulder, saw Sheila running to catch up.

"Were you just going to leave me?" she yelled.

"Hey, *you* got to go on the blimp rescue instead of *me*," Bill shot back over his shoulder.

They found the Coopers bunched at the back of the attack force, looking tiny and ridiculous. But they were functioning automobiles. As far as Mortimer was concerned, they might as well have been Cadillacs.

"Who's in charge here?" Mortimer shouted at the first line of Coopers.

A square-jawed man stuck his head out of the driver's side of the lead car. Three-day stubble, a cigar smoldering in his kisser. "I'm in charge of Yellow Group. What do you want?"

"Malcolm said you guys might have a job opportunity."

"Not us. Try Blue Group."

They went to the next line of MINI Coopers and yelled for the leader.

The driver's door of a glossy blue Cooper opened, and a lithe woman stepped out. She wore leather, hair standing up in wild burgundy spikes, a black patch over one eye. "Well, you just never know who you're going to meet along a sorry stretch of highway."

It took Mortimer a split second to recognize her. "Tyler!"

Bill whooped, and they rushed forward, shaking her hand and patting her on the back. She held up her hands, fended off a flurry of confused questions.

"One at a time."

"How did you get away from the cannibals?" Bill asked.

"Same as you two," Tyler said. "I ran my ass off and didn't look back."

Mortimer grinned. "So you decided to sign on with Armageddon, eh?"

"I've always worked for Armageddon," Tyler said. "Who do you think owned the Muscle Express?"

A man popped his head through the sunroof of another Cooper, holding a set of headphones to one ear. "They're starting engines, boss. We'd better crank 'em up."

"Good seeing you're alive," Tyler said. "Got to go."

"Wait," Mortimer said. "Malcolm said you might have room for us."

Tyler nodded. "I have room in my car. Jimmy needs a gunner too." She pointed to the Cooper all the way at the end of the line.

Sheila elbowed her way into the conversation. "Me too."

"Don't need anyone else," Tyler said.

"I'm *not* being left behind."

"You can sit in the passenger side of my car," Tyler said. "But if you get in the way of my driving, I'll pull over and dump your ass on the side of the road."

Bill laughed. "That's the charm school dropout I remember."

THE ROAD WARRIORS

LI

The semithunderous whine of fifty-one Toyota hybrids and ten MINI Coopers flying south on I-75 was surprisingly impressive. Mortimer had not traveled this fast in years. Even the Muscle Express hadn't topped more than forty miles per hour. The MINI Cooper, with the steely-eyed Tyler behind the wheel, ate up the highway at seventy.

"Isn't this a little fast for this fog?" Mortimer asked.

"Advance scouting reports the road clear of debris," Tyler said. "General Malcolm is hoping those underground people really threw off the Czar's schedule. If we swoop in fast enough we might catch them before they're set. Here, you're going to need this if you want to follow the play-by-play." She handed a set of headphones back over her shoulder.

Mortimer put them on, adjusted the microphone in front of his mouth.

Tyler's voice crackled in his ear. "The radio has been rigged with a few different settings. Right now we're just talking to each other. I can flip a switch to talk to the five Coopers in Blue Group, or I flip another switch and get the whole attack force, or hear Malcolm's orders or whatever. It's all plugged into the car's electrical system."

"What do you want me to do back here when the trouble starts?" Mortimer asked.

"The MINI is too small to mount a heavy machine gun," Tyler told him. "But there's an H&K full-auto 9 mm back there and a shit-load of ammo. They extended the moonroof to the backseat, so you can pop up and give them hell, especially if some joker gets on my tail. Just don't fly out if I take a sharp turn." To Sheila she said, "You can reload for him, make sure he's always got a fresh magazine."

Sheila gave the thumbs-up. "Okay."

"I'll need you to cut the chatter while I tune in the ball game. Maybe we can get the score." Tyler flipped to the main channel.

"—and get that first group in tight when you see them," came Malcolm's hard-edged voice through the headphones. "If we catch them in camp, then rip through and turn around for another pass as soon as possible. Don't let them mount up, whatever you do. If they've already hit the road, then we'll have to do it toe to toe, in which case keep your radios clear because I'm going to be issuing orders on the fly."

Mortimer slapped a fresh magazine into the H&K, stuck two more into his belt so he could grab them quickly. He reached into his shirt pocket for the cigar Bill had given him, bit the end and stuck it in his mouth. He tapped Sheila on the shoulder, gestured to the cigarette lighter. She pressed it in, waited, and it popped out a few seconds later. She handed it back to Mortimer, who puffed the cigar to life, then handed the lighter back to her.

Tyler smelled the smoke, wrinkled her nose and glanced in the rearview mirror. She put a hand over her microphone and said, "Those things will kill you."

Mortimer cocked the H&K. "Gee, and I'm usually such a careful guy."

A grin flickered at the corners of Tyler's mouth. Just for a second.

Mortimer stuck his head up through the moonroof, the wind ripping at him. He looked around to get his bearings. The Blue Group of MINI Coopers held together in a tight formation, Tyler's in the middle, one on either side, one in the front and one in the back. Mortimer looked at the MINI behind them, saw Bill's head sticking up through the moonroof, his Union hat tied on with a strip of rawhide under his chin. They traded thumbs-ups and Mortimer ducked back into the car.

The headphones crackled. "Big Duck, this is Silverfish, we have movement on the overpass just ahead, now we've passed it, looking back. Can't get a count, Big Duck."

Suddenly a flurry of voices on the radio. Mortimer could barely follow it.

—"I read you, Silverfish. Bullfrog, stay in formation. Slow it down, Dragonfly."

—"Big Duck, this is Dragonfly. I'm way in the back. Already going pretty slow."

—Malcolm cursed. "Well who the hell is this on my left?"

—"Willow Switch, sir."

—"I thought I was Willow Switch," came another voice.

—"We traded, remember? You wanted to be Iron Man."

—"Big Duck, this is Starfish. What about me? I can't see if I'm in formation or not."

—"This is Big Duck. I thought you were on point, Starfish."

—"No, that's Silverfish."

—"Babble Fish, here. Did you just radio to me? I was getting some apple juice."

—"Goddamn it, everyone shut the hell up!" Malcolm shouted. "I knew I shouldn't have let you pick your own call signs. Silverfish, stay on point."

—"Multiple sightings, multiple sightings, Big Duck. We have Red Stripes on the next two overpasses. I count at least a dozen, maybe—"

—"Everyone, tighten up," Malcolm ordered. "Keep sharp."

Far ahead, Mortimer saw a section of the fog glow bright orange with the sound of an explosion. Two more quick explosions followed.

—"Goddamn, Larry's on fire, I can't see—"

—"—mortars, I think. Where the hell did they get—"

—"Lost a tire, for Christ's sake, I can't steer this fucking thing—"

More explosions, almost on top of them now.

Tyler flipped the radio to the Blue Group setting. "Buckle up and spread out. Jimmy, I said spread out, but maintain speed, okay? You've got to keep up."

—"Sorry, boss."

Tyler switched back to the main channel.

—"—put some goddamn fire on those overpasses, make them duck their heads. The rest of you people spread out and keep going and we'll get through them as quickly as possible."

Another explosion to Mortimer's left. He winced at the flash. Two more mortar rounds chewing up highway to his right.

—"Silverfish here, I got headlights a hundred yards, a dozen pair easy, whoa! No, make that a lot more. Here they come, Big Duck."

—"Get back with the group, Silverfish. You can't do any more out there on point, and your ass is hanging in the wind."

A ball of fire erupted in front of them. Tyler yelled and swerved. A MINI Cooper from Yellow Group was tossed into the air, the flaming wreckage passing over Mortimer and obliterating the blue Cooper directly to Mortimer's left. The Cooper behind him swerved sharply, tires squealing, debris strewing fifty yards in a line of flame and smoke.

—"Jesus, that was Eddie."

—"Cut the chatter—"

—"Look out, they're already—"

—"This is Big Duck. Everyone shut the fuck up right now. I'm looking at trucks, V-8's, big stuff. Do not engage head-on, repeat, take 'em on the side streets if you can. You can't take these guys with speed or muscle, so it's going to have to be maneuverability. If you can—shit!"

Another series of explosions, machine-gun fire, flashes ahead in the fog. They passed a half-dozen demolished hybrids, still aflame. Mortimer's heart pounded in his throat. He saw Sheila sitting rigid in the passenger seat, Tyler's knuckles white on the steering wheel.

It came out of the fog like a charging bull, smashed through the left front quarter of a Yellow Group Cooper, sending it spinning off into the guardrail. A V-8 Mustang Mach 1. The engine roared. It had iron plates riveted across the front to guard the engine, more armor on the windshield, with only narrow slits for the driver to see through.

Tyler jerked the wheel, and the Mustang missed by an inch, passed them and immediately screeched the tires in a fishtail, coming back for them.

Tyler flipped to the channel for Blue Group. "Jimmy, you're with me. The rest of you stay with the attack force. You there, Jimmy?"

—"Right on your six, boss."

"This exit. Here we go."

She took three lanes sharply, barely making the off-ramp in time, scraping the curb as she took the turn at the bottom, flying past a defunct gas station and a doughnut shack. Mortimer looked behind. Jimmy was right there, the Mustang right behind him.

—"He's right on me, boss. Jesus, he's coming fast."

Mortimer saw Bill pop up through the moonroof. The machine pistol bucked in Bill's hand, a three-foot jet of fire pulsing from the barrel. The lead sparked off the Mustang's armor, doing it no damage, but apparently catching it by surprise. It swerved slightly, slowed its pursuit.

An arm came out the passenger window of the Mustang holding a weapon, rattled bullets at them. Mortimer ducked back into the car.

Tyler slammed on the brakes, fishtailed, turned suddenly down a residential street. Jimmy stayed right with her. The Mustang couldn't make the turn so sharply, went wide and chewed up a line of mailboxes before wrenching itself back onto the street.

"Split up, Jimmy!"

—"Bad idea, boss."

"We'll never get a good shot at the thing if we're both running away from it. Now go," Tyler ordered.

—"See you on the flip side."

Jimmy turned abruptly down a cross street. The Mustang never wavered, pushed the gas hard and came up behind Mortimer fast. Tyler turned, accelerated, turned again, zigzagging through what had once been a middle-class neighborhood. Malcolm had been right. The big bruisers had speed and muscle but couldn't maneuver so well, and every time Tyler took a sharp turn, the Mustang lost twenty yards.

But the muscle car made up for it on the straightaways, the big engine howling as the Mustang pulled within three feet of the Cooper's rear bumper, the faceless assailant in the passenger's seat shooting wildly.

Sheila had her hands over her eyes.

Tyler was a taut, wired mass of muscle and sinew. She jerked the wheel suddenly, and the Cooper whipped into a circular driveway. Tyler tapped the brakes, slowed the vehicle only slightly, and the Mustang shot past on the street. Tyler stomped the accelerator.

She shot out of the driveway, back onto the street, right behind the Mustang.

"Blast 'em," she shouted at Mortimer.

He popped out of the moonroof and unleashed the H&K, emptying a full clip in three seconds, ejecting it and slamming in a new one. He puffed the cigar like a lunatic locomotive. The Mustang had been modified for attack, not defense, and the exposed rear window presented an irresistible target. Mortimer fired, and the glass shattered. He fired again, and a neat row of holes appeared along the roof with metallic *tunk*s.

The Mustang slammed on the brakes.

"Shit!" Tyler hit the brakes too.

Not fast enough. The MINI slammed hard, crunching the front end. Mortimer pitched forward, managed to hang on instead of flying over the MINI's hood. The cigar flew out of his mouth. Tyler threw the car into reverse, backed up at full speed, headlight glass and the front bumper on the ground in front of them.

By the time the Mustang made its slow turn, the Cooper was flying back the way it had come. Soon the muscle car was on the Cooper's bumper again. Tyler resumed the zigzag strategy, but finally made a wrong turn into a cul-de-sac.

"Oh, fuck," Sheila said.

Tyler didn't slow down, aimed the Cooper at a narrow opening between a brick house and a wooden fence.

Mortimer tensed. "We won't fit. Turn it around. We won't fit."

"We'll fit, God damn it!" Tyler's grip on the wheel was iron, her whole face clenched and covered with sweat.

They flew up the driveway, across the yard and through the gap, each side clearing by less than an inch. Mortimer looked back, expecting the much wider Mustang to slam on the brakes.

The muscle car exploded through the fence, splintered planks sailing in every direction.

The Cooper scooted across the backyard, the Mustang gunning its engines behind, plowing jagged grooves into the soft lawn, kicking up dirt. The Cooper crossed over an already-down chain-link fence into the neighboring yard, dodging debris. The Mustang collided with patio furniture behind them, disintegrated ceramic pots, scattered pieces of a plastic swing set.

Mortimer emerged from the moonroof long enough to blaze half a magazine at the pursuer, bullets ricocheting in a shower of sparks. Tyler drove through a side yard, raced down another driveway and into a different cul-de-sac. Tyler stomped the gas.

A machine-gun burst from the Mustang shredded the Cooper's back right tire. The car skidded into a drainage ditch at full speed; the front end smashed into a telephone pole with a *pop-crunch*. This time Mortimer did fly, headfirst, forward and at an angle over the passenger side. He tried to roll with it, landing on grass and ending in a tangle of shrubbery.

He looked back, saw the Mustang rolling slowly, coming to a stop forty feet from the Cooper's rear bumper. It sputtered and conked out. There was a long moment of silence. Then the Mustang tried to crank the engine. It wouldn't turn over. It cranked again. Nothing.

Mortimer spotted where he'd dropped the H&K five feet away. He belly-crawled toward it through the grass, wincing at his sprained knee. He had minor cuts and bruises along his whole body. *Forget it. Go for the gun.*

The muscle car tried to crank one more time, and when it didn't, both Red Stripes climbed out, leveled their guns just as Mortimer reached the H&K. He pointed it with one hand, squeezed the trigger, let off two small bursts. He missed high, but sent the Red Stripes ducking behind the open car doors. Mortimer fired one more burst before the gun clicked empty. He felt at his belt for a fresh magazine, couldn't find one.

Shit.

Sheila rose through the moonroof, hair disheveled, bright blood streaming from her nose. She lifted her .45 automatic, fired five times fast.

They all heard the high-pitched revving of another car at the end of the street, accelerating, approaching fast. Machine-gun fire. The two Red Stripes looked at each other, turned and abandoned the Mustang, running full speed back among the houses. A second later, another MINI Cooper screeched to a stop next to the Mustang. A familiar face and a familiar blue Union officer's hat stuck through the moonroof.

"Over here." Mortimer stood and waved.

"You okay?"

"Yeah." Mortimer limped to the other Cooper. The knee sprain was minor. He bent to look into the driver's-side window. The kid behind the wheel was eighteen, twenty at most, red hair, freckles, buckteeth and leather driving gloves. "You Jimmy?"

"Yes, sir. What happened?"

Mortimer shook his head. "They just stopped. Maybe they threw a rod." Mortimer didn't exactly know what that meant, but he'd heard gearheads say it.

He limped to the Mustang, slid in behind the wheel. The interior smelled like beer and cigarettes. Mortimer turned the key in the ignition. The engine wheezed and strained but wouldn't turn over. He checked the gas gauge. The needle was square on the *E*.

He limped back to Jimmy's Cooper. "Can you get the rest of the battle on the radio?"

"Can't do it," Jimmy said. "I'm only rigged to hear the boss and the rest of the cars in my group. Group leaders get all the frequencies. You'll have to use Tyler's radio."

Mortimer went back to the wrecked Cooper, opened the driver's-side door.

"Oh, no. Damn." He sighed. "Damn."

Tyler was hunched over the steering wheel, half out of her seat, forehead smashed against the windshield. Mortimer eased her back into the seat. Her eyes were vacant, dark blood down both sides of her face. Mortimer felt for a pulse even though he knew there wouldn't be one.

"She hit so quick I don't think she felt a thing," Sheila said from the backseat.

Mortimer reached past Tyler's corpse, flipped the switch for the radio. He put on Tyler's headset. The confused chatter of battle assaulted him. He blocked it out and, into the microphone, said, "Malcolm, this is Mortimer Tate. You still out there?"

Confused static. Then:

—"I don't have time for you, Tate. I'm in the middle of a battle."

Explosions and gunfire in the background had almost drowned out Malcolm's voice.

"They're short on gas, Malcolm. You hear me? All that armor and those big V-8 engines. They're sucking gas fast. Are you getting this?"

A long pause.

—"Okay, you heard the man," Malcolm said. "We'll do a dog-and-rabbit on them. Let's run them dry, people. Engage only enough to get them to chase you."

"Good luck." Mortimer took off the headset.

He went back to the other Cooper. "Jimmy, I need a lift. There's something I have to do."

"No way, man," Jimmy said. "I've got to get back to the fight. Those are my people."

Mortimer started to protest, then stopped himself. It was the kid's right to get himself killed if he wanted. He looked at the wrecked MINI up against the telephone pole. "You think we can get that thing running?"

LII

Changing the tire had been the hard part. They pulled the battered Cooper out of the ditch. It started. It sounded bad, an arrhythmic clank coming from under the hood, but it would take them where Mortimer wanted to go.

They bade farewell to Jimmy, who took Tyler's body with him when he left.

The Cooper wouldn't go over thirty-five m.p.h. without the clanking getting bad, so they kept it slow, sticking to surface streets and avoiding the interstate. It took Mortimer, Bill and Sheila nearly two hours to reach the CNN Center.

They parked in front, sat in the car a moment and surveyed the scene.

Bill whistled. "What do you suppose happened?"

Mortimer shook his head. "I don't know."

Bodies. Wreckage. Flames. So much to take in all at once.

A large six-wheeled truck with an open-air bed was parked at an odd angle, one tire up on the curb, the driver's door open. The driver's legs were still in the truck, the rest of him on the ground, a pool of blood spreading out from his head. Forty feet away, a big Oldsmobile burned, the flames popping and snapping, a column of thick black smoke twisting into the air. A few dozen more bodies were scattered about, most in mismatched clothing, with the red armband the only thing they wore in common.

The stink of charred flesh made Mortimer's eyes water.

The front doors to the CNN Center stood wide open, hanging askew on bent hinges. A jam of bodies clogging the doorway.

"I'm going to have a look." Mortimer stepped out of the Cooper, drew the .38 revolver.

"I'll come with you," Bill said.

"Sheila, wait here and stay on the radio. If the battle shifts this way, honk the horn, give us some kind of warning."

Sheila looked at the dead. "Okay."

They had to climb over a pile of bodies three deep to get inside. Among the bodies were two men clad in the black suits of the Czar's secret police. One had a knife through his throat.

They entered the lobby, looked around. More bodies, many locked in the final throes of hand-to-hand combat.

"It looks like they were fighting each other," Bill said.

They walked toward the elevator for the other tower on the other side of the lobby, pressed the Up button.

The elevator door opened and a young man inside screamed, saw Mortimer's revolver and backed away, dropping a half-dozen cans of food and a head of cabbage. He wore jeans and a white T-shirt and a bloody apron.

"Don't shoot, man. I'm just the cook."

Mortimer lowered the pistol. "What happened here?"

The cook knelt, began scooping the cans into his apron. "I don't know, man. A bunch of those underground saboteurs hit while everyone was still asleep, really fucked everything up. Next thing I know all our own guys are killing each other. They're swarming into the kitchen and grabbing everything, cleaned the place out like fucking locusts, a bunch of them saying how they'll be damned if they're going to stick around here and get killed."

Bill snorted. "Looks like the proletariat bit the Czar in the ass."

"This stuff's mine." The cook clutched the cans and the cabbage to his chest. "I fought for it fair and square."

Mortimer waved his pistol toward the exit. "Get out of here."

He didn't need to be told twice, ran away and didn't look back.

Mortimer and Bill took the elevator to the top. The door opened and they leapt out, ready for action. They saw and heard no one at all. Another corpse sat crumpled in the corner with his head bashed to mush. They walked past him, opening doors and finding nothing.

Mortimer tried the last door at the very end of the hall. Locked. He jiggled the handle, thought he heard voices on the other side. He angled the revolver down, shot the lock with a single blast and kicked the door open.

A dozen women gasped at his sudden entrance, one screaming. They all wore lingerie or string bikinis. Velvet sofas and plush chairs. Soft music played from a DVD player. The Czar's harem. Mortimer was just thinking how cool it was to rescue a roomful of half-naked women when something smacked the back of his head.

The room whirled past his face in a blur and suddenly he was facedown in the shag carpeting. He felt a small hand grab a fistful of his hair, yank his head back. A cold knife blade against his throat.

"Wait!" shouted a familiar voice. "That's my husband."

.   .   .

"Sorry," Anne said after they'd moved him to one of the velvet couches. "We've been stuck up here for hours since all the shooting started, and we don't know what the hell's going on. We've been waiting for somebody to open that door so we could make a break for it."

Mortimer briefly related the pertinent details of the car battle and the apparent revolt among the Czar's men.

"But we don't know anything for sure," Bill said.

They headed out to the elevator, the scantily clad women with Bill and Mortimer in the lead.

When they reached the lobby, Anne saw the dead bodies and said, "Gather weapons and ammo, ladies. We may need them. For Pete's sake, Brandi, get rid of those high heels. We might have to run for it."

A stunning redhead in green panties and a matching bra kicked off her shoes. They picked through the dead, finding pistols and rifles. Anne found a Glock, checked the load and looked at Mortimer. "We're ready."

They ran out the door and were immediately set upon by a half-dozen Red Stripes.

"It's the women," yelled one of the Red Stripes. "Get them! We can have our way with them, then trade them for rat jerky."

Anne shot him in the face with the Glock.

The other women leapt into the action. An Asian girl in black stockings and garters kicked a Red Stripe in the balls. He went to his knees, and the girl stuck her gun in his mouth and pulled the trigger, the back of his head exploding in a spray of red gunk. Blonde twins in matching teddies had a Red Stripe on the ground, kicking him and smashing his skull in with the butt of a rifle.

In five seconds flat, the girls had disposed of the attackers.

"Holy shit," Mortimer said.

Anne barked orders. "Lisa, I want you on the street, shout if anything comes from either direction. Brandi, that truck looks big enough for all of us. Check it out."

The redhead who'd kicked the high heels away jogged to the truck, hauled the dead body the rest of the way out of the cab without thinking twice. She reached in, popped the hood, went around front and stood on the bumper so she could look down at the engine.

The rest of the girls climbed into the back of the truck.

Anne turned to Mortimer. "I was wrong. I'm glad you came to get me. We're square now, right?"

"Okay."

"The engine checks out and the keys are in the ignition," called Brandi.

"Good," Anne said. "Lisa?"

"All clear," said the girl from the road.

Anne patted Mortimer's cheek. "Thanks again. Really. Maybe we'll cross paths again sometime." She skipped toward the truck.

"Wait," Mortimer called after her. "Where are you going?"

"Back to Joey Armageddon's," she said. "That's were I belong. And I told you before, I'm responsible for these girls. I need to make sure they get back safely." She climbed behind the wheel and started the truck, backed it off the curb. Lisa came in from the street and jumped in the back.

The redhead—Brandi—hopped in the back too.

Brandi had found a pair of combat boots among the dead, stood tall and strong and straight in her green panties and bra, the butt of her AK-47 assault rifle resting against a cocked hip. The wind tugged at her red hair. A long streak of somebody else's blood down one leg. Her head was up, eyes bright. She looked like she owned the world.

There she goes, Mortimer thought. *The icon for a new age.* She could have been on the recruitment poster for the swingingest army in the world.

She met Mortimer's gaze and winked as Anne shifted the big truck into gear and kept going.

Bill said, "So that was your wife, huh?"

"Ex-wife."

Mortimer considered Anne's parting words. They were square. He'd found her. Saved her. The slate was clean.

Sheila's head came up through the moonroof. She held the headset away from her ear. "It's working, guys. Hey, they're doing it. They're running the Red Stripes out of gas."

They went to the Cooper. Mortimer took the headphones, listened but didn't hear anything. "What happened?"

Sheila took the headphones back and listened. "It was working a minute ago." She ducked back into the car, played with the switches. "It's working fine, we're just not getting anything."

"Maybe they're all out of range now," Bill said.

"The Czar has a shortwave radio setup in his lab," Mortimer said. "I want to know what's going on."

"Shit," Bill said. "Don't go back in there."

"They're all dead or ran away."

"You don't know that."

"Stay with Sheila," Mortimer said. "I won't be long."

. . .

The copper tang of blood hit Mortimer as the elevator door slid open on the top floor of the CNN Center. Lars lay dead in front of him, multiple bullet holes in his back. It struck Mortimer that he wore the same black suit working for the Czar as he did working for Armageddon.

Meet the new boss.

Same as the old boss.

Mortimer stepped over the body, crossed through to the "throne room."

The giant slumped dead in the chair, his chest and face caked with dark blood. He still clutched the caveman club in one hand. Around him lay half a dozen Red Stripes with their heads smashed open. Horace had gotten in his licks before he went down.

Mortimer picked his way around the bodies, trying not to step in too much gore, and entered the laboratory.

Freddy—the Red Czar—sat with his back to Mortimer. He wore a headset plugged into a ham radio. He chuckled to himself, shaking his head and taking gulps from a bottle of his terrible vodka.

He must have sensed Mortimer's presence, turned abruptly. "Oh, it's you. Asshole. You started all this."

"Not me."

"I attacked before I was ready. You made me think Armageddon was about to attack too, so I attacked first."

"I need to borrow your radio," Mortimer said.

This made Freddy laugh harder. "You want to hear what's on the radio? Here, have a listen."

He unplugged the headphones, and the speakers buzzed to life.

—". . . and I think they're dead too. I can't find any of the security people and—oh, hell, they're everywhere. They killed Nancy and the whole kitchen staff . . ." Static.

"Who was that?" Mortimer asked.

Freddy laughed again, eyes afire with madness. "That's your precious paradise. Joey Armageddon's is in ruins. Lookout Mountain is a slaughterhouse."

"You're a liar."

The static cleared, the voice coming in strong again. —". . . if you can hear this, if anyone's reading me at all. Repeat, the bicycle slaves are in revolt. They're apparently organized, maybe been planning this . . . I don't . . . they got weapons . . . so many dead . . ." It fuzzed to static again and didn't come back.

Mortimer felt his stomach twist, his fingers and arms and face going cold and numb.

Freddy slurped vodka, much of it spilling on his chest. He coughed, wiped his mouth. "Nobody wins. Only losers. Only more and more of the world dying faster and faster. I couldn't bring back civilization my way, and Armageddon couldn't do it his way."

Mortimer thought about the village around the incline station, all the bustling shops, the happy people singing along to "Walk Like an Egyptian." *It would have worked,* thought Mortimer. *We were so close.*

"So what's it going to be, Mortimer Tate?" Freddy belched, drank more vodka. "Are you going to shoot me now? Ha. What's that going to prove? Go ahead. You'd be doing me a favor."

Bang.

"Always glad to help."

. . .

Downstairs, Mortimer climbed behind the wheel of the MINI Cooper, started the engine. He felt light and insubstantial, like he might float up out of himself, get lost on the breeze. Or maybe he would faint. He wasn't sure.

"You find out anything?" Bill asked from the backseat.

Mortimer hesitated, took a deep breath. "No. No, I didn't find out anything."

"I'm sure it's all fine," Sheila said. "Last we heard General Malcolm had won. The Red Stripes ran out of gas."

"Yeah, that's right," Bill said hopefully. "They kicked ass. And we rescued those women. I'd say the good guys won the day."

"Right," Sheila said. "Yeah."

They looked at Mortimer, waited.

"I want to see Florida," Mortimer said. "You guys ever been to Florida?"

They scrounged a hose to siphon enough gasoline from the battlefield wrecks to get out of the city, kept heading south and finally slowed nearly to a stop when they spotted an unknown edifice in the center of the interstate ahead.

"Looks like a person," Sheila said.

Mortimer scratched his chin, blew out a sigh. "Just standing in the middle of the highway?"

"It's too big to be a person," Bill said.

Mortimer briefly pictured Horace, the shark-toothed giant. "We'll go slow. I'll toss it into reverse if something happens."

"Or run him over," Sheila suggested.

They edged closer, and the thing took shape. It was made in the form of a human, arms outstretched, legs bent. It stood atop a length of neon orange fiberglass that might have once been a car door or hood.

They parked the MINI, got out. The wooden plaque at the base of the sculpture read:

INTERSTATE SURFER
—ANONYMOUS

Upon closer examination, Mortimer saw the length of fiberglass had indeed been expertly shaped to resemble a surfboard.

"Huh." Mortimer sat on the front bumper of the MINI Cooper and looked at the metal surfer. The legs were axles banged and bent into submission, the arms strands of metal Mortimer couldn't identify, but the stubby fingers were spark plugs. The torso looked like a gas tank. The skull was some engine part Mortimer could only guess at, lightbulbs in the eyes, the wide mouth a car stereo. An orange highway cone for a hat.

Something in the body language kept the sculpture from looking completely comical. It must have weighed a ton but seemed perfectly balanced.

Bill sat on the bumper next to Mortimer. "It looks like the least little thing could knock it over, massive and fragile at the same time. I wonder how long it took him to do it."

"Beats me." Mortimer noticed a lack of bird droppings on the sculpture. Nothing rusted. This one was relatively new.

Sheila sat on the other side. "I'd have signed my name. Doesn't he want credit?"

They sat looking at the surfer a long time, nobody saying a word.

·   ·   ·

They ran out of fuel twenty miles north of Valdosta. They camped near the car that night, built a small fire and slept the sleep of the dead.

The next morning they sat around the campfire's cold coals, no gasoline, no food, no ideas and no coffee. If Mortimer had been granted only one wish, it would have been for the coffee.

Sheila spotted it first, a black speck in the blue of the sky. They sat and watched the speck grow bigger all morning until it was close enough to recognize as the Blowfish.

They yelled and jumped and waved as it passed overhead. Bill broke one of the mirrors off the MINI Cooper and tilted sun flashes at the blimp. Just when it looked like it would sail right on by, it made a slow, slow, slow, awkward turn and landed about two hundred yards down the highway.

Reverend Jake seemed happy to see them. They were sure as hell happy to see him. Sheila asked if he'd come looking for them. The reverend looked slightly embarrassed, admitted that he hadn't been searching for them. Instead, he'd been following the interstate south, intent on witnessing to the heathens in tropical Miami or Key West. He had, in fact, picked up intermittent signals on the radio that sounded vaguely like Jimmy Buffett music.

"Can you stomach some hitchhikers?" Mortimer asked.

The reverend cleared his throat. "'As you do unto the least of my children, so have you done unto Me,' says the Good Book."

Through clever and constant application of propaganda, people can be made to see paradise as hell, and also the other way round, to consider the most wretched sort of life as paradise.

—ADOLF HITLER

EPILOGUE

For three weeks they floated south. At first they used I-75 as a guide, but somewhere between Gainesville and Ocala, unseen snipers popped off a few shots at them. They veered east until they hit the Atlantic and followed the coast, always south.

They scavenged food, and with the onset of warmer weather, they also scavenged shorts and T-shirts and flip-flops. Bill didn't look right, the Union officer's cap and the six-shooters and the Bermuda shorts and the pink shirt that said MY HUS-BAND WENT TO FLORIDA, AND ALL I GOT WAS THIS LOUSY T-SHIRT.

Mortimer wore cutoff jeans and a white tank top that said TECATE, and Sheila switched between a glowing blue one-piece and a wispy-light sundress with spaghetti straps.

They stuck close to the beach so they could catch fish and crabs and oysters. Jimmy Buffett came in much clearer as they went south. Mortimer became obscenely fond of "One Particular Harbour," although Bill's favorite was "A Pirate Looks at Forty."

They got stuck in Boca Raton for a week when the Blowfish's little engine finally ran out of gasoline. They rigged an exercise bicycle to turn the propeller and took turns pedaling. This reminded Mortimer of the bicycle-slave uprising back on Lookout Mountain, but he quickly put it out of his mind.

He never told the others what happened.

They remembered what fear felt like as they passed Miami. The city looked just as decayed and haunted as Atlanta had, and they kept their distance.

If they'd tried to make Key West on foot or by car, they'd never have made it. Half the bridges were out, and Mortimer strongly suspected they'd been destroyed on purpose to keep away outsiders.

Too bad. Here we come.

They put down in a parking lot, several onlookers marveling at the sight of a blimp suddenly among them.

A man in his late fifties with a pierced ear, a gaudy Hawaiian shirt and a braided white beard introduced himself as the unofficial "sort of leader spokesperson guy" and asked for news of the outside world.

Mortimer said, "You don't want to know."

They were made welcome, and the locals showed them the ropes. They all got together about once every three months (give or take) to vote on whatever issues anyone wanted to raise, but nobody was obligated to abide by the outcome, so there wasn't a lot of stress about it.

Mortimer was told to find any old abandoned dwelling and help himself. He found a small, three-room place forty feet from the beach and moved in. Sheila moved in with him by unspoken agreement.

Reverend Jake set up a church. People came occasionally for a little fire and brimstone, the closest thing the community had to theater.

The public library had been set up on the honor system. You signed out a book and brought it back whenever. If you kept a book too long, somebody might occasionally show up on your doorstep and say something along the lines of "Hey, man, you done with *Potty Training for Dummies* yet?"

It amused Mortimer to check out Milton's *Paradise Lost,* but he quit reading halfway through and started checking out all the Harry Potter books instead.

They fished. They lounged in the sand and got tan. Mortimer made love to Sheila every night, often on the beach, sometimes in their lazy porch hammock. The Key West folks were easygoing, polite, helpful. Somewhere in the back of his mind, Mortimer knew that there was an ugly world out there waiting to crash down on these people. Sooner or later somebody would notice the island wasn't getting its fair share of misery, and they'd swoop in with pain and sorrow.

But not today. Maybe never. Mortimer planned to forget, to make himself as blissfully ignorant as the rest.

Six months went by like nothing at all.

He was lounging in the shade of his porch one day when he saw a figure walking up the beach toward his little house. Sheila swung in the hammock next to him, snoring lightly. It was late afternoon and hot.

The figure took shape as he got closer. Bill. His long Buffalo Bill/George Custer hair bleached almost white, long braids on either side, as was the style on the island. He carried his boots in his hands and walked barefoot in the sand.

Mortimer waved and waited. Bill stepped onto the porch, nodded hello. Mortimer put his finger to his lips in a *shhhhh* gesture.

"Go ahead and talk," Sheila said. "I'm awake."

"I'm getting a little restless," Bill said. "Thought I'd take off. nted to see if you'd come with me."

Sounds needlessly hazardous," Mortimer said.

"One of the guys I know has been working on a boat at the old navy base. It's rigged for steam. We've been on the shortwave radio to a lot of folks willing to trade. Thought we might get some commerce going."

Mortimer shrugged. "I don't know. I can't really think of anything I need."

They had plenty of fish to eat, and mild weather, and fish, and people in Bermuda shorts who wanted to talk about how good or bad the fishing was on any particular day, and Jimmy Buffett music, and fish, and lots of swimming in the warm ocean, and fish, and plenty of goddamn fish.

"We're heading for South America. Thought we might swing by Colombia, pick up some coffee."

Mortimer stood, stretched lazily. "Guess I'd better get packed."

"Me too," Sheila said. "Don't leave me stuck in paradise."